Run Dog Run

by

Kathleen Kaska

Run Dog Run

Cover Art by *Kristian Norris*

The Wild Rose Press, Inc.
PO Box 708
Adams Basin, NY 14410-0708
Visit us at www.thewildrosepress.com

Publishing History
First Edition, 2022
Trade Paperback ISBN 978-1-5092-4095-1
Digital ISBN 978-1-5092-4096-8

Published in the United States of America

Kate and Rosa Linda left the Jeep in the middle of the road and ran toward the wreck. It looked as if the pickup had plowed through a barbed-wire fence and nose-dived into a utility pole. It rested precariously on the embankment. The front end was smashed in like an accordion, and the right rear tire hung in mid-air. The driver's side door hung loose on its hinge.

"Stay here," Kate said. She climbed down into the ditch and up the other side. The engine was running. Kate looked inside afraid of what she might find. The dashboard had buckled and smashed into the passenger seat. Glass shards that had once been the windshield covered the seat bench and floorboard. The back window was shattered as well, but the front seat was empty. "There's no one inside."

Rosa Linda scanned the pasture. "Jesús!" she called. "Why didn't he stay put and call for help?"

Kate reached inside to cut off the engine. That's when she saw blood pooled on the floorboard, more splattered across the seatback.

"Give me your cell," Kate said.

"Why?"

"I'm calling the sheriff."

"No, Kate. You can't—"

"Rosa Linda, Jesús did not walk away from this mess. Give me the cellphone."

Praise for Kathleen Kaska

"Kathleen Kaska uses both tightly-knit and directed dialogue and passages replete with detailed descriptions to bring her characters and scenes to life. Her crisp narrative draws her readers into the realm of animal abuse and in particular the controversy surrounding greyhound racing. Kaska masterfully weaves in vivid depictions of not only the breathtaking landscape of Africa, but also the Texas Hill Country. Kate Caraway is a gutsy protagonist who faces challenges head-on."

~ Feather Quill Book Reviews

Dedication

To Becky

Chapter One

Wondering how her life could have unraveled so quickly, Kate Caraway waited at baggage claim for British Airways to locate her last piece of luggage. The events of the past few days fogged her mind—no time to make a rational decision, just get the hell out of the country while there was still a chance, before things got really ugly. Her stomach tensed and she drew in a deep breath. Bad coffee and stale peanuts were the only reason she had not passed out.

Tired of watching the same CNN news report for the fourth time, Kate looked over at her husband. Jack had finally dozed off, his chin resting on his chest. She wanted to pull him close, to place his head on her shoulder and make him comfortable, but she dared not wake him. Neither she nor Jack had slept since they left Nairobi forty-eight hours ago. He was snoring lightly, like a child. Kate watched for a moment longer. A gentle pulsing from a small vein in his temple made her smile, but only for a brief second.

How in the hell did I manage to screw things up so quickly? Kate chided herself. Jack had assured her that she had done the right thing. But she had discovered a frightful side of herself and was terrified that it would emerge again the next time she became outraged, the next time she was pushed too far. She could not live with that.

1

The aroma of freshly baked cinnamon rolls wafted in, bringing with it a feeling of comfort, yet sadness. Her chest ached for home. Since setting up her research camp and moving lock, stock, and barrel to Kenya, Kate had thought very little of what she'd left behind. Kenya had become her home even before the idea for the research camp had taken hold. She'd first gone to East Africa twenty years earlier as part of a work/study program during her second year at the University and remembered an odd sensation as the wheels of the plane touched down at the Nairobi Airport. She felt as if she'd returned home after years—after eons of time—to the place of her birth. Was the home she longed for the place she'd left, or the place to which she'd just returned? That question, she feared, would not be answered anytime soon.

Giving in to hunger pangs, Kate made her way to the food court where a line had formed in front of Cinnamon's Bakery. She smiled at the thought of that universal sweet smell grabbing hold of travelers and pulling them like a magnet to the counter. She ordered two cinnamons rolls and two cups of coffee. Jack was awake and stretching when she returned.

"I honestly believe you could sleep right out there on the runway," she said. "Come on. There's a table by the window. I have breakfast."

"This isn't a roll," Jack said when he opened the box. "It's a cinnamon mound and I plan to eat every bite. Sorry I dozed off."

"Don't be silly. I'm surprised we're both still standing."

As Kate cut into her roll, she noticed Jack set his coffee down and lean back in his chair, a puzzling look spreading across his face.

"What?"

He smiled. "You look…peaceful."

"That's what they say about the dead right before they close the lid."

They finished their meal when they heard their names announced to come to British Airways Baggage claim. "That was close," Jack said. "We have less than an hour before our flight to Austin."

"You think we made the right decision, then?" Kate asked.

"About why we left or where we're going?"

Kate stood to leave and suddenly grabbed her stomach as a sense of terror washed over her. She closed her eyes and tried to steady her breathing. Until two days ago, she'd never understood the meaning of panic attacks. Now, they hit frequently and without warning. She felt as if she'd stepped up to the lip of a cliff, and only blackness showed below. It took all her energy not lose control and topple over the edge.

"Kate," Jack cried. "Sit down."

"I'm okay. It just…hits."

"Take it easy. I'll get you some water."

"No. Don't leave me."

"Try to relax. Once we get to the ranch, you can rest." He pulled his chair up next to her and waited until her hands stopped shaking and the color returned to her face.

****

When Kate and Jack landed at Kennedy that afternoon, they debated about where to go next. They talked about spending a few weeks up on Cape Ann where they had often vacationed after baseball season ended. Chicago was always a possibility. It had been their home for seventeen years before they moved to Africa. The old baseball crowd would welcome them back, but they'd be curious, and too quick with questions Kate couldn't answer. The most logical place was Texas, Kate's home state, where she was born and lived until she finished college. Although most of her friends had moved, Max and Olga Rodriguez had put down stakes in nearby Wimberley and showed no signs of leaving. They were the closest thing to family Kate had left.

"We made the right decision," Jack said. "I can't think of a better place to be than with Max and Olga. And you haven't seen your goddaughter in more than five years."

"I know. I can't wait to see them, but I wonder if it might be better to have a few weeks to ourselves. You know how crazy things can get on the ranch. And when I talked to Olga about coming she said that Rosa Linda was up to her old tricks and was giving her father fits."

Jack laughed. "Well, when isn't she? Beside, a little distraction right now might be better than having too much time on your hands. Come on. Let's collect our bags and head to the gate."

****

Surprisingly, Kate slept most of the way to Texas, waking only when she felt the cabin pressure change and the plane descending. The muscles in her neck had cramped from leaning in the same position for three hours, but otherwise, she felt an awareness of her body, a feeling of wholeness that offered a little hope.

"Are we there yet?" She smiled at Jack.

"I snuck a sedative into your water," he said.

Kate gasped and realized he was joking. "Well, I'm grateful to whatever was in my water. I actually feel normal."

"Enjoy it." He laughed. "What we're about to feel is anything but normal. It's ten in the evening and the temperature at the Austin airport is ninety-three with ninety percent humidity. We're going to need bathing suits."

****

Kate's heart gave way to tears when she spotted Olga standing by the baggage carousel. She ran over and threw her arms around the woman who was the closest thing to a sister Kate had ever had.

"Welcome home, *chica*," Olga said. "If you didn't come visit soon, I was going to go to Kenya to get you. The bungalow's ready. I filled the fridge and turned down the AC. Jack, what a sight you are."

"I hope that's a compliment," he said. "You're as gorgeous as ever. Don't I get a hug, too?"

"Of course, but don't look too closely or you'll see streaks of grey in my hair and, believe me, they're not due to my age."

Kate laughed. "Uh oh. What trouble's my goddaughter brewing up now?"

"You'll find out soon enough. Why didn't you tell me you were coming sooner? I get a call before I finish my first cup of coffee this morning, telling me you and Jack are back in the states. What's going on? Is everything okay?"

"Nothing a little rest won't cure," Jack said, glancing at Kate.

"I'll tell you the sordid details later," Kate said.

"Whenever you're ready," Olga said, "but don't expect much peace and quiet. When I left the ranch, Rosa Linda was making plans for you."

****

On the drive from the Austin-Bergstorm Airport to the small town of Wimberley west of Austin, Kate sensed another panic attack coming on. She took a few deep breaths and, remembering what Jack said about her needing a distraction, Kate brought up the subject of Rosa Linda.

"*Dios mìo*. That girl is about to give Max a stroke. It's her latest cause. Rescuing greyhounds from abusive owners."

Kate wasn't sure what she expected, but this was the last thing she needed to hear. Jack reached from the backseat and placed his hand on her shoulder. She squeezed it, reassuring him that she was okay. It had been years since Kate investigated animal abuse cases for the Humane Society in Chicago. Her work was never rewarding and the investigations always ended badly. Sometimes they arrested the abusers, rarely were they convicted, and nine times out of ten, the animals were euthanized.

"Sounds like a good idea to me," Jack said.

"It is, except the man she's going after happens to be our good friend and neighbor Guy Fordyce. One of Guy's ranch hands contacted Rosa Linda with some story about the dogs being neglected."

"You don't think it's true?" Kate asked.

"I'm not sure. Max is convinced it's a bunch of hogwash. It all started when Rosa Linda became involved with a local greyhound adoption program. You know how she is. Once she seizes on something, it's full steam ahead. Maybe you can talk some sense into her. Lord knows I've tried. I don't want her getting in over her head and causing more trouble than she can handle."

Jack laughed. "Are you talking about Rosa Linda, your only daughter, the one whose middle name is Trouble?"

"Yeah, I see what you mean. Fat chance she'll listen to anyone, but I'm sure Katie can make her listen." She glanced over with a weary smile.

By the time they arrived at the bungalow, it was close to midnight and fatigue had replaced what excitement Kate had felt upon seeing Olga after five years.

"Here's the key," Olga said. "Relax and settle in. Max is in Dallas and won't be back until tomorrow. See you in the morning."

"I can't thank you enough for this," Kate said.

"Then don't." Olga laughed. "By the time Rosa Linda gets ahold of you, you'll wish you were back in Africa."

They walked into an icy cold room. Jack snapped on the light and sat the bags down. "I'll never get used to going from extreme hot to cold by simply walking through a door, but then I'm not a Texan."

"It's not easy for us, either."

"You asked me something earlier today." Jack adjusted the thermostat and turned to his wife. "Now I have to ask you the same question."

"About what?"

"About making the right decision to come here. An animal abuse case—that's the last damn thing you need." He pulled her close. "If you want to change your mind, Olga will understand after we tell her what's happened."

"Let's try to get a good night's sleep. We'll have time to talk it over in the morning."

****

The morning for Kate came later than usual and, for that, she was grateful. She took her first cup of coffee and stepped onto the porch, disturbing a mockingbird perched on the porch rail. She seated herself in the rocking chair as the bird fussed and flitted over the intrusion.

"Sorry, I'm sure you weren't expecting visitors, but we'll be here for a while so you'll have to put up with us."

"Tell me you're not talking to yourself," Jack called from inside.

"No, just a mockingbird who's not happy over having his territory invaded."

"That's almost as bad. Want some breakfast?"

"As long as you're cooking, sure." Kate rose to go inside for another cup of coffee when the sound of a car approaching much too fast caught her attention. Rosa Linda pulled up in front and laid on the horn.

"What the hell?" Jack went to the door. "Hey, young lady. Last time I saw you, you were just learning how to drive. Come here and give your godfather a hug."

"Later, Jack. Kate, get in. Hurry!"

Kate rushed out. "What's going on?"

"I'll explain on the way."

Kate went inside and grabbed her camera bag.

"What are you doing?" Jack cried.

"Weren't you the one who said I needed a distraction?"

"Yeah, but not before breakfast. Do you want me to come along?"

"Hurry!" Rosa Linda called again.

"I'll be fine. If I'm not back by sunset, call in the guard," Kate joked.

Kate hopped in and before she could slam the door, Rosa Linda gunned the engine, spraying gravel across the drive.

"Do I even get a hello?" Kate said, grabbing for the seatbelt.

"Oh, Kate, I'm so sorry, but when Mom called me and told me you were coming, I was so relieved. I need help and I knew you'd listen to me."

"Where are we off to?"

"You'll see."

The Jeep bounced and skidded down the gravel road and soon they turned into the back entrance of Guy Fordyce's ranch. Rosa Linda gave no consideration to slowing down over the cattle guards. Kate braced herself to keep from slamming her head against the roof. Along pastures thick with flowering alfalfa, they drove right into the heart of the ranch. Rosa Linda pulled over and stopped on the side of the road.

"We're supposed to meet Jesús here." Rosa Linda cut the engine. "Mom told you about the greyhounds on Fordyce's ranch. Jesús Flores works for Guy. He contacted me a few weeks ago. He said some of the dogs are living in disgusting conditions and they're treated like garbage. I've been trying for days to get onto the ranch to see for myself. Then he called this morning and left a frantic message for me to get to the ranch quickly. Something about having proof. This is the chance I've been waiting for."

"Why didn't Flores report the abuse to the authorities?"

"And lose his job and get sent back to Mexico?"

"Is he an illegal?"

"No, he has his work visa, but he's afraid if he

causes trouble…well, you know the story. Ever since he first contacted me, I've been trying to get the Blanco County Humane Society to investigate, but Fordyce has connections, and I'm not getting anywhere. He's running for state senator, and he has a bunch of influential good old boys backing him. All I need is evidence and I'm about to get it. Then I'm alerting the authorities and calling the press. I'll have him arrested."

"Hold on. You need to take things one step at a time." Kate knew Rosa Linda well enough to err on the side of caution.

Her hotheaded goddaughter was not beyond overreacting. From her work with the Humane Society, Kate knew the importance of having all her ducks in a row before she made any reports.

"If Fordyce has been racing dogs for years, why has the abuse issue arisen all of a sudden?" Kate asked. "You'd think that he wouldn't want any bad press, especially now."

"The Fordyce ranch hasn't been running all that smoothly lately. Guy's dog trainer, Diego Gomez, died unexpectedly not long ago. A new guy, Wayne Brody, took over the training. Jesús says Brody also uses live lures, which are illegal."

"Live lures?"

"Small animals: rabbits, hamsters, gerbils, and any small mammal they can get their hands on." Rosa Linda uncapped her water bottle, leaned over, and tossed a generous amount over the back of her neck. She straightened up and let the water run down her back. Standing just under five feet, Rosa Linda's hundred pounds were tightly packed into a tiny, muscular frame. Her thick, black hair, cropped above her ears, gave her the look of a featherweight boxer. "I plan to do all I can to close down the racing track as well."

"I know you feel strongly about this, but closing down a well-established racetrack won't be easy," Kate said.

"It won't happen overnight. But it will happen." Rosa Linda smiled. "You can bet on it."

Ten minutes later, they still waited. The drone of heat-aroused cicadas pulsating through the air sounded like bacon sizzling in a hot pan. Kate sat on the Jeep's bumper and pressed the palms of her hands over her eyelids, trying to ward off an approaching headache. Sweat rolled down between her breasts and tickled her sternum. Her jeans stuck to her legs.

"He should have been here by now." Rosa Linda flipped over her iPhone and punched the numbers. "No answer. I don't understand. I told him to call if anything went wrong. We don't have much time to search those pens."

A shadow sailed across the road. Kate looked up to see a red-tailed hawk soaring overhead, its brick-red tail feathers shining brilliantly in the late morning sun. Kate watched as the raptor dipped and rose, drifting effortlessly on a warm air current. *At least someone is enjoying this weather*, Kate thought. The bird circled and landed on a utility pole not thirty feet away. It watched its intruders for a few minutes, and then started preening its feathers.

Kate's patience began to wane. If Jesús's claims were true, and Guy Fordyce was responsible for the abuse of his greyhounds, she would soon become a major thorn in his side. Right now, all she could do was sit and wait while the window of opportunity slipped away.

"Here he comes." Rosa Linda jumped down from the bumper of the Jeep and brushed dirt off the seat of her shorts. Kate looked up the road and saw a cloud of dust rising over the hill.

"Damn!" Rosa Linda said. "It's Garrison, Guy's brother."

A banged-up Mercedes sputtered to a stop in front of the Jeep. The car's once golden color had faded to dirty-shit yellow. The paint on the hood looked as if it had been blasted off in a sandstorm. The man who stepped out looked in worse shape than his car. His scrawny frame and prune-like skin gave the impression of an old man. As he got closer, Kate was surprised to see the youthfulness in his eyes. He could not have been more than forty-five. Kate wondered what misfortunes of life had contributed to his ragtag appearance.

Garrison Fordyce removed his cowboy hat, exposing a crop of sandy hair. The gesture was not an act of chivalry. Instead, he wiped the sweat off his brow. Using his tongue, he shoved a wad of tobacco to the back of his cheek. He propped his foot on the bumper of the Mercedes and draped his shotgun over his knee.

"Well, look who's here. Little Rosa Linda Rodriguez. Didn't your daddy ever teach you not to trespass?" He gave Kate the once over, chewed, and spit a brown stream that landed less than a foot from her boot. Kate caught the odor of stale beer mixed with the tobacco and had to swallow hard not to gag.

"I didn't think Guy would mind if I drove Kate around the ranch and showed her how your brother has improved the place," Rosa Linda lied. "We stopped to photograph the hawk."

"Your daddy might be chummy with my brother, but

don't think you can go snooping around the ranch whenever you want. We've got expensive breeding stock on this side of the property and if you hit one while cruising around like some damn tour-guide, you'll have hell to pay." His warning was cut short when his cell beeped. "Yeah…not yet. I'm on my way." He opened the car door and laid his shotgun on the back seat. "Besides, little lady, bad things happen to people who snoop." He got back into his car and drove away.

"Nice guy," Kate said.

"Garrison's an asshole. Guy lets him hang out here, since he's never been able to hold down a job. He tells everyone that he's the vice-president of Fordyce Enterprises. What a laugh. Rumor has it his third wife left him about six months ago, and took what little money Garrison had. Now he's sponging off his older brother."

Knowing that Rosa Linda could very well stay put on this hot, dusty road until the sun scorched the life out of her, Kate suggested they head back to the ranch and formulate Plan B before their efforts resulted in a bullet in the backside. Rosa Linda reluctantly agreed. On their way out, she drove to the top of the next hill to give Kate a view of the Fordyce ranch house and the facilities that sat nestled alongside a lush grove of live oaks.

Kate focused her binoculars on the property.

"Can you see Jesús's red pickup? He usually parks it next to the bunkhouse, that long white building to the left of the barn," Rosa Linda said.

"Nope. No red pickup around."

Rosa Linda turned the Jeep around and they left.

****

The beauty of the Texas Hill Country never failed to

astonish Kate. Old cowboy movies portrayed the Lone Star State as a dry desert, sprinkled with cacti, or with tumbleweeds rolling down a lonely street flanked by wooden sidewalks. Except for a few historic small towns in the remote western region of the state, nothing could be further from the truth. With its lush terrain covering an ancient limestone plateau, this land supports cedars, junipers, big-tooth maples, and record-size live oaks, all vying for water from the streams and creeks that carved canyons through the earth. It was evident to Kate that the dry summer had indeed taken its toll on the pastures. But the native vegetation still flourished, coloring the land in dusty greens.

In the distance, a dirt devil spiraled a mound of dust into the sky. Kate had often seen small whirlwinds near her camp in Kenya. She suddenly realized how similar this area of Texas was to East Africa. The wide-open spaces were just as overpowering. Except in Kenya, red oat grass replaced tall wispy bluestem and acacias substituted for live oaks. And the high altitude at the base of Mount Kilimanjaro brought crisp, cool mornings, which gave way to pleasant afternoons. The late African sun filtered through the dust and painted the sky a faded pink, giving the land an illusion of softness in an otherwise precarious existence. Kate's first pang of homesickness butterflied somewhere deep inside. Not yet ready to deal with her recent plight, she turned her mind to the situation at hand. Work was always her best painkiller.

Suddenly Kate noticed a flash of crimson down one of the rutted tracks leading off the main road. "Stop!" she shouted. "Is that Jesús's truck sitting in the ditch?"

Rosa Linda slammed on her brakes. The Jeep

skidded sideways, spraying gravel across the hood and windshield before sliding to a stop.

"He's had an accident!" Rosa Linda cried.

Kate and Rosa Linda left the Jeep in the middle of the road and ran toward the wreck. It looked as if the pickup had plowed through a barbed-wire fence and nose-dived into a utility pole. It rested precariously on the embankment. The front end was smashed in like an accordion, and the right rear-tire hung in mid-air. The driver's side door hung loose on its hinge.

"Stay here," Kate said. She climbed down into the ditch and up the other side. The engine was running. Kate looked inside afraid of what she might find. The dashboard had buckled and smashed into the passenger seat. Glass shards that had once been the windshield covered the seat bench and floorboard. The back window was shattered as well, but the front seat was empty. "There's no one inside."

Rosa Linda scanned the pasture. "Jesús!" she called. "Why didn't he stay put and call for help?"

Kate reached inside to cut off the engine. That's when she saw blood pooled on the floorboard, more splattered across the seatback.

"Give me your cell," Kate said.

"Why?"

"I'm calling the sheriff."

"No, Kate. You can't—"

"Rosa Linda, Jesús did not walk away from this mess. Give me the cellphone."

Chapter Two

Kate untied the laces of her hiking boots and slid them off with one hand while pulling her belt off with the other. She placed her watch on the nightstand, and leaned back on the pile of pillows propped up on the king size bed.

"Don't get too comfortable. We're due on the verandah in a few minutes for cocktails." Jack seated himself at the foot of the bed, picked up his wife's foot and started massaging.

Kate closed her eyes for the first time in what seemed like forever. "Five minutes on each foot. I'm sure Max and Olga will forgive us if we're a bit late."

"If we're more than a bit late, do you think they'll get suspicious?"

Kate opened one eye and looked at her husband of twenty-one years. A clean shave and a rest had taken ten years off his appearance. Except for the slight graying around his temples and a few crows' feet around his light brown eyes, Jack seemed to have aged very little. His hundred and sixty pounds had evolved from muscle into harder muscle. It never ceased to amaze her how he maintained his physique without lifting a finger. Kate had to work harder with each passing year to stay in shape.

"Stop grinning. While I've been out sweltering in a damn pasture, you've had a chance to shower and catch a few winks." As her tension began to ease, another wave of unwelcome emotions rushed in.

"What is it?" Jack asked.

"I've known for a long time I needed to leave Kenya. I knew you needed to come home as well. I'm sorry it happened like it did."

"It wasn't your fault. You did what you had to do under the circumstances, but you do scare me sometimes." Jack smiled, pulled Kate's socks off her feet, and escorted her to the shower. "Max is chilling a bottle of champagne. While you're in the shower, I'll see if I can find something to soothe that sunburned nose."

****

On the way to the Rodriguez house, Kate and Jack walked through the garden Olga had been cultivating for the past twenty years. Raised beds of native plants lined the perimeter. Texas sage and verbena grew in Mexican pottery. Autumn aster, still in bloom, formed purple mounds over the terraced area along the western side. Mountain laurels and redbuds grew tall, blocking the view of the front drive, and the dusty-purple flowers of several rosemary bushes lined the south wall. The sound of trickling water from a small fountain added to the tranquility. In the middle of the lush oasis, a swimming pool caught the breeze drifting in from the hills, cooling the entire garden. A spicy aroma wafting in from Olga's kitchen made Kate realize how hungry she was. As they approached the verandah, they heard raised voices.

"You had no business going over there," Max said.

"I made it my business," Rosa Linda cried.

"That entire notion is absurd!"

"Jesús would not lie to me."

Kate and Jack climbed the spiral staircase up to the

verandah where a sweeping vista of the Hill Country came into view. Kate walked over and gave Max a hug. His once thick, black hair had turned gray. A recent expanse of belly hid his belt buckle. His mid-fifties seemed to have taken a toll on her old friend. Kate wondered what had sped up the aging process.

"You look terrific," Max said, and kissed her on the forehead.

"Stop giving your daughter a hard time." Kate teased. "You created a monster and you have to live with her."

"Why is it when you come to visit, I can't help feeling I need therapy?"

Kate laughed. "I've been telling you that for years."

"I never get a break with you. Hey, what happened in Kenya that sent you hightailing home?"

"Max! She hasn't even had a chance to say hello." Olga chastised her husband and rescued Kate by placing a glass of champagne in her hand.

Kate's stomach twisted into a knot. She forced a smile. She was not ready, however, to bring the incident up for a friendly discussion.

"That's okay, Olga. Max is the only person I know who can put life in perspective as easily as taking a breath," Kate said.

"Max, you promised to give me a baseball update," Jack said, changing the subject.

"You haven't missed much. The Cubs were tied for last place the last few weeks of the season." Max chuckled. "It's that damned curse. You need to get back into the game and straighten things out."

Until his retirement from major league baseball, Jack had worn the Cubs' uniform and catcher's mask for almost twenty years. And Max took every opportunity to remind his old friend that the team hadn't won a World Series title once since 1908.

Grateful that Jack had stirred the conversation to baseball, Kate took a sip of champagne and seated herself on a rattan sofa next to Olga. If Max seemed to have aged since their last visit, Olga had stopped time. Her long, black braid, the only style Kate had ever seen her wear, was as bright and shiny as ever. Her ruby-red lipstick contrasted her natural, creamy complexion. On most women, the look would seem artificial, but on Olga it was striking.

"So, tell me, what luxuries did you miss most while you were living in the bush?" Olga said.

"That's easy," Kate said. "Nachos, good wine, shoe stores, and Antonio Banderas movies."

Olga laughed. "I can fix that."

It seemed like no time had passed since their last visit. Kate met Olga and Max Rodriguez while attending the University of Texas at Austin. Max was a young associate professor, teaching in the anthropology department with her father. Ted Caraway was Max's mentor, and Max and Olga spent many evenings at the Caraway home. When Kate's father suddenly died, she found herself completely alone. If it had not been for Max and Olga's friendship, Kate might never have finished college. Visiting them on their ranch in Wimberley was like coming home. They merely picked up at whatever point life presented itself.

The sun began to slip behind the hills, but the hot, humid temperature seemed to hang in the air. As the last remnant of light disappeared, the evening ushered in the musty smells of juniper and cedar, which mixed with the aroma of Olga's cooking. Kate finally began to relax. But the reunion and promise of comfort food did not calm Rosa Linda. She sat pouting, shooting angry glances at her father. Kate knew that her goddaughter was waiting for the right moment to bring the conversation back around to the greyhounds. As if on cue, a fawn-colored greyhound slunk onto the verandah. She spotted Rosa Linda, skittered over, and tried to hop up in the chair.

"Down, girl," Rosa Linda said. The dog hesitated, then turned around three times and folded her lanky legs in a neat little package under her thin, sleek body next to Rosa Linda's chair.

"Who's this?" Jack asked.

"Her name is Luna. She's a rescue dog." Rosa Linda nuzzled the dog's ears. "I can't imagine what she went through when she was a puppy. She was one of the slow ones. She wouldn't have lasted long that's for sure."

"Rosa Linda, this subject is closed," Max said.

"Dad, in case you don't remember, Kate's here to help with the investigation."

"Kate and Jack are here to relax!" Max retorted.

"I'm here to do both," Kate said, but her attempt at diplomacy did not subdue Rosa Linda.

"And now Jesús has disappeared, and may be dead!" Rosa Linda's eyes flashed.

"You don't know that, young lady!" Max shouted.

"It doesn't look good, Max," Kate said.

"Then where is he?" Max said.

Good question, Kate thought.

"Maybe you should ask your friend," Rosa Linda retorted. "I'm sure Guy's involved."

"This is none of your business, Rosa Linda." Max

rose to fill his glass.

"I can't stay out of this, not now, Dad." She stood up, and Luna ducked under the patio table.

"Guy Fordyce is our neighbor and has been raising greyhounds for years. I refuse to believe—" Max shouted.

"Weird things are happening on that ranch!" Rosa Linda interrupted. "You won't believe what these dogs go through during training. I've read stories about owners who club the young dogs who can't cut it or worse yet, leave them to starve."

Kate rubbed her temples then took a swallow of champagne, trying to quell the bile rising in her esophagus. Her thoughts went back to earlier days when, not long after finishing college, she had become involved in animal rights issues. She had taken an abnormal psychology course to understand why some people abused animals. Thinking that understanding could make her job easier was naive on her part. Instead, understanding their psychoses only made the picture uglier, and her job more difficult. That realization was all too clear in Kate's mind.

"Stop it, you two!" Kate cried out, louder than she intended.

Everyone in the room fell silent. Jack walked over and gave Kate's shoulder a tender squeeze.

"You okay?" Jack asked.

"I'm fine. Just tired. Listen, Max if there is a case of animal abuse, we'll go through the proper channels to see that it's stopped." Kate took a deep breath and continued in a softer voice. "We can't do anything tonight."

"Katie's right," Olga said. "Let's eat dinner and give Katie and Jack a chance to unwind."

"I'm sorry," Max said. "But Guy's been a friend of mind ever since he moved here."

Suddenly he stopped in mid-sentence and clamped his jaw shut. Kate turned to see the source of Max's distress. A new guest had joined the party. Rosa Linda welcomed him with a kiss.

The handsome young man looked scrubbed and polished from the silver buckle on his cowboy hat to his black boots that poked from under the hems of his creased jeans. His starched white shirt added a sophisticated contrast. He stood a couple of inches taller than Rosa Linda, and, side-by-side, they seemed the perfect match.

"Jack, Kate, I want you to meet my fiancé, Daniel Martinez," Rosa Linda said.

"Fiancé?" Jack said. "You're full of surprises, young lady."

"Daniel and I met a few months ago on a rafting trip through Big Bend. Daniel was photographing Santa Elena Canyon."

After the introductions, Luna bounced over to Daniel and placed her front paws on his shoulders, meeting him eye-to-eye. "Guess who will be the flower girl?" Daniel laughed. "We plan to tie a pink ribbon around Luna's neck and hang a little basket of rose petals under her chin." When he smiled, his eyes disappeared. Kate liked him immediately.

"You're a photographer, Daniel?" Jack asked.

"It's sort of my hobby. I'm finishing up my master's in sociology at UT. Photography adds a nice balance."

"We'll have the wedding in the garden," Rosa Linda said, "and of course, Mom will cater."

"I thought you retired," Jack said.

"I thought so too, but my daughter and husband are always finding reasons for me to get back into the kitchen."

"Daniel, are you sure you are ready for this?" Jack said extending his hand. "I know what it's like to be married to a high-spirited woman. Never a dull moment." Jack gave Rosa Linda a hug.

Daniel grinned. "I heard about the adventure your wife and Rosa Linda had today. If you have any suggestions, Mr. Ryder, I could sure use them. I know Max has tried to tame his daughter for years. I'd be a fool to think I could do a better job."

"Call me Jack. The only advice I have is to stay out of her way and give her space."

Max snorted into his champagne glass and walked to the edge of the verandah for a smoke.

"The date is set for three weeks from tomorrow," said Rosa Linda.

Another snort from the shadows, and Kate discovered that not everyone was excited about the upcoming event.

"Rosa Linda's not the only one who needs your assistance," Olga said. "Before I can even think of the wedding, I have a catering event here on Sunday. I could use an extra hand with the cooking. Max and I are sponsoring a fundraising brunch for Guy's senate campaign. You'll get a chance to meet him then."

"I'd love to help cook. In camp, cooking was something I couldn't be bothered with, unless you call mixing formula for orphaned animals cooking."

Max chose to rejoin the party as the conversation changed from wedding plans to a topic he was more interested in. "Guy's running for state senator." He gave his daughter a stern look. "I'm sure he's unaware of any problems with the greyhounds, if there are any. Besides, Jesús Flores has worked for Guy only a short while, Rosa Linda. You don't know anything about this man."

"I know enough," Rosa Linda said, turning to Kate. "He's an honest man trying to make an honest living. I've been helping him with his English. When he found out about the abuse, he was afraid to go to Guy with the information. He didn't want to cause trouble, lose his job, and have to return to Mexico. Jesús knew that I was involved with greyhound adoption, so he contacted me."

"Max, whatever happened on the ranch today doesn't look good," Kate said. "After the Hays County sheriff arrived, he called every hospital from San Marcos to Austin. Neither Jesús or any unknown injured person had been admitted."

"That's not our concern," Max said. "I'm sure Guy can handle whatever happened." Having heard enough talk about missing persons and abused greyhounds, Max steered the conversation to ranching. He was explaining a new method of land conservation when Maria, their housekeeper, came out onto the verandah. She walked up to Olga and whispered in her ear. Olga looked toward the door and her smile disappeared as a tall lanky man, wearing a tan uniform walked in. Sheriff Holden McCrae was no stranger to Kate. He had arrived at the scene of the wreck on the Fordyce ranch earlier that day. He removed his hat and ran his fingers through a mess of thick gray hair. The solemn look on his face indicated bad news.

"Hate to break up the party," McCrae said. "We found Jesús Flores about an hour ago. Some high-school students out for a beer party at the old Driftwood

Cemetery near Cypress Creek stumbled upon his body. Mrs. Caraway, Rosa Linda, I'm afraid I need to ask you a few more questions."

Chapter Three

Kate stood by the window in Max's office, watching streaks of purple fade across the western sky. Rosa Linda sat in her father's desk chair with her head buried in her hands.

McCrae closed the door behind him and strolled over to the desk, the sound of his boots muffled by the thick rug. He picked up a magazine, studied the cover for a moment, and tossed it aside. "Tell me again what Jesús said when he called you to meet him on the Fordyce Ranch."

"Like I said before," Rosa Linda huffed, "he was upset. Said he couldn't talk and to get to the ranch as soon as possible."

"Then he hung up?" McCrae said, flipping open a small notebook he'd taken from his shirt pocket.

"That's what I said, didn't I?"

"Rosa Linda." Kate went over and placed her hand on the girl's shoulder then turned to the sheriff. "You said Jesús was found in the cemetery. Surely he didn't get there on his own."

"His body was moved," McCrae said.

"So it wasn't an accident?" Kate asked.

"Hardly. If those kids were looking for some fright to add to the excitement of their beer party, they found it."

"What do you mean?" Rosa Linda said.

26

"His body was strung up and tied to a cross."

"Oh, my God," Rosa Linda cried.

"Was he dead before that happened?" Kate asked.

"We won't know until we get the ME's report," McCrae said.

"Did you check out his story about the dogs?" Kate asked.

"After we found Jesús, I went back to the Fordyce ranch and checked every kennel. Those dogs looked fat and happy."

Rosa Linda slammed her fist down on the desk. "Jesús was telling the truth. Why would he lie?"

"Rosa Linda, if you believe Jesús, that's good enough for me," Kate said. "But we have no evidence, and now Jesús is dead. Go back to the beginning and try to remember everything he told you."

McCrae nodded to Kate in gratitude and continued with his questions. "When did Jesús first call you with this abuse thing?"

"About three weeks ago," Rosa Linda said. "And I immediately called the humane society."

McCrae waited.

"They said they'd check into it," she continued. "But as far as I know, they haven't done a damn thing. Then Jesús called yesterday afternoon. He'd found lures that had been discarded. They were still alive."

"What time was that?"

"About four-thirty."

"Did you see these lures?" McCrae said.

Rosa Linda hesitated. "I was supposed to visit the kennel today at lunch while Wayne was gone."

"But you got there before noon," McCrae confirmed, reading from his notes.

"Jesús called this morning. This time he sounded really frightened, and said something about finding their bodies. Said that he couldn't talk, but urged me to get out there as soon as possible. That's all I know."

"Why did he call you and not me?"

"Isn't that obvious? He doesn't trust the authorities."

"He was an illegal?" McCrae said.

"No! He had his green card."

"What happened after you got the call?"

"I picked up Kate and we rushed to the ranch."

"What time did you get there?"

"Around eleven-thirty. We waited for half-an-hour and then tried to call him, but got no answer."

"I suggested we leave because something had obviously gone wrong, and we had nothing to gain by waiting around," Kate said. "That's when we found Jesús's truck and called nine-one-one."

"Did you see anyone else?"

"Garrison came by," Rosa Linda answered. "He told us to get off the property."

"Did you tell him why you were there?"

Rosa Linda glanced at Kate. "No, I made up a story about showing Kate around."

"He bought that?"

"You know Garrison. He's not too smart. I told him we were leaving. Then he got a call and had to rush off."

"But not before he threatened us," Kate added.

"Sounds like Garrison," McCrae said. "The guy's full of hot air. I wouldn't take anything he said seriously."

"Maybe you wouldn't, Sheriff," Kate said. "But I get kind of testy when someone threatens me with a shotgun."

****

After McCrae left, Kate and Rosa Linda joined the others on the verandah, but no one had much to say. Dinner was quiet and that too-familiar knot had taken up residence in Kate's stomach, causing her appetite to disappear. Finally, Jack broke the silence. "It's been a crazy day. I, for one, am dead on my feet and I'm sure everyone else is too."

No one debated Jack's assessment, and the solemn party broke up. On the way back to the bungalow, Kate reached for Jack's hand.

"Do you want to talk?" Jack said.

"You mean about what happened to Jesús?"

"No, that's not what I mean." He kissed her hand.

"Not right now. Let's just walk."

The path leading to the bungalow was marked by flagstones and bordered by tall, well-sculpted mountain laurels, creating a leafy corridor of dark green and purple. Before reaching the house, it wound through a grove of Althea trees. Purple, pink, and white blossoms that had fallen from the delicate branches now littered the flagstones. There were still enough flowers on the trees to satisfy the tiny, white butterflies that darted through the grove. Kate and Jack had stepped onto the porch when Rosa Linda ran up behind them.

"Kate, wait. Can I talk to you?"

"Sure, honey."

"Let's talk out here," Rosa Linda said.

"I can take a hint," Jack said. He wished them goodnight and went inside.

Kate sat down on the steps. Rosa Linda paced along the walkway. Anxiety rolled off her like churning waves on angry water, leaving Kate with little patience. She was about to prod her goddaughter, when Rosa Linda pulled an envelope from underneath her shirt. "Here. You need to see these."

"What are they?"

Rosa Linda didn't answer. It wasn't necessary. Kate shifted through the photos. "Where did you get these?"

"From the disposable camera I'd given Jesús. I took it from his truck this morning when you went to call the police. I had them developed this afternoon."

"What?"

"Don't be angry, Kate."

"Rosa Linda, we have a murder here. You should've given these to McCrae. You could be charged with evidence tampering."

"I was so desperate for something to prove that Jesús was right. You don't know how hard it is to get something on these guys."

"Are these Fordyce's dogs?" Kate looked at another photo.

"I'm afraid so."

Some showed several greyhounds crammed into a kennel. One shot showed dogs being loaded into a traveling kennel in the bed of a pickup. Others showed bodies of dead greyhounds, emaciated, heaped in a pile on the ground, and other shots were obviously taken of the Fordyce ranch.

"What's this?" Kate said.

"The lures I told you about earlier. They use them to train the younger greyhounds. It's not only the dogs that are mistreated. They tied the lures to a mechanical pole that hangs just out of reach for the dogs. They use the lures over and over until they are near death. Sometimes the greyhounds get close enough to nip at the lures. The dogs wear muzzles, but they can still snatch small bits— limbs, tails, ears, tearing away at the animal piece by piece." Tears flooded Rosa Linda's eyes. "Kate, this is proof. I know I should have told Sheriff McCrae, but I don't trust him. Daniel and I talked about it, and he suggested that I bring the photos to you."

"I'm giving these to McCrae tomorrow."

"I know. But I wanted you to see them first. Daniel's waiting. See you tomorrow." She darted back down the path and was gone in a flash.

****

Kate had no trouble accepting Jack's laid-back attitude when she found out, after their third date, that he was also an early riser. Often up by four-thirty herself, Kate's internal clock ticked best in the morning. Having a partner that did not mind her rooting around in the kitchen at that hour of the day was comforting. After the stress of the past few days, they managed to sleep late. Six o'clock found Kate sitting on the front porch of the bungalow, enjoying her first cup of coffee. The stars in the sky were fading as a faint, pink glow rose from behind the hills, silhouetting the line of big-tooth maples that grew along the distant ridge. The majestic trees, stark in their blackness, reminded Kate of the tall Maasai warriors who she had hired to guard her camp. A frogs' symphonic choir sounded on the bank of the stock tank nearby, lulling Kate back to the time when she first arrived at Amboseli National Park to study elephants and was overcome by its illusory tranquility.

The caffeine worked its way to her brain and brought Kate's mind back to the ranch and to yesterday's events. She tried to make a mental agenda for the day, but her thoughts were constantly interrupted by visions of Jesús's grisly death and the place where his body had been discovered.

Lights flashed from the inside of their bedroom. Kate's sullen mood lightened when she realized that Jack was probably watching last night's baseball scores scroll across the screen of a muted TV. A few minutes later, he joined her on the porch with a kiss and a coffee refill. Sometime during their two decades of marriage, they had fallen into a pattern of enjoying their coffee in silence, and starting their day with minimal conversation.

"Cubs are out of the running," Jack said.

"Too bad."

"There's always next year. Plans?"

"Jog, cook, snoop, visit the morgue. You?"

"Sports pages, nap, read, nap, return calls."

"Give Gary my best."

As soon as Kate and Jack had arrived on the ranch, Jack wasted no time in calling his old friend Gary Palmer. Jack and Gary had played together on the Cubs' team for most of their baseball career. After they retired, Gary stayed with the team as manager. Jack received several offers to manage other teams, but he chose to accompany his wife to Africa instead. Kate was reminded, again, of how important it was for Jack to be back home and in contact with his old baseball buddies. For his benefit, she vowed to make their return a good thing for herself as well.

****

Kate's four-mile jog took her through the ranch, down the main road, and back again. Taking in the sights along the way provided her with a distraction from the morning heat. Springtime in the Hill Country threw a blanket of wildflowers over the landscape, but late summer, in its simple starkness, was an annual reminder that nothing lasts forever. Soon the leaves of maples and redbuds would turn rusty red in preparation for nature's closure on another year. At times like these, Kate thanked her father for the camping trips when she was young, giving her an appreciation for the outdoors. Growing up in the city offered opportunities, but urban living also tended to skew one's perspective on life. She covered the four miles in under forty-five-minutes. *Not bad for a forty-two year-old woman*, thought Kate.

Kate walked into the bungalow to find Jack dressed and on his way out.

"Max called. He's going into Austin and wanted me to come along. Need anything?"

"Not that I can think of. Have fun."

"And you be careful. I'll be back to join you for the sunset and a glass of wine."

"It's a date."

Kate showered, changed, and started rolling enchiladas in Olga's kitchen by eight in preparation for tomorrow's brunch. "I really miss cooking," Kate said. "I think it's my only natural talent."

"I remember when your father was alive," Olga said. "You and I would hole up in the kitchen and try out one new recipe after another. Some were disasters."

"We'd open up a bottle of wine, shove in an opera cassette, and go to town. You'd just started your catering business."

"It's too early for wine and opera. You'll have to settle for more coffee and Edith Piaf."

"You'll get no complaint from me."

"How many chicken enchiladas have your made?"

"About two dozen."

"Here, use the shredded beef for another two dozen, and then use the mushroom and onion mixture for the rest."

"Olga, do you really think Guy knew about the mistreatment of his greyhounds and chose to ignore it?" Kate said.

Olga stuffed small bell peppers for the chili rellenos, and laid them neatly in a row in a baking pan. "Guy and Meredith have had a pretty rough time lately. Their daughter died a few months ago. She had been into drugs, and before they could get Victoria into treatment, she drowned in their pool. The autopsy showed that she had taken a large quantity of Valium."

"How horrible."

"Meredith still hasn't recovered."

"How do you get over the death of your child?"

"I don't think you do. Running for state senator is Guy's way of coping—or not coping—with what happened. I think he hopes his efforts in public office will make a difference somehow. I'm not sure Meredith is up for all of this. There's something else, too. Meredith was attacked a few months ago."

"Attacked?"

Olga grabbed a kitchen towel and wiped her hands. "Meredith's a member of the Hays County Historical Society. They've taken charge of restoring historic sites around the area. She was alone cleaning up one of the sites when she was robbed."

"No wonder Guy has ignored the dogs, not that the abuse can be excused. Here, let me cover those chili rellenos and put them in the refrigerator." When Olga failed to respond, Kate looked up. "What?"

"Meredith was attacked at the old cemetery where Jesús's body was found."

"You don't say. What do you know about him?"

"I've only met Jesús a couple of times. He seemed honest, and Rosa Linda trusted him. He wanted to make a better life for his family here in the States. I don't know what he stepped into, Katie, but I can't help but feel concerned for his family back in Mexico. I'm sure you will find out what is going on." Olga placed another platter of tortillas in front of her friend and the conversation returned to cooking as they roasted red peppers and peeled the skin off in preparation for Olga's famous salsa.

"How many are we cooking for?"

"Thirty. I'm pulling out all the stops for this one. We're charging five hundred a person—a boost for Guy's campaign fund."

Kate had had almost twenty-four hours to form a preconceived notion of Guy Fordyce, and waiting another day to find out whether her judgments were accurate was difficult. Patience was not one of her attributes.

With the big food items prepped, all that they needed to finish were the condiments. Three hours after Kate had rolled her first enchilada, she took off her apron. "Can you do without me?"

"Maria can help with the rest," Olga said. "Where are you off to?"

"I might have to wait until tomorrow to meet Guy, but there's one thing I can do today. Where do I find Jake's Tavern?"

"You're kidding."

"According to your daughter, Guy's dog trainer,

Wayne Brody, does lunch there."

"How my daughter knows these things is beyond me." Olga made the sign of the cross. "Want me to come along?"

"You have too much to do here. Besides, Brody might be willing to talk if it's only him and me."

"You're not exactly paying a visit to the local country club." Olga grabbed her laptop and wrote down the address to Jake's. "It's easy it find, right off Highway 12. Be careful."

"If one more person tells me to be careful, I'll scream."

Olga smiled. "Maybe one day you'll listen."

****

Kate did not bother to change clothes for her surprise meeting, a decision that proved wise, for the smoke in the tavern, mixed with a smell of rancid grease, was as thick as cotton. The door stood wide open with the help of a huge brass sand-filled cowboy boot that served as an ashtray, spittoon, and whatever else happened to fall into it. Country music twanged from the jukebox. As soon as her eyes adjusted to the dim light, Kate noticed that except for a bleach-blond bartender whose dark roots had almost overtaken the bleach job, Kate was the only woman in the place. The patrons watched as she made her way to the bar. Being a pushy woman in the African bush, Kate had become accustomed to stares and to people telling her that she didn't belong. Their efforts only resulted in intensifying her determination to stay and make her project work.

But no one said a word, and as soon as Kate sat down at the bar, the men turned back to their beer and grub. Kate ordered a grilled cheese and a Coke.

"Women don't usually come in here alone," the bartender said.

Kate removed the paper wrapper from the straw. "You're here," she said.

"Out of necessity. It pays the rent. Name's Bev." She lit up a cigarette. Kate was definitely going to have to burn her clothes when she left here.

"My name's Kate. This must be a tough job."

"Na. Now that I work days, it ain't so bad. I used to work weekend nights. Talk about hell raisers. Six months ago, I got between a beer bottle and a guy's head."

Without meaning to, Kate glanced at a scar under Bev's left eye. Bev merely laughed. "Yeah, that's how I got this. A little too close for comfort. The tips ain't as good during the day, but the worst thing that happens is some guy falling asleep in one of them booths." She took a drag off her cigarette and blew the smoke from the side of her mouth. "And I got a working kid that don't mind helping his momma. He drives a truck for a living, and sends home part of his paycheck."

"Lucky you. I had a dog once, but he had a difficult time holding down a job."

Bev's laughter caught the attention of a scruffy-looking fellow sitting at a nearby table. He sauntered up to the bar and bummed one of Bev's cigarettes. Stringy blond hair, tied in a ponytail, hung down from the back of a faded blue and gold cap that sported an "Eagle Scout" logo. Despite the second-rate tattoos decorating both forearms, and the gold-cross earring in his right ear, Kate had a strong feeling that the tough-guy image was a mere facade. She wondered where he found the cap. The guy standing next to her was no more an Eagle Scout than she was.

"Wayne, you're always nosing around where you don't belong," said Bev. "Can't you see that the lady is wearing a wedding ring?"

"That's okay with me. I plan to die an old man, shot by a jealous husband."

"You'll get shot by a jealous husband all right, but it won't be when you're old." Bev handed him another Tecáte, and went to attend to another customer.

"What's a classy lady like you doing in Jake's?" He took a seat next to Kate.

"Looking for you," Kate said, extending her hand.

Looking more cocky than surprised, he shook Kate's hand and held on longer than polite society allowed. "This is my lucky day. I don't know who you are ma'am, but any woman who comes looking for me without a shotgun gets my undivided attention."

"My name's Kate Caraway. I'm here to find out about Jesús Flores." Kate detected a slight crack in Brody's tough-guy veneer. "Rosa Linda Rodriguez and I had an appointment with him yesterday, but his murder prevented him from keeping it."

Brody downed half of his beer in one gulp. "Yeah, that was a real shocker. The cops have been buzzing around the ranch all morning."

"Any idea what happened? Jesús called Rosa Linda yesterday morning upset."

"Why are you interested in all this?"

"Rosa Linda's my goddaughter. She asked me to help. She's concerned about Jesús's family."

"That guy was nothing but trouble. Always sneaking around. Always looked like he knew something you didn't. I told Guy that Jesús was up to no good, but whoever listens to Wayne Brody?"

"Jesús was concerned that some of Guy's greyhounds weren't treated well. He said something about finding their discarded bodies."

Brody took a wad of bills from his pocket, and emptied his bottle. "Yeah, well. That stupid son-of-a-bitch Jesús shouldn't of ever swam across the river. If you ask me, Guy made a big mistake hiring that guy. That Mexican would do anything to stay in this country. Anything." He glanced at the Budweiser clock hanging over the bar. "I gotta get back to work." Brody slammed the money down on the bar and left.

"What's your secret? I've been trying to get rid of that joker for months." Bev picked up the cash, noticed that it didn't include a tip, and stuffed the money in the register. She reached for her cigarettes and came up empty-handed.

"Why do I get the feeling that seeing you three times in two days is no coincidence?"

Kate looked up as Sheriff McCrae took the stool Wayne had vacated. "I know you're not here for the food."

"You missed him," Kate said.

"Good. You can fill me in and make my job easier."

"Not much to tell. I asked him about Jesús and the dog abuse. He became a bit huffy when I mentioned dead bodies. I guess I frightened him off." She turned and looked directly at McCrae. "About this time I usually get a lecture for meddling where I don't belong."

"And where do you belong?"

The question was benign, but cut deep. Kate chose not to answer.

"Listen, I can't keep you from asking questions about the dogs, but if you're the kind who listens to advice, and I don't think you are, you'll stay away from the Fordyce ranch. Finding out what's going on there is my job." Then he flashed his Andy Griffith smile. "Hey, I'll be in Houston next month. Maybe your husband can get me tickets to the Cubs-Astros game. If you want to help, that's where I need it." He paid for Kate's lunch and left.

"For being a stranger around here, you make friends fast," Bev said as she refilled Kate's glass.

"It only seems that way. I usually just piss people off." Kate rose to leave.

"What's your hurry?" Bev said.

"I need to visit a dead man before he returns to Mexico.

****

An afternoon heat-fired storm was blowing in from the south, dropping the temperatures into the comfortable mid-nineties. These dark, heavy clouds rarely produced rain, but at least they provided a short respite from the heat.

"I hate this rain-tease weather," Rosa Linda said. "I wish it would rain and get it over with."

"Be careful what you wish for. Once it starts, it doesn't seem to stop."

Rosa Linda and Daniel turned off the main highway to the road that led to Molly Gibson's Greyhound Adoption Kennels.

"I think we should tell Kate what we're doing," Daniel said, as he pulled up to a sprawling ranch house.

"Let's wait. We have to be careful. The fewer people who know, the better. In the meantime, we'll keep her busy with the dogs."

Daniel parked in front of Molly Gibson's house and

blew the horn. When she didn't appear, they walked around the house to the kennel where Molly spent most of her time tending to her wards. They found her sitting on the ground in front of an opened pen. Dressed in oversized overalls, and with her bright red hair tucked up under a floppy straw hat, Molly looked like a twelve-year-old kid. Her leg was curled up under her and her chin rested on her other knee. A small greyhound quivered in the corner, seemingly not tempted by the food Molly held in her hand.

"Bradford brought her in this morning," Molly said. She held up her hand signaling them to approach cautiously. "She raced at River City on Friday and strained a femoral muscle so badly that it separated. She took a nasty tumble and chipped a bone in her hip as well. Luckily, Bradford was on duty. The owner wanted her euthanized." Molly scooted over and Rosa Linda joined her. "Bradford offered to treat her, but the owner said that he would not pay for unnecessary vet bills. When Bradford asked for her papers, the asshole tried to get him to fork over money for the dog."

"Does Bradford think she'll recover?" Daniel asked.

"Physically, yes, but she's pretty traumatized. I hope she'll be adoptable," Molly replied.

"I hope so, too," Rosa Linda said. "Otherwise your threesome in the big house will have to make room for one more sibling."

Their laughter caused the greyhound to rise up and wag her tail, but the resulting pain caused her to lower her head back down.

****

Kate drove up and parked in an oil-stained lot behind the Austin Police Department. She needed a convincing story in order to view Jesús's body. She'd thought about asking McCrae to call ahead on her behalf, but decided it was better to ask for forgiveness rather than permission.

The sign on the door read "Medical Examiner." Kate walked into a room that smelled as if the same air had been circulating for decades. A man with unruly gray hair sat behind a metal desk, studying crime-scene photos on an iPad. His eyebrows grew together in the middle of a protruding brow, giving him the look of an ancient humanoid. Specks of dry skin had sprinkled down onto his black-framed bifocals. The cigarette, which hung loosely between his lips, propelled him from the Neanderthal era to the present.

"Dr. Mallory?"

He stubbed out his cigarette. "Who wants to know?"

"I'm Kate Caraway. I'm…assisting Sheriff McCrae with an animal abuse investigation."

The guy gave Kate the once-over. "He's the sheriff of Hays County."

"I know who he is."

"I'd like to see the Flores body."

"What does that have to do with animal abuse?"

"It's part of the murder investigation. I was an investigator for the Humane Society of the United States for many years. McCrae asked for my help," Kate lied.

"Sure, he did. You look familiar."

Kate found it hard to believe anyone would recognize her from her book jacket even though the book's publication celebrated a modest success.

"You from Chicago?" he asked.

"I lived there for almost twenty years."

"You're Jack Ryder's wife."

"And you must be a Cub's fan. My husband gets recognized often, but how did you know I was his wife?"

"I spent eleven years in that city. The only good thing about Chicago was the Cubs. I had season tickets. You sat in the next section. I soon figured out you were Ryder's wife. I remember one particular game against the Astros. Your husband clearly made an out at the plate. The umpire didn't see it that way and called the runner safe. The game was over. The Astros won. You went ballistic. In fact, you were often more entertaining than the game."

"Whoever said baseball was boring was an idiot."

He closed his iPad, found his pack of cigarettes, and said, "This way."

He led her to a cold, sickly-smelling room where he slid out the drawer that held Jesús's remains. As soon as Kate saw the deep gash in the left side of his skull, she was certain as to the cause of death.

"He must have slammed hard against the dashboard," Kate said.

"True," Mallory agreed, "but that's not what killed him. "

"What do you mean?"

"Take a closer look." Mallory slipped a pen from his shirt pocket and used it as a pointer. "A blow to the head, even a powerful one, would not splinter the skull like this. He was shot with a .22. The bullet's what killed him."

Jesús looked older than his twenty years. Kate thought of his family in Mexico, waiting to join him for a better life here in United States. Rosa Linda said that Jesús's youngest brother was in and out of trouble, and Jesús wanted to bring him to Texas as soon as possible.

What would happen to his family now? Kate stared down at a face that hadn't even had a chance to wrinkle.

"What do you think happened? He was run off the road, knocked out during the collision, and then shot? That sounds pretty absurd."

"It does. My guess is that someone shot at him while he was driving. That would have caused him to lose control of the pickup. See here," Mallory pointed again. "This side of his face is peppered with glass."

"Someone shot him as he drove by?" Kate asked. "Out there on the ranch?"

"Hey, I'm only telling you what I see here. I can only speculate what happened on the ranch."

On the way back to his office, Mallory said, "What's your husband doing now?"

"Hanging out with me and missing baseball."

Kate thanked him, and as she turned to leave, he called after her, "The Astros are playing the Cubs soon." He handed her his card, winked, and went back to studying his photos.

"Oh, what a tangled web we weave," Kate thought. Maybe, if the Cubs won today, Jack would be too overjoyed to be aware that she was using him. Kate laughed to herself. Jack had once told someone that their relationship was successful because they knew how to use one another. That memory always comforted her. The tension of their early years of marriage had been smoothed by Jack's sense of humor.

Kate took Mallory's card and promised to get back to him about the baseball tickets. Then she looked at her list. It was only two-thirty and she had already rolled several dozen enchiladas, pissed off Wayne Brody, and told a whopper of a lie. She had three and a half hours before she agreed to meet Jack for a glass of wine on the front porch of the bungalow. If she hurried, she could manage a second visit to Guy's ranch and a second meeting with Wayne Brody. Kate looked forward to rustling his feathers again. She wasn't sure what a psychologist would say about this quirk in her intrusive personality, but being a pain in the ass sometimes gave her great joy.

Kate worked best alone and was glad that Rosa Linda had her upcoming wedding to plan and her new fiancé to fuss over. Except for Jack, having people around during an investigation distracted Kate. Her husband kept her feet planted firmly on the ground and her head pointed in the right direction, whether she liked it or not. He had a way with stubborn, irrational people. Maybe Kate could convince Jack to have a talk with Max and find out why he did not like his future son-in-law, but first she needed to find a convenience store and buy a six-pack of Tecáte.

Finding the ranch entrance was easy. Kate drove past an ornate gate marking the main drive. An iron sculpture depicting rolling hills with a river meandering at the base and the words "Fordyce Ranch" etched above the scene hung over the gate. A quarter mile down the road, Kate noticed the service entrance gate was open. She drove in, crossed the cattle guard, and followed the road around the orchard to a huge complex of corrugated tin buildings. There were several vehicles parked in a circular lot, including a trailer filled with cattle. Kate parked out of the way, under the shade of a live oak, and walked over to a group of men getting ready to unload the new arrivals.

A man who looked as if he had spent every waking

moment outdoors stood with a clipboard in hand. He had an unlit stogy clamped between his back teeth as he barked out orders to two young ranch hands. "Make sure you search the east pasture before you turn them out. I don't want to lose any more cattle. Do you hear me?"

"We spent all day driving through that pasture last Monday, boss."

"Well, do it again!"

Kate appreciated the distraction. The boss looked in no mood to socialize with an uninvited guest.

"I'm busy, ma'am. What do you want?"

"Wayne Brody?" Kate asked.

The man pointed his thumb in the direction of the chain-link cages located behind the cattle pen. The sound of barking and whining led her in the right direction. She found Wayne, followed by another guy who was parading a greyhound on a lead.

Wayne unhooked the lanky dog and shoved it into a kennel. "I don't have time for this. If her time doesn't improve, I'll send her down." He stormed off to open another cage. "Guy wants to send these three to River City next week. Run them through again and see if their time improves. If not, I'm sending them down as well."

Wayne's mood looked as if it hadn't improved since lunchtime. Kate wondered if she was the reason.

"You could always put her up for adoption." Kate held up the six-pack. "I'm sure you're not supposed to drink on the job, but it looks as if you need one."

Wayne spun around and the look on his face changed from shock, to pleasure, to suspicion in the two seconds it took him to recognize his visitor. The frustration and uncertainty disappeared, and the tough guy facade returned. He accepted her offering without a second thought.

"I don't drink alone. Come on." He nodded for Kate to follow. They walked behind the kennels through a barn door into a shabby tack room that doubled as an office. The place smelled of horsehair and old leather. Bridles, ropes, straps, and all the tools necessary to keep a ranch in working, order covered every inch of wall space. On the other side of the room, several beat-up file cabinets lined the wall. To the right of the door, two double-drawer file cabinets sat about three feet apart. An old door resided on top of the cabinets, bridging the gap and forming a desk. A sardine can, oil and fish long gone, overflowed with cigarette butts. A few manila folders and half a dozen nubby pencils and leaky pens lay scattered across a desk surface that looked as if it hadn't been dusted since the dawn of man. On the left side sat an old black phone, the type that rang rather than buzzed. Kate looked around at the makeshift office and wondered why Guy Fordyce did not provide his trainer with a more accommodating facility.

While Wayne pulled two beer cans from their plastic holder and stacked the rest in a mini-fridge, Kate walked around the work area. On the other side of the room was a utility kitchen and shower stall. The rod that once held a shower curtain was bent in the center, causing the rings to slide down into the crease. Various cans, bags, bottles of food, and supplements were stacked on shelves. On the drain-board of a stainless-steel sink, a sticky jar of honey sat next to an old, dirty blender stained green from whatever concoction Wayne had mixed up.

Wayne noticed Kate's curiosity. "This place was a real mess before I took over. Seemed like everybody on the ranch used this room at one time or another. I'm still working on cleaning it up. Gomez, Guy's other trainer, was a slob." He handed Kate a beer. "There's a lot to taking care of these dogs."

"I'm sure it's quite a responsibility," Kate said.

"Yep, but I get some of the ranch hands to help when I get too busy. To tell you the truth, working with the dogs is a pain in the ass." Wayne gulped his beer. "Listen, ma'am, I don't know what Jesús's problem was." Wayne parked one hip on the edge of his desk and pulled Bev's pack of Salem out of his shirt pocket. "I've only started working with the greyhounds a short time ago. It ain't my idea of ranching. But when Gomez died of a heart attack a few weeks ago, Guy turned the operation over to me. Guy's been good to me, and he was in a real pinch. But I'd much rather be working with the herd. Cows are stupid. They don't yap or have to be hosed down, or attended to like whiny kids. Guy's considering getting out of the dog business. If he ever stopped long enough to ask my advice, I'd tell him to get rid of the whole dang lot all at once."

"Jesús said the greyhounds are living in poor conditions. Do you know what he was talking about?"

"Mrs. Caraway. You're welcome to look around. If I treated Guy's dogs poorly, he'd fire me in an instant." He dropped his empty beer can in the trash next to his desk and took another from the refrigerator. "Jesús worked with Gomez, and I often saw them arguing. Jesús had a soft spot in his heart for the dogs. From what I could gather, Gomez took good care of the dogs as long as they were winning and earning a good amount."

"What about the slower ones?" Kate asked, not sure that she wanted to hear the answer.

Wayne reached into his pocket and pulled out a

pocketknife. He unfolded a blade and started cleaning his fingernails. "Guy told me that when the dogs started losing to send them to an adoption kennel."

"Okay, but what about Gomez, what did he do with them?"

"Gomez had been with Guy for a long time. He's dead—let's leave it at that. Jesús was a troublemaker. He should have never gotten Rosa Linda involved."

"What do you mean?"

"I mean Jesús and Gomez didn't get along, so Jesús could have been making all of this up. He drank. He lied. I didn't trust him, and I'm not sure what he and Rosa Linda were up to."

"She was helping him with immigration problems involving his family."

"You believe what you want, but if you want to know my opinion, I think Jesús was using her and Guy."

"Using them, how?"

"Like I said before, Jesús was desperate to move his family to the US. At first, I felt sorry for him. I mean, I got a mom in a nursing home in my hometown. She sort of went off her head when my father died. I wish I could afford to bring her here. My sister takes care of her. She works as a secretary at Sul Ross University, but doesn't make that much, so I send her what I can. So, I know how Jesús felt. But something wasn't right. I got the feeling that he was trying to come between Guy and Gomez. You know—stir up trouble and then be the one to put out the fires. Kinda like crying wolf. I tried to talk to Guy once—"

Suddenly the office door few open and Garrison walked in.

"Dickson told me a woman was here nosing around.

You don't listen none too well, do you?" Garrison pointed his finger a few inches away from Kate's face. Beads of sweat glistened on his upper lip.

"Don't you ever knock?" Wayne said.

"You shut the hell up." Garrison turned his gaze to Wayne and noticed the beer. "This ain't no social club. You got work to do, and you—" He pointed back at Kate. "—you were told to stay off this ranch."

Garrison turned on his heel and left.

Chapter Four

Kate and Jack strolled from their bungalow through Olga's garden to the Rodriguez home to attend Guy Fordyce's campaign brunch. The sound of Mariachi music and the spicy aroma of Olga's cooking drifted in on a slight, but welcome, breeze. Kate's hopes rose with anticipation that today might bring some relief from the sweltering temperatures. Then she remembered summertime discomfort in this part of the state did not usually break until mid-autumn, and what she was feeling was merely a tease from the fickle Texas weather.

An eclectic mix of luxury machines crowded the drive. Several four-wheel-drive SUVs, all big and all expensive, dwarfed a Miata, two brand-new Mercedes, and one BMW. Two valets bickered over parking someone's Hummer. Garrison's antiquated vehicle was parked front and center, blocking the steps leading to the front door—clearly not the work of a valet. It amused Kate to think that Garrison had a passive-aggressive way of making his presence known at a brunch that honored his esteemed older brother.

Jack reached over and fastened the hook at the top of Kate's dress. "It's not as quaint as having all of the suspects gathered in the drawing room, but I'm sure that you will have a field day with your investigation."

"My list of suspects is short, and I'm getting conflicting stories," Kate said. "Whoever killed Jesús knew him, and I suspect Jesús knew something and he died because of that information. But murdering someone over an animal abuse situation really puzzles me. Would that be a motive for murder?"

"If someone stands a chance of losing a lot, it would be," Jack said.

"You mean Guy Fordyce?"

"I mean anyone."

"Where did you get that sports coat?"

"I bought it yesterday afternoon. Like it? I didn't exactly have time to mull over my packing before we left."

"I like it very much." Although she rarely shopped for Jack, Kate felt a twinge of guilt. They had been back in the United States only a few days, and all Kate could think about was returning to Kenya. But it was becoming clear to her that Jack was happier to be home than he let on.

"Speaking of new clothes?"

"The dress is Olga's. I haven't had time to shop."

A man and woman whom Kate figured were the guests of honor stood in a receiving line at the entrance to the garden, greeting some of Central Texas's wealthy democrats. Expecting a tall, slender, stereotypic Texan, she was surprised to see that Guy was about her height. His stocky frame appeared too bulky to fit comfortably under his Italian-made jacket. Dark eyes enhanced by his fair complexion and set deep within his weather-beaten face, showed the fervor and passion of a man with a lengthy agenda for life. His throaty laughter carried across the garden and sounded to Kate too forced to be real. Laughing at bad jokes, she guessed, was part of a politician's job, and campaigning for senator looked natural on him.

Meredith Fordyce stood close to her husband, holding on to his arm as she smiled and greeted their guests. She was model-thin and stood a couple of inches taller than Guy. Her auburn hair matched her sunbaked skin, both nicely reflecting the rose color of her Hermes suit. A pearl necklace draped over the neckline of her cream silk blouse. Her Jimmy Choo heels were the exact color of her outfit. No doubt, this woman spent a lot of time on her wardrobe, but the dark rings under her eyes made her otherwise flawless appearance seem a bit worse for wear.

As the last guests arrived, Olga ushered Meredith to a table of equally well-dressed women whose jolly conversation waned when Meredith sat down. What does one say to a woman who had recently lost a child? As she accepted a glass of champagne from an accommodating waiter, her frozen smile set the tone at the table.

"Dr. Caraway? I recognize you from the photos in your book."

So engrossed with watching Meredith Fordyce, Kate was not aware that Guy had joined her and Jack.

"And the famous Jack Ryder. I was in the stands the day you caught your last game in Chicago. Sure hated to lose you. There's serious talk about your name being on the ballot for the Hall of Fame."

"Mr. Fordyce, glad to meet you. I think the only thing I gained after twenty years behind home plate are bad knees." Jack laughed and shook hands with the guest of honor. "Max and Olga have been singing your praises since my wife and I arrived a couple of days ago. So, you're a baseball fan?"

"I follow the Astros when they're winning. Meredith and I were in Chicago on business and we decided to take in a game. I was surprised to learn that you were retiring, but—" Guy looked at Kate. "—I can understand why a new life in Africa looked appealing." He extended his hand to Kate. "No offense, Mr. Ryder, but I have to admit that I am more a fan of your wife. Dr. Caraway, your book, *The Politics of Poaching*, read like a thriller. I'm happy to see you two survived the poaching wars."

"Nice to meet you, Mr. Fordyce. Please call me Kate. The war is far from over, though. We only won a few battles."

"In my naivety, I assumed elephants living in a national park were protected."

"For the most part they are, but during times of drought, they wander away from the preserve in search of food where they are often shot."

"The park rangers can't prevent that?"

"In some cases, the rangers are the poachers. I established my program to document relationship dynamics within family units. Jack and I soon learned we had to keep our subjects alive before we could conduct research."

Kate had a dozen questions for Fordyce, but knew this wasn't the right time. Jack always reminded her that any decorum she possessed dissipated quickly when she became anxious. As much as she hated to admit it, he was right.

Before she could decide on her approach, Max interrupted them. "Guy," he said, "you are wanted elsewhere."

Max raised his eyebrows at Kate as if to remind her

that this was a campaign brunch, not a murder investigation.

"Not quite what I expected," Kate said, taking a glass of champagne from Jack.

"What did you expect?"

"The good old' boy type. Not someone so polished."

"Mr. Ryder," Maria touched Jack on the arm, "you have a phone call. You can take it in Mr. Rodriguez's office."

"Be nice." Jack left, and Kate had a few moments to peruse the crowd before she saw Olga waving her over to the table of once lighthearted, but now stoic, women trying to make small talk with Meredith Fordyce. As Kate walked over, she noticed the waiters bringing out the last of Olga's dishes, and Kate hoped that the buffet line would begin soon.

The humidity was rising and her feet were beginning to hurt. Shorts, T-shirts, and hiking boots made up the entirety of her African wardrobe. If someone had told her last week that she'd be dressed in heels, rubbing elbows with the cream of Wimberley's crop, Kate would have never believed them. She sat down, and Olga made introductions.

Meredith Fordyce was not as talkative as her charming husband. Pretending to listen to the conversation, her painted-on smile gave her away. As the women chatted about socially polite issues, Meredith nodded occasionally to show her agreement. Even though they spoke of benign and harmless topics, the tension in the air was thick. Kate wondered about the death of Meredith and Guy's daughter. Do parents ever recover from losing a child? The incident was too recent not to be foremost on everyone's mind. Small talk was like placing a blanket over the rubble left by a house fire, too flimsy to hide the smoldering remains. No one spoke of life's misfortunes. Not a word mentioned about Meredith's attack, Jesús's murder, or children who strayed and were lost forever.

Kate, wishing she were anywhere but at this table, looked around and noticed that Rosa Linda and Daniel had arrived. Ever since her conversation with Wayne, Kate felt that Rosa Linda had not told Kate the complete story of Guy and his greyhounds. As Kate rose to join the young couple, Olga started moving people toward the buffet table.

"You need a real strong hint, don't you? You got a lot of nerve to be on the ranch drinking beer with the help."

Startled, Kate turned to see Garrison Fordyce standing behind her. His eyes were as red as the stripes on his tie and although sober at the moment, the bourbon and coke he was drinking would soon take care of that.

"I made my presence known this time," Kate said.

"Known, but not welcomed. It's my job to look after things. Guy can't be bothered with trespassers, and I plan to see to it that his operation runs smoothly. Snooping around the ranch can be dangerous."

Knowing that Garrison was blowing smoke, Kate couldn't resist playing his bullshit game. "That's some job, overseeing the operation of a five-thousand-acre ranch. Guy's lucky to have you."

"Damn right. If it wasn't for me, things would turn to shit."

"From what I've heard, the ranch has been plagued with problems recently. Tell me, Garrison, how did you manage to straighten things out so quickly?"

Garrison's face turned a deep crimson, and his jaw clinched so hard Kate expected to hear his molars crack any second.

Feeling a bit ornery, Kate pushed a little harder. "Looks like your job isn't finished, seeing as how a man was murdered on the ranch two days ago."

Garrison choked on his bourbon, and before he could catch his breath, Kate left while she still had the last word.

Kate sauntered to the buffet table and grabbed a plate. Jack joined her in the serving line. They worked their way across a sea of exquisite food: shrimp ceviche with poblano peppers and fresh cilantro, black bean and corn salad, enchiladas Verde smothered in white cheese sauce, and chili rellenos topped with raisins and green olives. Alongside the main courses, were dishes of queso dip, guacamole dip, mole sauce, and chopped jalapenos. And finally, small dishes of Olga's famous espresso flan sat ready to cool palettes after the spicy meal. Punch bowls of mimosas, mango-vodka punch, and watermelon rum decorated the end of the buffet table. Under a blanket of ice, a variety of Mexican beers cooled in a huge ceramic vat. A bartender, dressed in black slacks and a white shirt with a serape draped over his shoulder, served drinks.

Kate piled a heap of tortilla chips on her plate beside a fruit salsa, and reached for a glass of mango punch. Jack brushed her cheek with the back of his finger and said, "Can you behave yourself for a couple of days?"

Those resident butterflies fluttered in her stomach, and she forced a smile. "Going to Chicago?"

"Only for two days. Bill Summers wants to visit." He moved a step closer, touched her elbow, and with that sincere look that could melt away her tough veneer, he said, "We can't go back to camp now. The staff will handle everything in the meantime. Besides, we need a break." He tucked a wayward strand of her hair behind her ear. "I'll return to Africa with you whenever the time comes. You know that, don't you?"

She did, without a doubt. "And if Bill offers you a position on the team," she said, "you must take it."

Kate squeezed his arm. Life's conflicts always strengthened their relationship. She only wished that they didn't come with such a healthy dose of anguish.

Over coffee and dessert, Guy started his campaign speech. He spoke of bridging the gap between the environmentalists, who believed they have a natural claim to the Hill Country's beauty, and the developers who want the entire world to enjoy it. The battle between the two factions began in the seventies when Austin and the surrounding countryside made the headlines as one of the best places in the country to live. The quality of life received high marks in almost every category. The environment was clean, the music and cultural world had put Austin on the map, and the cost of living was inexpensive. In the past forty years, a steady stream of new arrivals, to the tune of a thousand people a month, transformed this quaint university city of three hundred thousand into a metropolis of more than a million people.

The countryside west of Austin, spreading out into the Hill Country, had been scalped and developed to the point that one subdivision flowed into the next. Huge, expensive homes dotted the landscape, what was once a vast green expanse of trees was now home to some of the wealthiest people in the county. At one time, driving west of Austin meant a leisurely trip to view the wildflowers and a chance to commune with nature. Now the bumper-to-bumper traffic flowing into the city snaked all the way from Lake Travis twenty miles away. Ironically, the quality of life that had lured people here was disappearing as fast as the influx of humanity flowed in.

The small communities of Wimberley and Dripping Springs had managed to retain their charm, but with the encroaching development, it was only a matter of time before they became swallowed up in a sea of luxury homes. In his speech, Guy promised to save what was left of the Hill Country surrounding Wimberley, the one problem that concerned everyone in Hays County.

Listening to his speech, Kate had almost forgotten why she was here. She could almost see herself voting for him if she had been a registered voter. Although she saw the sincerity in Guy's face and heard the passion in his voice, something seemed out of place. Could this man be as concerned for the needs of his neighbors and the environment, and still neglect his greyhounds? These days the media scrutinized politicians down to the minutest details of their lives. Was Guy so naive he believed his earnest desire for making a difference would overshadow such skeletons in his closet? Kate didn't think so.

When the party broke up, Olga invited a few friends to stay for more coffee and conversation. Guy, Meredith, Rosa Linda, Daniel, and two other couples whom Kate had not yet met went up to the verandah while the staff cleared away the buffet. Max seemed pleased with the event and could not speak Guy's name without preceding it with "our next state senator."

Rosa Linda grabbed Kate's hand and brought her

over to meet a man who looked as if he had played fullback in his younger days. His gold-rimmed glasses and thinning hair did not take away from his appearance. In fact, it added a sense of intelligence and integrity. "Kate, I want you to meet one of my favorite people, Bradford Gates. He's a vet and has volunteered a great deal of time and medicine to the greyhound-adoption program."

"Dr. Gates, thanks for assisting my goddaughter in her new endeavor," Kate said.

"Call me Brad. Rosa Linda told me why you're here." He lowered his voice. "Tomorrow's my day at the dog track. I supervise the races and take care of the dogs if there's an injury. I can arrange for a guest pass for you." He glanced at Rosa Linda. "The first race is at eleven."

"I'll be there," Kate said and turned to Rosa Linda for a clue to the clandestine nature of his invitation, but received none. "Think we can make that first race? I want to ask—"

"Daniel and I are driving to Laredo in the morning," Rosa Linda interrupted. "He wants to shoot some scenes around Casa Blanca Lake near the Rio Grande. We won't be back until Tuesday."

Before Kate could respond, Guy Fordyce was on his feet, and heading in their direction. Rosa Linda wasted no time in making her retreat. "Excuse me, I need to help Mom. She hasn't sat down all morning." Rosa Linda turned and was gone again.

Kate had learned to trust her intuition a long time ago, and now she was certain that Rosa Linda was avoiding not only Guy, but Kate as well. She was here to get answers, but, so far, she was coming up dry. She turned to speak to Brad, but he had disappeared also.

Too many secrets and even more questions. What had Jesús discovered on the Fordyce ranch two days ago that led to his murder? Did it have anything to do with the greyhounds? And the most perplexing question, why was Rosa Linda holding something back if she was so anxious for Kate to get involved? Questions left Kate feeling uneasy and suspicious. She hated not knowing—it brought on a barrage of loathsome baggage and frightful feelings from her childhood.

When life became overwhelming, she would remember a recurring dream-turned-nightmare that started right after her mother's death. Kate was stacking blocks, arranging them according to size, much like she did with the bones in her father's anthropology lab. The sense of order gave her a feeling of safety and security. All of a sudden, an intense loneliness enveloped her, and the task grew too enormous for a little girl.

Then darkness swallowed the room, shocking her awake into a cold sweat and the painful reminder that her mother was gone.

It had been years since she had thought about that nightmare. Looking around and taking instant stock of her situation, Kate suddenly became aware there were no neatly stacked blocks in her life right now.

Laughter broke her reverie, and she looked around at the people on the verandah. Now that the formalities were over, they all appeared more relaxed, even Meredith Fordyce seemed to breathe a little easier. Was it because she was no longer in the limelight, or because the alcohol had soothed her nerves?

"Well, how did I do?" Kate turned around and saw Guy, minus his suit-jacket and tie, looking more like a

Central Texas rancher.

"I'd vote for you," Kate said.

"That's all I wanted to hear. Running for state senator is a real chore. I have to say the right things to the right people, make everyone happy, and enjoy doing it. Sometimes I wonder if I have what it takes."

"And what does it take?" His candor surprised Kate.

"I'm not always sure. You start off passionate about your beliefs and want to make a difference then quickly discover that it's not that easy. Compromise comes into play, and the game's off and running." He unbuttoned his shirtsleeves and rolled them up to his elbows. "You have to remember what you've promised and why. And you promise a lot of things. But I guess honesty is the main quality, and the most difficult to maintain."

"Why is that so hard?"

"Because politicians lie. Not that they mean to, but it happens, and the reason behind it is often a noble one. I'm not making sense." He rubbed his hands across his face. "But I'm sure you've experienced the same thing."

"How's that?" Kate said defensively.

"With your operation in Kenya. Your intention was to save elephants, and you end up in the middle of a political struggle."

"I like to think I maintained my integrity."

"We all do. It's been a crazy two days. Holden McCrae told me that you and Rosa Linda were on the ranch Friday, and that you found Jesús's pickup."

"Jesús seemed to think that some of your greyhounds were mistreated. He said something about finding their bodies."

"Dogs die, Dr. Caraway—Kate. That doesn't mean they've been mistreated. We had a situation recently where a few young dogs came down with parvo. We lost three."

"They weren't vaccinated?"

"Not in time. That was probably what Jesús was referring to when he spoke to Rosa Linda. He had not been around long enough to know about raising dogs. He overreacted."

"People aren't brutally murdered and tied to a cross for overreacting."

"Jesús was a troubled young man. Like I told Holden, if he wants to find out why Jesús was murdered, go to Mexico and start looking there. I don't seem to have my checkbook with me, but come by the ranch this week. I'd like to make a donation to your wildlife organization. I believe in what you're doing. You not being a voter proves that."

Kate welcomed the chance to speak with Guy alone, even if she suspected his interest in her foundation was not as sincere as he let on.

But if Guy thought he could buy her off, Kate had no problem playing that game as well.

Guy left to join his wife, and Daniel sat down beside Kate.

"Man, it's so hot, I'd like to strip down to my shorts and jump in that pool. I guess if I did that I wouldn't be making a good impression."

"Speaking of which, why does Max cringe when you walk in the room?" Kate said.

"You get right to the point, don't you?" Daniel did not look perturbed by her question, which was a good sign, since he was marrying into a family that wore their abruptness on their sleeves. "Would any man be good enough for Max Rodriguez's daughter?"

"I think that Max would give anything to guarantee Rosa Linda's happiness. And you seem to make her happy."

"Yes, but can I make her wealthy?"

"I think you have Max all wrong. He doesn't care about that."

"Yes, he does. Sociologists don't get rich, and migrant workers don't leave their children an inheritance. He had hoped for better for Rosa Linda."

"Did he tell you that?"

"Not in so many words. Do you know what my parents are doing as I sit here drinking champagne with wealthy Mexicans, Dr. Caraway? They are picking tomatoes in the Valley. I come from a family of migrant workers. Do you know what it is like to pick someone else's land for barely enough money to live on? Look at Guy Fordyce running for senator and talking about the environment. Is he aware that illegal workers are pouring into this area to work on ranches like his? How could he possibly know what it's like for the less fortunate?" Daniel paused and looked around. "I'm sorry, I know that you are not like many of these people."

Kate looked around too, and it was apparent that not one person in the room likely ever had to worry about financing their education. And for the first time, Kate noticed what seemed like a natural ability to finesse his way around any crowd was only a method of survival, for it was clear Daniel Martinez had an underlying feeling of not belonging.

"Give him a chance, Daniel. Max will come around."

"He's never even asked about my family, my father's name. How he feels about me being the first

Martinez to go to college. He's never even asked. He turns up his nose and walks away as if he smells something bad when I walk into the room, as if—" Daniel stopped in mid-sentence, and Kate turned to see Holden McCrae, accompanied by two other officers, walking up to the verandah.

The chatter stopped as he approached Guy Fordyce. "Mr. Fordyce, can we go inside?"

"Right now?" Guy asked.

"It can't wait."

Everyone watched as McCrae and his officers followed Guy into the house. Max, Olga, and Meredith were close behind.

"What's that all about?" Daniel asked.

A few minutes later, Olga rushed over.

"Katie, help me with Meredith. Guy's been arrested for Jesús's murder."

Chapter Five

Kate had considered renting a car while she and Jack were in Wimberley, but the Rodriguez household had more vehicles than drivers. When Kate asked if she could borrow Rosa Linda's Jeep to drive Jack to the airport, Rosa Linda had graciously offered her wheels for Kate's service as long as she needed.

Kate and Jack started out early, and she hoped to use the hour's drive to the airport to discuss the inevitability of living in Chicago again if Jack returned to major league baseball. Sensing his excitement, she wanted to share in his good fortune, but with the situation on the ranch heating up, she needed him here.

Besides, contemplating a major lifestyle change was not something she wanted to deal with just yet, and maybe not for a while. But the events of the previous evening spun around in her mind, and she wasn't able to find the words.

They made the drive in silence and as they approached the airport, Kate said, "Call me as soon as you hear something, and good luck."

"I will." Jack placed his hand on her thigh and gave it a tender squeeze. "You okay with this?"

She covered his hand with hers and squeezed back. "Sure. Tell everyone that I said 'hi,' and make sure Gary buys you dinner at Shaw's. Don't let him off cheap."

She exited onto Terminal Drive and started to pull

into the short-term parking lane.

"Don't park. Drop me off. I know you're anxious to get back and find out what happened to Guy."

"Are you sure?"

"Kate, I'll be back in two days. I know it's useless for me to tell you to get some rest, but your healthy glow is beginning to look a bit tattered."

She pulled up to the curb. Jack grabbed his bag, gave her a kiss, and started toward the terminal. Kate slid down the window. "Hey, come back here."

Jack leaned in the window.

"You're wearing new jeans."

"Do they make my butt look big?"

"I don't think that's possible. You look terrific."

"So do you. Promise me you'll wear those shorts every day for the rest of your life."

"Thanks for being a low-maintenance husband, and bring me something from Chicago. Maybe Anthony Rizzo's signature on a baseball."

"He's been traded, honey, sorry." Jack winked.

Kate watched as Jack wove his way through the crowd of travelers. Her dark mood lifted when he turned around and blew her a kiss. She laughed and left the airport.

Kate had two hours before her scheduled meeting with Brad Gates at eleven, enough time to drive to Austin for breakfast and a newspaper before driving to the River City Racetrack. The last time Kate visited the state capital, Olga had taken her to the Magnolia Cafe for an Austin-style breakfast. The thoughts of that fabulous down-home, Tex-Mex meal brought on hunger pangs. Then she recalled the long line of patrons that snaked around the outside of the restaurant and knew that she would be late if she had to wait for a table. She needed a restaurant where she could be sure to get in and out in a short amount of time. Remembering Katz's Deli from her college years, she drove down West Sixth Street, turned onto Rio Grande, drove back around and realized that the Austin institution was gone. Angie's Bar and Grill beckoned Kate with its sandwich board announcing breakfast. She parked in the back lot, grabbed the *Statesman* from the newspaper rack, and walked inside. A waitress—who had the entire surface area of both ears pierced, hole punched, and studded with metal—seated Kate immediately. Her bagel and cream cheese arrived shortly thereafter. Glad that she had opted for a lighter meal, Kate smeared cream cheese on her bagel and then stopped in mid-bite.

The bold, blocked-letter headlines read loud and clear. "Senatorial Candidate Arrested for Murder." She put her bagel down and read further. It was all there—motive, means, and opportunity. According to the Hays County Sheriff's Department, Jesús Flores had been blackmailing his employer. The authorities found Fordyce's gun near the murder site, and a reliable witness overheard Fordyce threaten to kill Flores a few minutes before the murder. Fordyce could not account for his whereabouts at the time of the murder, and, according to Sheriff Holden McCrae, "We had no choice, but to pick him up." The *Statesman* reported that Fordyce had returned to his ranch after being released on bail. He could not be reached for comment.

Blackmail? *What reason would Jesús have for blackmailing the one person who could help him stay in this country?* Kate thought. Jesús needed Guy. And who was this witness? Kate needed answers and she wouldn't find any sitting here. Washing her bagel down with large gulps of coffee, she gathered up the newspaper to leave.

"You're a crazy fool."

A shriek of laughter caught Kate's attention. A woman doubled over in a fit of giggles sat in the booth near the kitchen. She looked as if she had just come off duty from the Gentlemen's Club in South Austin. Her breasts poured out the sides of a red sports bra, slightly hidden under a droopy tank top. She wore a black spandex skirt too small for her butt, and, with her legs crossed, her leopard-print panties peeped out at the top of her thigh. Across the table, laughing as hard, and starting to choke, sat Garrison Fordyce. The skimpily clad Miss Florence Nightingale jumped up and, stumbling over her stiletto heels, reached over, and slapped him on the back. The gesture caused them to laugh harder. He finally caught his breath, and the woman darted toward the bathroom, swaying and careening off the chairs like a steel ball in a pinball machine.

Garrison waved his empty glass at the waitress. "Two more bloody marys."

It seemed that the younger Fordyce was not too upset over the arrest of his older brother. Kate grabbed a coffee-to-go, and left the restaurant before Garrison noticed her.

****

As Kate drove down Fifth Street to pick up Interstate 35, she feared she might have miscalculated the time needed to drive to the racetrack. Even at this time of the morning, traffic moving east through downtown inched along like a slow-moving caterpillar. As she reached Congress Avenue, movement in all four lanes stopped—

a construction crane creeping across the intersection had blocked traffic.

Kate prayed for patience. Being late for an appointment threw her into a frenzy, and if traffic was this bad in the heart of the city, I-35 promised to be worse. One mile and twenty minutes later, Kate finally saw the south entrance to the interstate.

She nosed her way between a cattle truck and a Ford Escort, and entered what was known as the suicide gauntlet—the eighty-mile stretch of pavement between Austin and San Antonio. The traffic eased, and as soon as she reached the outskirts of the city, she accelerated to seventy-five and set the cruise control.

Before she left the bungalow, Olga instructed Kate how to access the iTunes on the radio. Kate scanned her choices and made a selection—Bruce Springsteen's latest release. She sipped her coffee, and tried to relax, letting her mind sort things out in the quiet of her enclosed mobile world.

Guy certainly did not act like someone who had committed a morbid murder. If the greyhound abuse became public, the bad press would tarnish his reputation and possibly cause him to lose the election, but it would not ruin him. Kate was certain that the greyhound issue would not lead to murder. Perhaps Jesús had tried to blackmail Guy for another reason.

Then it occurred to her that considering all of the misfortunes Guy had been through lately, this might have been the push that toppled him. What happens, she wondered, when someone has "gone over the edge" as they say? Does that person enter a world of serene complacency—a place where conscience no longer exits, where the primal instinct to survive is so strong that it destroys millions of years of moral and ethical evolution? Had Jesús pushed Guy too hard? Desperate people kill, but killing Jesús was not enough. Hanging him from the cross proved the act of a madman. None of this made sense. Kate wondered if living in the bush for the past few years had dulled her ability to read people.

She took a sip of her coffee, and as she reached over to place the cup in the holder on the console, she glanced up into the review mirror. Her heart jumped into her throat. In a split second, a full-ton pickup swerved from the left lane and edged so close behind the Jeep she couldn't see the pickup's grill.

"What in the hell are you doing?" she shouted.

She slammed down on the accelerator to put some distance between them, but the driver, invisible behind tinted windows, stayed on her bumper. She looked over and found that the traffic in the left lane had thinned. She swerved to the left and the driver of the pickup followed. Kate sped up and turned sharply back into the right lane, only to have this maniac mirror her every move. Her pulse beat hard in her veins, and panic started to surface. If she attempted to brake and slow him down, he'd plow into the back of Rosa Linda's Jeep. Kate flicked on her blinker, hoping he would ease up if she began to pull over. No luck. He stuck to her as if the two vehicles were tethered. Then the driver did the unthinkable, he edged even closer, and nudged her bumper. Kate jolted forward as the speedometer hovered near eighty-five. She gripped the wheel, and for a second time in as many seconds, terror struck like a lightning bolt. Up ahead, a flashing sign warned of a right-lane closure, and the traffic was backing up. Soon she'd be boxed in between a row of cars on her left and an embankment on her right.

As she fast approached the barrier, her only choices were to slam on the brakes and brace herself for a rear-end impact, hoping her neck would withstand the force, or veer off to the right shoulder, praying that she would stay on the pavement long enough to slow down and not careen off into the ditch. Behind the road barrier sat a transportation department truck loaded with hot asphalt. If she hit the barrier, she'd plow into the truck and Kate Caraway would be a thing of the past. She tapped her brakes, and veered to the right.

The driver of the truck slammed on its brakes and swerved into the left lane, causing cars to scatter like billiard balls. Then the driver plowed across the median, jumped into the northbound lane, and disappeared.

It was too late for Kate to brake safely. As she jerked the Jeep to the right, her hot coffee flew into the air and onto her thigh.

Too numb with fear to feel pain, Kate's only intention was to hang on and keep the Jeep from rolling. She was driving too fast to stay on the shoulder and after the coffee left its cup, the Jeep left the road. The force pitched the Jeep upward, and Kate was airborne.

After what seemed like an eternity, the vehicle landed hard, jarring every bone in her body. Her brain shook in her skull and she felt as if her teeth had cracked on impact.

She was still unable to gain control. The Jeep careened up to the other side of the embankment, and, as quickly as she left the highway, she was on pavement again, heading south on the service road. But the Jeep remained upright and, although still swerving, she was able to regain control.

Kate pulled over onto the shoulder of the service

road and stopped. Too stunned to move, she dropped her forehead onto the steering wheel.

She wasn't sure how long she sat there when she heard someone shout, "Ma'am, are you okay?"

She looked up to see three men from the highway crew running over.

"Someone call nine-one-one. I think she's hurt."

Kate uncurled her fingers from the wheel, and opened the door. "No, I'm fine, just a bit shaken up."

"Lady, when we saw you heading toward us, we thought we were all goners. How you kept from rolling over is a miracle. That guy behind you in the white truck was a lunatic. Are you sure you're okay?"

Every muscle in her body shook. She tried to stand, but her knees buckled. "I just need to sit here for a moment."

"Are you sure you don't want me to call for help? Besides, that guy needs to be reported to the police."

"He's long gone by now. I'll be fine in a minute." Then her voice froze deep in her throat. As shock started to set in, everything disappeared from Kate's mind. The only thing she could focus on was the coffee splashed all over the inside of Rosa Linda's Jeep. Unable to control her emotions, she started to cry.

Against her protest, the guy unclipped his cellphone from his belt and called the highway patrol. Within minutes, a state trooper was taking down their statements. "Get the license-plate number?" he asked.

"Are you kidding?" the guy said. "He was racing around like a madman."

"How about you, ma'am?" he asked Kate.

"He was so close to my bumper, I couldn't even see the grill. But the pickup was a white, late model Dodge-

Ram dually."

"Yeah," the guy said. "It also had a red and white *Succeed* bumper sticker on the left rear bumper."

"Anyone see the person driving?"

The three men shook their heads.

"The windshield was tinted," Kate said.

"I'll radio in the information, but there's not much chance of finding this guy unless he causes another accident. Are you okay to drive, ma'am?"

"I'm fine."

"I'll be off then." He walked back to his patrol car and drove away.

Kate regained her composure and thanked the highway crew for their assistance. Before she pulled back on the highway, she called the racetrack and left a message for Brad that she was running a few minutes late. Still a bit shaky, she held on to the Jeep and walked around looking for dents and scrapes. Amazingly, it appeared that the only damage came from the coffee stains on the floor mats. Feeling a bit silly for letting her mind wander while driving on the interstate, she pulled back into the line of traffic, and was glad to see a stream of cars creeping along at thirty miles-per-hour. The lane closure continued as far as the eye could see, which suited Kate. She had no desire to travel any faster.

Half-an-hour later, as she approached the outskirts of San Marcos, Kate spotted a billboard advertising the River City Racetrack. The turquoise building stood just off the service road. A flashing marquee announced the time of the next race, while neon greyhounds sprinted down the track. Surprised to see so many racing fans here on a weekday, Kate had to park several rows away from the entrance, as the massive parking lot was almost full.

Before entering the gate, she purchased a program from a woman whose curly gray hair was held atop of her head by a purple scarf and a River City Racing Staff visor. A builder's apron, wrapped around her thin waist, bulged with coins. As Kate fished change out of her pocket, the woman greeted her with a friendly Texas drawl. She spoke from the left corner of her mouth, while dangling a lit cigarette from the right.

"First time here, hon?" She looked down at Kate's blistered leg. "You may want to spend a few extra bucks and buy a ticket for a seat in the Club House, so you can stay outta the sun. It's only four bucks. No use burnin' that pretty face as well. The first race just got started."

Kate smiled. Her fellow Texans had a way of making strangers feel at home without being intrusive. "I'm fine. Hot coffee and interstate driving don't mix. Bradford Gates has arranged for a guest pass for me. Do you know where I can pick it up? I also need directions to his office."

"Sure, hon. Go to the first ticket window." She pointed with her cigarette. "Your pass should be there. At the end of the betting windows, you'll see a row of offices on the right. The second door is the "PR" room. They'll call Dr. Gates for you." She took a deep pulled on her cigarette. A precarious ash fell off the end and dusted the right side of her apron. "Good luck, hon."

Kate thanked her and walked toward the entrance of the track. It was a few minutes after eleven, and Kate was eager to see the dogs run and get a feel for the world of greyhound racing. Instead, obligation and curiosity led her in search of the vet. She found the door marked Public Relations, and walked inside a cool air-conditioned room.

A young girl, who looked to be of high-school age, sat behind a counter reading a paperback with a bare-chested, muscle-bound vampire on the cover. A smiley face was hand-drawn on a nametag that read Tammy. She shifted on her stool, aware that Kate had walked in, but continued reading for a moment longer. Then she reached for a used ticket stub, marked her place, and reluctantly closed the book.

She looked up at Kate with clear blue eyes that sparkled with a vacancy that told Kate that Tammy's heart was clearly in her romance novel rather than in her job.

Tammy sighed and folded her hands over the cover of her book. "May I help you?"

"Can you tell me where I can find Dr. Gates? I had an appointment with him at eleven. I'm afraid I'm late."

"Sure, I'll call him." Tammy picked up the phone and punched in the numbers.

Kate took the opportunity to look around the room. A huge window in the back overlooked the track, and Kate noticed the results of the first race flashing on the board.

"He's on his way, ma'am," Tammy said. "You can watch the dogs from the window if you want. I've seen them run so many times, that I get bored...well, you know? Is this your first time to the track?"

Did Kate look so out of place? Tammy was the second person who had asked her that question in the past five minutes. "I can arrange for a personal tour before you leave, you know, explain the betting process and the works," Tammy said.

"Thanks for the offer. I would like to see a few races. The park seemed fairly full today, but you don't seem very busy here."

"Yeah, well most of the people who come to bet on the races are regulars, and even though we have many visitors—tourists that stop by in the summer—they come to watch a few races. It's easy to find your way around the park. When we first opened, we had several tours a day, you know, press and that sort of thing."

"That's not true any longer?"

"The Louisiana casinos have been drawing a lot of gamblers across the state line. Some of the horse and dog tracks in Texas have closed, but the River City track is doing fairly well."

"Kate, thanks for coming." Bradford Gates walked in and wasted no time with handshakes. He ushered her out of the office as if this were the last place he wanted her to be. "I felt bad about the sudden invitation yesterday, but I know why you're here, and I want to help. We can talk more in my office."

Getting the message, Kate turned the conversation to small talk. "I had no idea that the dog races drew such a crowd."

"A lot of people don't know what to do with their time, or money. Throwing it away on a few moments of excitement is their choice."

On the way to his office, Brad waved and greeted several people by their first name, but as soon as he closed the door, his friendly facade turned serious.

He pulled a folding chair out for Kate, and sat behind his desk. "I have to be very careful around here— for several reasons. Lately, I've had to remind myself why I became a vet. My career is hanging by a thin thread, I've lost a lot already, and…well, after what's happened recently, I'm prepared to lose a lot more. I hope you understand."

"Understand?" Kate felt every tense moment in the last few days crash down on her head, losing what little patience she had left. "I came here to investigate an animal abuse case, so my recent unemployment wouldn't get the best of me. I've been here for three days. I have not seen any suffering dogs. Instead, a man's been murdered, and a dog owner and senatorial candidate has been arrested. Forgive me if I sound impatient, but I almost rolled my Jeep on the way over here. I've scalded my leg with hot coffee, and my husband is off planning a new career. Some days I wake up, and I'm not sure what country I'm in."

Brad laughed. "Sounds like you've had a bad morning. Forgive me. I guess I shouldn't have laid all of that on you." He walked over to a cabinet and took out a tube of ointment. "Here, try this. I use it on the dogs, but it's a basic antibiotic-inflammatory gel, and it will cool that scalded skin. But be careful when you go to sleep tonight, you may have a strong desire to curl up at the foot of the bed."

"Thanks. Sorry about that outburst. I promise to quit whining and listen."

"Let me back up. Until this last year, I spent much of my time at my animal clinic. The vet who worked here at the track left for greener pastures, and they asked me to fill in until a replacement could be found. Actually, Guy was the one who asked me. At the time, he sat on the River City board of directors. To make a long story short, I didn't like what I saw—dogs running in the heat of the summer and collapsing during races, dogs living their entire lives in cages at the track. I also began to hear rumors about the abusive training of some of the dogs. I had had it with one particular trainer whose dogs saw more time in this office than on the track. This guy broke every rule in the book. I reported the infractions to the Board, but because of the political nature of this business, nothing happened, and the trainer continued to run his dogs, and the dogs continued to incur injuries and worse."

"Couldn't you get him banned from the track?"

"I did more than that, unfortunately. I finally went to the press with my findings, and all hell broke loose. A reporter conducted an investigation that ultimately led to the trainer's arrest, but in the meantime, my name became associated with the so-called bad guys at the dog-racing track. You know how rumors get started. Many people assumed that I was part of the abuse. Then my appointment book at the clinic began to have too many blank spaces. My accountant wants me to consider bankruptcy. Partly out of guilt, but mainly because there weren't any vets lined up outside anxiously waiting to take over as track vet, the Board hired me part-time under the condition that I kept my mouth shut."

"Why didn't Guy speak up on your behalf? After all, he was responsible for getting you into this mess."

"By that time, Guy's term on the Board had expired, and he had begun planning his senatorial campaign. But that's not what I wanted to talk to you about."

"I didn't think so. I'm listening."

"Several of the Fordyce dogs have died in the past few weeks."

"I know, Guy told me about the parvo."

"That's not what I mean. Dogs here at the track." He unlocked a desk drawer and pulled out a small notebook.

"Everything's officially recorded here in the office,

but for my own benefit, I've started keeping personal notes. Four dogs in the past two weeks. Three died while racing and one was found dead in the kennel right before a race."

"What happened?"

"I can't explain it. Two of the dogs that died on the track actually collapsed while running, the other soon after. They had convulsions and died a few minutes later."

"What does Guy have to say about it?"

"Not much."

"Have any of the other dogs died here at the kennel?"

"No. Guy doesn't keep his dogs at the track kennel, though. Since he lives nearby, his trainer brings them up the morning of the race."

"That's kind of unusual from what I've learned about greyhound racing."

"Yeah, well, Guy Fordyce is used to making his own rules."

"Any ideas what—" Before Kate could ask her question, the phone rang.

"Excuse me." Brad answered, and wiped a hand over his face. "Right, I'm on my way. We have another dog that's collapsed. Here's my card, call me at my clinic later."

"Not so fast. I'm coming with you."

The back of Gates's office opened up to the track-yard where dozens of dogs looked out at the world from their confinement. A dog handler hurried toward Gates, carrying a greyhound. The dog was convulsing. Its legs flayed so wildly, the handler had a difficult time holding the animal.

When Kate saw the greyhound, she stopped dead in her tracks. At first, she thought she was looking at Luna. The dog had the same coloring.

"Put her down on the table in my office, Mike." Brad quickly removed the muzzle and palpated the dog's neck and chest. He reached for a vial and injected a needle into the dog's neck. But by that time, the dog's body had gone slack. Brad picked up the stethoscope and listened to its chest, then raised its eyelids and examined them with a light scope. "We're gonna lose this one. Bring me the dog's papers, and tell the owner that I'll call him this afternoon. I want to perform an autopsy this time."

"Probably the heat again. I'll call the trainer." Mike said.

"Mike, bring me this dog's papers." Brad's exasperation sent the handler out immediately. He left in a huff.

Kate walked over and brushed the dog's head. "Why do they have to race these animals in this heat if this is the result?"

"I'm sure the heat did not cause the seizure."

"How do you know?"

"Because this dog came from the Fordyce kennel."

Chapter Six

After a day of dead dogs and doubletalk, Kate had only one thing on her mind when she returned to the bungalow. She threw off her hot, sticky clothes and turned the air conditioning down to sixty-five for the sole purpose of chilling the room and then enjoying a hot bath. This place felt like the Taj Mahal compared to what she had been used to for the past five years in camp. Constructed in the early 1900s, Olga's bungalow was once the home of the original owner of the ranch. Olga had remodeled it, carefully preserving its charm, while adding modern conveniences and enlarging the windows. The fireplace and walls were constructed of fossiliferous-limestone blocks with native pine framing the windows, doors and forming the baseboards. Polished granite mined from the Granite Shoals Quarry, located on the northern cusp of the Hill Country, replaced the cracked tile counter tops in the kitchen. With all its modern conveniences, the bungalow still had the look of an old, country lodge, reflecting the natural resources of the area.

Olga had stocked the place with several bottles of Texas wine. Kate uncorked a Fall Creek Merlot and headed for the bathroom. Not even this room had escaped the native Texas stone. A huge ammonite fossil, alive more than a hundred-million years ago when a shallow sea covered all of Texas, was embedded in the white limestone wall directly over the tub. Unobtrusive gallery lighting shown perpetually on the fossil, giving it a delicate glow.

Within minutes, steam filled the room. Kate eased into the hot bath and smiled as she envisioned their living quarters in Kenya. This room alone was larger than their entire boma, where the centerpiece stone was not an ancient fossil, but a concrete floor, and heating the bath water involved throwing dried cow chips on a stone-lined pit situated under a forty-gallon water barrel, which stood just outside. The preparation took all the luxury out of bathing.

The sunken tub, large enough for two people, was also framed in granite, but this rock was cut from a deeper, richer shade of pink. A dimmer switch at arm's length allowed for instant twilight. Olga had decorated the shelves surrounding the tub with myriad scented candles molded in every size and shape imaginable. A skylight made stargazing on a clear night possible.

Kate had carried the phone into the bathroom anticipating Jack's call. She had taken her first sip of wine when the phone rang. "Hi, sweetheart," she said.

"I'm on the landline at the office. How did you know it was me?"

"I could tell by the urgency of the ring."

"Are you in the tub, or did I call too early?"

"You always call at the right time. I wish you were here. Things happened so fast that we haven't had time to enjoy this beautiful place. Jack, we *do* need a vacation—time to ourselves without trying to solve the world's problems."

"Sounds like you've had a rough day. You want to tell me about it?"

"Yes, but first tell me about Chicago. How's old the gang? Have you been fitted for a Cubs' uniform yet?"

Jack laughed. "No, not yet, and the old gang is no more. I hardly know anyone. Besides, I'm not the only one the organization is interviewing, but I'm the only one who's been out of the game for a while. I think Bill asked me up here more out of consideration for an old friend."

"Don't underestimate yourself. If you take the job next spring, I'm sure Max and Olga wouldn't mind if we stayed on the ranch until then. We could relax here and spend some uninterrupted time together." The pause on the other end of the line dampened Kate's hopes before she had time to enjoy the idea. "Jack—what is it?"

"The position's available immediately. Roger Franks, the pitching coach, is retiring. His back is giving him a lot of trouble, and they want his replacement on the bench as soon as possible. Sort of like on-the-job training. You remember Roger—he used to say that he'd sell his soul for your seafood bouillabaisse." Apparently sensing Kate's disappointment, he brought the subject back around to vacationing on the ranch. "But after the season's over, we could spend the winter on the ranch and be in Chicago next March. Besides, you're busy with this investigation and by the time you wrap it up, I'll be back."

"You mean if you get the job, you're staying?"

"I'll come back for a few days, but I'll need to return to Chicago as soon as possible. Let's not worry about that now. Tell me about your day. I'm sure it was more exciting than mine."

Feeling her vacation idea grow tepid with her bath water, Kate told him of the incident at the track and her visit with Guy at his ranch later that afternoon.

****

After the greyhound had died, Gates had work to do, so Kate left him to the unfortunate task of dealing with track officials who wanted to avoid publicity at all costs, and owners who were so far removed from their racing property that another dead dog was another dead dog.

Kate wanted to tour the track and learn how it operated before she watched her first race. With some background information perhaps she could have a better understanding of what had become known as the "Sport of Queens." When she returned to the PR room, Tammy was hanging up the phone.

"Dr. Gates just called and told me to give you the VIP tour. Ready?"

"Lead the way."

Wearing the official turquoise blazer and a smile deserving of her title as tour guide, Tammy escorted Kate to the trophy room where photos and plaques of dozens of champions covered the walls. Kate noticed Guy Fordyce in several of the photos and took the opportunity to generate some gossip if Tammy was willing.

"Guy Fordyce seems to know what he's doing. It looks as though he has raised quite a few winners."

"Mr. Fordyce is a very important man around here. He has a great breeding stock of greyhounds." Tammy hesitated, and then pointed to a photo on the wall. "Last year his dog, Ranger, won the Champion Stakes."

"I guess you heard that Guy was arrested this morning."

"I can't believe that he would do something like that. He's one of the nicest men I know." Kate could see that Tammy was caught between the urge to say more and the obligation to stick to her well-designed presentation. Kate was not going to let Tammy off the hook that easily. Pretending she had not noticed Tammy's discomfort, Kate said, "I read in the newspaper that he was released on bail this morning. I'm sure he has already hired the best lawyer money can buy. I visited his ranch yesterday and it is obvious that he is a fairly wealthy man."

"Do you know the Fordyce family?" Tammy pointed to another photo of Guy and a young girl with long blonde braids, standing on either side of a greyhound. "Ranger was Victoria's dog. She raised him herself."

Kate looked at the photo and was overcome with a deep sadness. Victoria Fordyce, clearly the apple of her father's eye, had inherited his fair coloring and strong build, along with her mother's height, Victoria looked like a Nordic goddess. She did not look like a child hooked on drugs.

"Did you know her?"

Tammy bit back tears, barely able to keep the quiver out of her voice. "Vicky was a few years younger than me, but I've known her for a long time. But it wasn't until I started working here that we really became friends." Tammy stared at the photo. "She went to this private Catholic school where a lot of the rich kids go, and I always thought she was a rich snob. But when I started working here last year in the concession stands, she'd always come visit. There are not many young people who hang around the track, and she would come over to talk." Tammy turned to look at Kate, and with a valiant effort, forced a smile. "I'd still be selling soda and popcorn if it weren't for her. She talked her father into getting me this job as a tour guide. I'm trying to work my way through college."

"When was this picture taken?"

"About a year ago. I know what you're thinking. You should've seen her before she died. She was a totally different person. I don't know what happened. One day she was her usual happy self and…well…she was the type of person who always looked out for the underdog, always there to help no matter what. Then she seemed to change overnight. I think it had something to do with some new boyfriend. Vicky stopped coming by and the next time I saw her, she looked bad. You know—stressed, sort of bad. I began to see less and less of her. They said she killed herself. That's so hard to believe."

Two official looking men strolled in and Tammy quickly resumed her role. "Let's walk over to the parade ring before the next race. You can pick out a dog. I'll show you how to place a bet."

"I'll just watch this time."

Kate had been to a few horse tracks in her time, and although she did not believe in racing for profit, it was easy to understand the attraction that drew so many spectators. Thoroughbreds were some of the most powerful animals alive, and once they shot from the starting gate, it was impossible not to get caught up in the excitement. Kate looked around the clubhouse, but failed to understand what drew these fans to the dog track. The air of excitement was absent, replaced by a sense of languor, as if many of the racing fans were here only to kill time.

The next race was about to begin as the lead-outs, those in charge of handling the dogs during the post-parade and placing them in the starting boxes, paraded the dogs onto the track, giving the public a last-minute look at the racers. But the serious gamblers, noses in their tip sheets, did not seem interested in viewing the dogs. Thirty seconds after placing the greyhounds in their starting boxes, the mechanical rabbit rounded the track, the doors flew open, and the dogs burst out. Racing up to forty-five miles-per-hour, the greyhounds made short time of the quarter-mile stretch to the finish line, and in a blink of an eye, the race was over.

People began maneuvering their way to the betting windows, some to collect their winnings and others in hopes of recapturing their losses on the next race. Kate looked down at the dogs still on the track where the lead-outs were attempting to leash their wards. Hopping around the artificial lure, the greyhounds appeared to be the only ones excited about their performance. Kate watched as the handlers led the dogs off the track. They removed the racing blankets, hosed them down, and then walked them back to the kennels.

"These dogs are bred to run. They can't wait for the doors to open so that they can chase the lure." Tammy explained as if she had read Kate's mind and felt the need to add some excitement to the event. "What's neat about dog racing is that it's the only spectator-betting sport in which no live person participates in the actual competition. The dogs are on their own, and all they want to do is run," Tammy said.

"What happens to them when they no longer win races?"

Tammy relied on her well-rehearsed spiel to explain to Kate that if the dogs failed to win a certain required number of races, they were sent down to lower-grade tracks, and then often to adoption organizations. "Many of the owners work closely with several groups in the area and they're great about finding homes for most of the dogs."

Kate wondered about those that were not adopted, but did not voice her concern to Tammy.

Kate left the track shortly after two. Her only consolation for getting back on the interstate was to exit at San Marcos and take the scenic route down Highway 12 across Devil's Backbone, a road that snaked over a ridge of the Hill Country. The two-lane winding road was precarious in places, but at least she would not have to deal with insane interstate drivers.

In San Marcos, a quaint college town situated on the San Marcos River, Kate located a car wash. As she cleaned Rosa Linda's mats and scrubbed the inside of her Jeep, Kate remembered the photos Rosa Linda had given her. The Fordyce ranch was next on Kate's list, and the photos might give her a good reason to visit. She tossed the mats in the back of the Jeep to dry and walked over to the Pac-N-Go for a bottle of tea and a granola bar. Then she drove to City Park, found a picnic table in the shade near the river, and opened the envelope to have another look. When Rosa Linda had given Kate the photos on Saturday night, she'd been too tired to examine them closely. Here in the bright sunlight, she took the time to study them. A closer look at the more disturbing photos told her that she had wasted her money on the granola bar.

Kate wondered if the dead greyhounds could have been the ones that Guy spoke of—the ones that supposedly had died of parvo. She was familiar with the disease—a mammalian/avian illness that spreads like wildfire. Domestic dogs were usually vaccinated, but if the virus attacked animals in the wild, there was not much hope. Last summer, Kate watched helplessly as canine parvo wiped out an entire family of African wild dogs living near her camp. But if the dogs in the photos were indeed the parvo victims, why did Jesús feel compelled to take these pictures? Then another thought occurred to her, had Guy's disinterest led to ignoring the greyhound's health? The photos of the dogs being loaded onto the truck seemed innocent enough. They appeared healthy and even eager. Fordyce bred and sold greyhounds, and these dogs could very well have been on their way to a new home.

Kate debated whether to show them to Guy. She needed to get them to Sheriff McCrae as soon as possible. It had been almost forty-eight hours since she had taken them from Rosa Linda.

She decided a few more hours would not hurt. Kate placed the photos back in the envelope, finished her tea, and picked up the cellphone to call the Fordyce Ranch and announce her visit, then hesitated. She had no right to press this man for information. True, he had invited her to the ranch to give her a donation, but that was before he had been arrested for murder. Kate dropped the phone back in her bag and opted for a surprise visit.

Years ago when she was an official investigating abuse cases, she had to be cautious in her questioning. Citizens had rights, and gaining information often required a carefully planned strategy. Being a regular citizen gave her a license to snoop and become generally obnoxious if necessary. Arrest or no arrest, she decided to continue with her intrusive ways.

Kate drove up to the Fordyce Ranch around four, and was surprised to find things rather quiet. After ringing the doorbell the second time, she suspected that the Fordyces were probably at home, but choosing not to receive visitors. She considered walking around to the back patio when Meredith Fordyce suddenly opened the front door. She did not seem surprised to see Kate. Though impeccably dressed in starched jeans and a white sleeveless sweater, Meredith's countenance today rivaled that of the living dead.

Before Kate could explain her intrusion, Meredith invited her in and ushered her into the den. "Guy is with his attorney. He shouldn't be much longer if you didn't mind waiting. Would you like something to drink? Coffee or tea, or how about lemonade?" Meredith asked, sounding like a Stepford wife.

Kate accepted the lemonade. Meredith smiled and left the room. Kate assumed the lady of the house would join her. But after several minutes, a maid whose width seemed to match her height, waddled in carrying a tray on which sat a small pitcher of lemonade, a plate of cheese and crackers, and one ice-filled glass. She smiled at Kate and waddled out of the room.

Glad to have time to herself, Kate considered how she would approach Guy. Unless the events of the last twenty-four hours had changed the Texas rancher, she should have no problem getting Guy to talk. Kate looked around the gallery-sized den—just what one would expect to find in a wealthy rancher's home. The stone fireplace, big enough to spit a cow, was the focal point. Bookcases filled with books on ranching, business, investments, and myriad other subjects formed the walls on each side. A wrought iron grate, delicately sculptured to resemble the Fordyce ranch sign that hung over the gated entrance to the property, shielded the front of the unused hearth. Beyond the center of attraction, the elegant but rustic style continued across the den. Redwood beams supported the vaulted ceiling and the same dark wood framed the windows and bookcases.

Dozens of framed photographs stood everywhere: between collections of books, lined up in a straight row along the mantelpiece, tastefully arranged across the top of an antique rosewood library-table—the only piece of furniture in the room that dated back to the nineteenth century. The pictures told a story of a happy Fordyce family. Meredith and Victoria seated on both sides of a young replica of Guy, mother and daughter holding the squirming boy while kissing his cheeks, a young Victoria and little brother astride a brown and white pony with a braided mane. One photo caught Kate's attention more than the others. Meredith was wearing a simple white cotton dress and summer sandals. She was bending over to look at her toddler daughter's pouting face, which was partly shaded by the ten-gallon hat perched on her tiny head. Kate picked up the picture and examined it closely. Meredith was beaming with a joy that can only be felt by a doting mother. The smile was genuine, not the pasted-on version that covered her face now. No wonder Meredith chose not to join Kate for refreshments. She could easily understand why this woman avoided the den with its cheerful reminders of the past. Kate replaced the photo on the rosewood table, and scanned the collection for pictures of prized greyhounds, but found none.

She poured herself a glass of lemonade. Too impatient to sit, Kate took her glass to the bookcase to peruse Guy's collection. As she leafed through a book on holistic ranch management, Guy Fordyce became even more of a conundrum. Kate replayed parts of his campaign speech in her mind. His concern about saving the surrounding environment sounded sincere. There was something about him that did not ring true, but she could not put her finger on it.

Voices in the hall and the closing of the front door alerted Kate that she would soon have another opportunity to gather fodder for her, so far, fruitless investigation. A few seconds later, Guy walked in.

"Sorry to keep you waiting. Please, sit down. Man, what a mess." Guy settled into a well-worn leather chair. Kate opted for the granite bench that extended from the front of the fireplace.

"I hope you don't mind my coming unannounced," Kate said.

"Not at all. I need to talk to a normal person after listening to that legal mumbo jumbo from my lawyer. I have your check here." Guy handed her the envelope.

"That's not why I came."

"I know, but this ol' West Texas rancher always keeps his promises."

"West Texas? You're not from around Wimberley?"

"Moved here a few years ago from Alpine, beautiful county, the Trans Pecos, but too isolated to raise children. I was in the banking business back then, and to tell the truth, I was ready for a change. Meredith is from around here and I always loved the Hill Country, so when Victoria was little, we sold our ranch near Alpine and moved to Wimberley. Go ahead, use this check for your research."

"Thanks." Kate folded the envelope and stuck it in the pocket of her shorts. She envisioned the money going for salaries, supplies and medicine, but she feared that her staff might have to use it to pay the bribes demanded by the government that would most certainly come after the disaster that she had caused.

"The *Statesman* painted a pretty grim picture," Kate said.

"Well, for whatever it's worth, I didn't kill Jesús. I don't know why I am telling you this. My attorney tells me that I should keep my big mouth shut, but why should I when I'm innocent?"

"You don't have to tell me anything. But I'm here to find out why Rosa Linda, and evidently Jesús, believed that some of your greyhounds had suffered from some sort of abuse. Within a couple of hours of my arrival, Jesús was dead and two days later, you're arrested for his murder. I might be wrong, but the two seem to be connected. Maybe I can help—that is, if you want my help. I have a propensity for sticking my nose in other people's business to the point where they tell me what I want to know to get rid of me." Then she let all pretense fall away. "Why was Jesús blackmailing you?"

"Let's back up a minute, Kate. I'm not as involved with the dogs as I used to be, but I would know if any unethical practices had been occurring. After we talked at the party on Sunday, I spoke to Wayne, and he assured me that no dog is suffering in any way. I inspected the kennel as well, and everything was up to snuff."

"Is it possible that he's using live lures to train the dogs?"

"I asked him about that too, and he said no. And I believe him. About a year ago, Wayne wandered in looking for a job. He told me straight off that he didn't have a lot of credentials. While growing up, he had worked on his family's ranch, but other than that, he had no experience. I appreciated his honesty. I told him I'd give him a shot. Besides, he arrived at the right time. He helped Victoria with training Ranger, and he became like an older brother to my son Guy Junior. I know he doesn't especially like working with the dogs, but I really needed someone since Diego died."

"Jesús confided in Rosa Linda," Kate continued, "claiming he saw Wayne using live lures."

"Well, we have two different stories here, don't we?"

Kate could hear the slight strain in his voice. There was no use pursuing that subject any further, at least for now.

"How about the blackmail note?" Kate said.

"I never saw a blackmail note."

"I don't understand. The newspapers said the police found a blackmail note in your office. Actually, it was in the trashcan. It had your prints on it."

"I know. I know. It was written from a note pad on my desk, but I'm telling you like I told the sheriff, I never saw that note. Even if I had, would I throw it in the trash? Does that make sense? Don't you think I'd probably hide it or destroy it, rather than leave it around for someone to find?"

"What did Jesús come see you about the morning he was killed? He called Rosa Linda about finding the bodies of dead greyhounds. He was agitated and wanted us here immediately."

"He was upset when he came to see me, but it wasn't about finding dead dogs. He wanted money. I refused and he got pissed off."

"Why did he need money?"

"He was anxious about bringing his two brothers and a cousin over and impatient with the process. I think he believed that I was preventing it somehow, taking too much time. He asked me for money to send to his family. Don't get me wrong. I helped Jesús many times. I paid him well, and he had free room and board here. But I began to wonder where all of his money was going, and if he was really sending it home like he claimed." Guy massaged the back of his neck and arched his back. "Man, I tossed around all night. I finally got to sleep around four o'clock only to wake up with a back strain. Anyway, I'd pretty much had it and lost my temper. With Diego dying all of a sudden and the stress of the campaign, and…well…my family has had its share of tragedy lately. I got angry, but I didn't threaten him. Why would I?"

"A witness heard you threaten to kill him."

"Nora, my maid, speaks very little English. She heard us arguing and became upset. I spoke to her and she denies saying that to the sheriff. I think they took advantage of her and read into her statement what they wanted. Like they did with that note."

"Wayne believes that Jesús was running from something in Mexico."

"So do I. Wayne worked with Jesús and knew him better than I did. I don't know what the hell's going on here. Up until a few months ago, everything seemed fine. Then Victoria became involved in drugs, and before I could get her any help, she died. Now my wife stays sedated, my son's running around like a wild thing, and now this."

"I'm sorry. I can't imagine what you and your family have been through. It must be hard."

"It is. Much worse for my wife. Sometimes I wonder if she'll ever recover, but I guess one never totally recovers from something like that. Anyway, I have no idea why Jesús called Rosa Linda. He left here madder than a scorpion backed into a corner. But like I said, we didn't discuss the greyhounds."

"Something must have happened after he left your office. Any idea where he was off to?"

"I know what you're getting at. I left after he did, but I didn't go *after* him. I took a ride around the ranch. I went to check on some cattle."

"No one saw you?"

"Hell, no. It's a goddamn big ranch. Had I known that I'd needed an alibi, I wouldn't have gone alone." Guy stood up and paced the room.

Kate had the feeling that their visit was coming to a close, and decided at that moment to show him the photos.

He sighed. "Pardon my outburst."

"Understandable. What do you think of these?" She handed him the envelope. "Jesús took these pictures of your dogs." Kate was not yet ready to divulge the fact that Rosa Linda had given Jesús the camera.

Guy flipped through the photos. "Why do you think that these are my dogs? They could be anyone's."

"That's true. But look at that photo. It's a shot of your entrance gate with the Fordyce sign."

"You're right, and that's one of my ranch trucks. Looks like Wayne was transporting some dogs we sold several days ago. Those dead dogs are not mine, though."

"They weren't the ones that died from parvo?"

"No. They didn't die all at the same time. It was over the course of several weeks." Guy studied the inside of the envelope as if to find the answer to the mysterious pictures. He shook his head, and handed them back to Kate.

"They must mean something," Kate said.

Guy walked over to the bookshelf. Thinking that he was reaching for a book, Kate was amused to see him slide the shelves on the right of the fireplace into a blind wall, exposing a small, but well-stocked bar. He plunked a couple of ice cubes in a crystal glass and added a generous amount of Glenlivet.

"To be honest, Kate, I don't know what the photos mean. They're the least of my worries. I don't suppose you'll join me."

"Too early in the day. I'd fall asleep before I made it back to Max and Olga's place." Kate wasn't sure, but she got the feeling that Guy was relieved when she declined his offer. Either she had overstayed her welcome, or Guy enjoyed drinking alone.

Guy set down his glass, and ran his hands over his face. "Why don't you leave them here, and I'll let Wayne take a look at them?"

"I plan to turn them over to Sheriff Holden."

"I don't know what good that would do, but that's your decision." Guy glanced at his watch. "My son has an archery tournament this afternoon. Garrison has been giving him some pointers, and I had better get out there while Guy Junior still has a fighting chance of winning a trophy. My brother means well, but…" Guy left it at that and walked Kate to the door.

On her way out, she remembered one more question. "Have any of your dogs had epilepsy? One of your dogs died during a race today. Brad said it was a seizure. Three similar deaths occurred in the past two weeks."

"Probably the heat. I'll have another talk with Wayne." Guy wished her well and closed the door.

The Texas heat was often blamed for everything

from ill-tempered children to ill-mannered adults. Was it also the blame for ill-fated greyhounds? Kate doubted it. She walked back to the Jeep and when she opened the door, the heat hit her in the face like a jet stream from hell. For the second time that day, she had forgotten to park under a shade tree, a Texas summertime survival necessity. On the asphalt in the parking lot of the racetrack and here again parked on Guy's white-bricked drive, the inside of the Jeep was hot enough to bake a turkey. Maybe Guy was right. Maybe it was the heat.

She reminded herself to crack her windows and locate some shade next time she parked. Saying a prayer that this heat wave would break soon, Kate lowered the windows, turned on the air-conditioner, and enjoyed the artificial wind blowing on her face. When she could touch the steering wheel without burning her hands, she put the Jeep in gear and left the ranch.

On her way back, Kate turned over in her mind the information she had learned. Brad was suspicious of the treatment of Guy's greyhounds. Except for the recent deaths of his dogs while at the track, Guy's dogs seemed to be well treated. Was Brad's concern legitimate? He had good reason to get back at Guy. Guy started the ball rolling that eventually led to Brad's troubles. Kate also noticed that Brad was quick with the injection when the dog was brought into his office. This sort of thinking got her nowhere. She was exhausted and hungry. Nothing made sense.

Driving through Wimberley, Kate stopped by the Wimberley Bread Basket and loaded up on groceries. Too hot to cook, she purchased seasoned olives, soft spreadable goat cheese, and a loaf of Italian bread. As a long-needed treat, she selected a bottle of Ruffino

Chianti Classico.

Kate needed a quiet evening to contemplate the day and consider her next move.

****

Her phone conversation with Jack helped. He left less than twenty-four hours ago, and she already missed him. After she hung up, she promised herself that she would enjoy the evening. Think, relax, and try not to feel too sorry for herself for having to dine without her husband.

Kate drained the water from the tub, slipped into a pair of cool pajama pants and a light tank top, and poured herself a second glass of wine. It was time for a priority list. She jotted down tomorrow's schedule with the precision and forethought of Sherlock Holmes. Rosa Linda and Daniel would be back from the border tomorrow, and Kate planned to get to the bottom of her suspicions, visit Sheriff McCrae to compare notes, and call Brad to find out about the autopsy results.

Feeling better about the day, Kate took her wine and Tuscan picnic to the front porch to watch the sun set, and hoped that a cool western breeze might find its way to Central Texas. No such luck. The sun disappeared, but the heat and humidity lingered. Kate finished her meal, remembered to crack the windows in the Jeep, and returned to the air-conditioned bungalow. She closed the door to the outside discomforts and picked up a book that Olga had given her.

She smiled as she read the title, *The Moor*, one of the books in Laurie King's Mary Russell and Sherlock Holmes series. Kate had been away too long. How did another Sherlock Holmes author arrive on the scene without her knowing? She crawled in the king-sized bed and felt like a small tumbleweed on a vast desert. Big beds were great as long as she could wave to Jack on the other side. Less than a dozen pages into the novel, the words began to blur. She slumped down on her pile of pillows and fell into a deep, much-needed sleep.

Chapter Seven

Kate bolted upright as the scream echoed in her head. She started running before she realized the danger of her actions. Then her foot caught on a rock and she stumbled, but by the grace of God, she managed to catch herself before she fell. The tiny slice of moon that had lighted her way only moments ago, was now hidden behind clouds, making it impossible for her to see. Despite the darkness, Kate ran, breathless with fear and desperation. She would not lose him this time. The path made a sharp turn to the left. She heard his labored breathing up ahead. Then suddenly the beast stopped dead in its tracks, jerked its head back in her direction, and stood its ground. Slowly, deliberately it crouched down, head low, teeth bared. A fluorescent glow shone from the inside of its mouth. Kate slowly reached into her pocket only to discover it empty. What a fool she was for taking up the chase without so much as a thought for her own safety, for she had not remembered to grab her Derringer before she left the bungalow.

Keeping her eyes on the animal, she stepped to the side of the path, hoping to take cover behind the sparse vegetation, which grew on the heath. Suddenly her breath caught. It was too late. She had underestimated her enemy. She recognized the signs. Prey had become predator. The hound let out an ear-piercing wail and charged. As Kate turned to run, the ground crumbled beneath her feet and she slid face down into a steep ravine. The fall knocked her breathless. Her head was spinning, but she managed to roll over onto her back. She must get up while she still had the chance, but her legs felt like stone. She groped around the ground for a stick, a rock, anything she could use to defend herself. Then she looked up and saw the hound looming over the precipice. Red beams of light shot from its eyes—its drooling lips curled up exposing a mouth full of jagged teeth. Kate tried to rise up on her elbows, her heart pounding hard in her chest. In slow motion, the hound leapt, and with a loud thud hit the ground next to where Kate was lying. The dog circled slowly, each step echoing louder and louder.

****

Kate tumbled out of bed—her pajamas damp and clammy against her skin. Unsure of where she was, she knocked the bedside lamp over. The loud pounding continued. She fumbled around, righted the lamp, and found the switch. Light flooded the room.

Silence.

Kate sat and listened, but all she heard was the hum of the air conditioning unit. Unsure if the pounding noise was a reverberation from her nightmare, or if she really heard something, Kate walked over to the window. She pulled back the curtain and scanned the porch. She had forgotten to turn off the porch light. The front of the bungalow and the few flagstones leading to the hedged path to the Rodriguez home were illuminated. Beyond that, darkness swallowed the landscape.

All was quiet.

As she dropped the curtains, Kate caught a glimpse of the Mexican hammock swinging on the edge of the porch. She stepped outside hoping to feel the first hint of a cool front. Instead, the still air, hot and stifling, hit her in the face. She walked over to the hammock and peered around the bungalow, looking for the culprits. Raccoons. Kate remembered Olga telling her how they conducted nightly raids on her garden. The tenacious little buggers had stolen a variety of small objects that weren't nailed down, uprooted potted plants, climbed the wisteria vines, and on one occasion, when feeling rather festive, had taken a dip in the pool. But no furry creatures lingered about tonight, and all seemed right with the world.

Taking a deep breath and swallowing away her unfounded fears, Kate looked up at a clear starlit sky. She caught sight of a satellite drifting above the horizon and watched as it passed under the Big Dipper. A familiar tune entered her head about Texas's stars at night. *It's true*, she thought. There was no sky like a Texas sky. Maybe it was the feeling of enormity in a state whose east-west borders were wider than the distance from El Paso to San Diego. More stars, more sky, more space. They were all part of the magic that made her proud to call this state her home.

As Kate tried to recall the next line of the song, she was startled by the sound of something moving through the dry grass. She turned around and the movement stopped. She walked around to the side of the bungalow, keeping herself in the shadows. If the raccoons were still around, she planned to crash in on their fun as a payback for waking her. A border of Texas sage grew in a long bed that stretched the length of the bungalow—a great place for the nighttime raiders to hide.

"Kate, it's me."

The voice from behind was familiar enough, but the

suddenness caused her to jump and let out a scream.

"Are you okay? I'm so sorry. I thought you saw me. You looked like the dogs have been after you."

With both hands, Kate brushed her damp hair from her face. Her breathing returned to normal. "Yes, I'm fine. I thought you were a raccoon. Too little sleep, too much wine, and a murder mystery have frazzled my nerves."

"A fictional mystery or a real one?"

"Both actually." Kate laughed. "Come in, Max. What time is it? It must still be ninety degrees outside."

"It's nine-thirty, ninety-two degrees, and ninety-five percent humidity. Come to think of it, I should be asleep as well. There's not much to do on a night like this. They keep promising rain, but it ain't gonna happen unless we get some hurricane activity in the Gulf. I saw the porch light on and hoped you were still awake. I can come back tomorrow, if you want," Max hesitated. "If that would be better."

"Don't be silly. I have a half-empty bottle of Chianti."

They went inside where the air was cool and breathable.

"If you were thinking positively, you would say a bottle half full."

"There's nothing positive about half the wine gone. Would you like a glass?"

"Only if you'll join me."

"I never drink after a nightmare. What's up?"

"We haven't had a chance to really visit since you've been back. I wanted to see how you were doing."

"Bullshit. I've known you too long. I repeat. What's up?"

Max helped himself to the wine and sank into a cushy lounge chair. "I was hoping to live to be an old man, but I gave up on that idea a little over twenty years ago when my daughter was born. That girl is going to send me to an early grave."

"She's not a girl any more, Max. You should be proud of her. She's smart, determined, and she'll be successful in anything she does. And soon she'll be married to a fine young man, I might add."

"I don't want to talk about that."

"Oh, yes you do. That's why you're here. Daniel is going to be your son-in-law soon. Don't you think you should settle your differences?"

"I don't trust him. He comes around every weekend and then he and Rosa Linda disappear. They're in Laredo or Del Rio or somewhere visiting friends along the border. Rosa Linda doesn't know anyone in these places. Or they're at Big Bend taking pictures. He claims to be photographing nature, but I've never seen any of his work. If I question Rosa Linda, she gets defensive and accuses me of meddling. We've always been able to talk. She'd tell me everything, and now, well…I feel like a stranger."

Kate laughed, walked over to Max, and gave him a kiss on the forehead. "You're not experiencing anything that all fathers haven't experienced before they gave their daughters away. If you don't want to lose her, Max, you need to let go and start treating her like an adult."

"I agree, but there's something else I haven't told you. Don't chastise me, but I had someone look into Daniel Martinez's background. I know he comes from a poor family in the Valley. Despite what he thinks, I don't hold that against him. In fact, I admire a person who can pull themselves up by their bootstraps. But he claims to be in graduate school at UT, and he was, up until a few weeks ago. For some reason he dropped out in mid-semester, but he's lied to me about it and I'm worried that he's lied to Rosa Linda as well. The wedding is planned for two weeks from Saturday, and if this guy is lying to my daughter," Max stood up and set his glass on the end table, "you can bet as sure as the sun comes up, there won't be any damn wedding on this ranch. She looks up to you. Could you talk to her—you know—woman to woman?"

"I had planned to do that tomorrow when they return." Kate wasn't quite ready to expresses her concerns about Rosa Linda's sudden lack of interest in the greyhounds. At this point, it would only add fuel to Max's fire. "How does Olga feel about this? Has she talked to Rosa Linda?"

"Olga thinks that I'm over protective. She's really taken in by Daniel, and is already planning to childproof the swimming pool for our future grandkids. I'll let you get back to your nightmare. Let's talk again tomorrow. When's Jack coming back? I'm not finished giving him a hard time."

"A couple of days. Promise me that you'll try to be objective about Daniel until we know what's going on. Remember, you haven't heard his side of the story."

"You're right. I'll stay calm and see what he has to say."

Kate smiled, ignoring the slight sarcasm in that statement. After Max left, she was unable to fall back to sleep, so she surfed the channels for an old movie, trying to still the onslaught of thoughts that raced through her mind. Did Rosa Linda know that Daniel had quit school?

Maybe they had decided together that Daniel would set aside his education and focus on supporting a wife. He seemed the kind of person who would not accept financial help from a rich father-in-law.

Kate hoped that whatever the reason, it was as innocent as planning for the future.

Kate found the classic-movie channel. The original *Sabrina* had started. Preferring Humphrey Bogart and Audrey Hepburn to hounds and moors, Kate watched the movie until sleep overcame her once again.

****

Determined not to let the weather intimidate her, Kate slapped on her running shoes for her morning jog. The sun was rising over the hills, but the humidity felt like last night's unfinished business. Kate called McCrae, left a message with his dispatcher, and then took off. Despite the discomfort, the exercise cleared her mind. By the time she returned, her jogging clothes were soaked, and the sun was well on its way to keeping its promise of another scorcher.

She had stepped from the shower and was considering cheese and toast from last night's dinner when the phone rang.

"Mrs. Caraway? This is Lisa, the sheriff's dispatcher. He finally decided to check in. Hold on. Here he is."

"What's up?" McCrae said.

"I have something to show you."

"On the Fordyce ranch?"

"No, it fits nicely into my bag."

"Good. Meet me in town. Haven't yet had breakfast. The Haystack has the best greasy breakfast around, unless you're concerned about your arteries."

"I can do without grease."

"That's what I figured." McCrae chuckled. "There's one of those new-age coffee shops in town, the type that has the nerve to play classical music and sell lattes and tofu salads here in Central Texas. My wife drags me in there, trying to get me to eat better."

"If they have espresso, you're on."

"It's on Main Street next to the post office, called Micah's. You can't miss it. It's the only place in town that has a "Join the Green Party and Save the World" banner displayed in the window."

"See you in half-an-hour." Kate hung up and called Olga to find out if Rosa Linda and Daniel had returned from Laredo. Olga said they had come in around one, exhausted and a bit worse for wear. She tried to talk Daniel into staying the night, but after the confrontation with Max, she understood when he turned down her offer. Besides, Olga reported, Daniel wanted to make his early morning class. Rosa Linda was still asleep, but as soon as she awoke, they had plans to work on wedding stuff all day.

Kate didn't say anything to Olga about Daniel no longer being enrolled in school. That was between her and Max, and if he had not told her yet, Kate would keep quiet for now. Surely, Rosa Linda must know. Last night's slight feeling of uneasiness had grown into a knot in Kate's stomach the size of Texas. She wondered why her goddaughter, who had been so passionate about exposing Guy Fordyce for dog abuse, had suddenly dropped the entire investigation in Kate's lap. That was fine with Kate. Rosa Linda didn't need to get involved, since the situation was tangled up in a brutal murder. Nevertheless, it was out of character for Rosa Linda.

Then Kate reminded herself that her goddaughter was in love. It was not so long ago when Kate could still remember how she felt when she first met Jack. Regardless of how independent and determined she was to develop her own life and career, falling in love put her brain on hold for the first few weeks until she and Jack had their first spat.

Now that Kate was here, did Rosa Linda relax, knowing that Kate could handle the situation, or was Rosa Linda hiding something and avoiding Kate? Romance or no romance, Kate feared it was the latter. Since Rosa Linda planned to run errands with Olga, Kate could visit with her goddaughter later this morning. Right now, she planned to show McCrae the photos and find out what he had uncovered.

Kate showered and dressed in cool, comfortable clothes, a short-sleeved white linen blouse, and a nylon skirt. She'd keep her hair loose until it completely dried, pulling it back into a ponytail would come later as the day heated up. To keep the sun off her head, she donned on a wide-brimmed straw hat. She turned the air conditioner down to keep the room chilled and stepped out to another muggy day.

The discussion she had last night with Jack helped to clarify the events of the past few days. Jack had agreed to call again this evening, and she hoped to have more information to feed his levelheaded brain. Then she wondered what news he would have for her. Even though he tried to downplay his chances at getting the job in Chicago, she knew how important it was to him. She had to agree that living in Chicago for a while would be nice. Kate made a mental note to express her enthusiasm. She and Jack did not need the money, but he needed the job.

When they pulled up stakes and moved to Africa, Kate was apprehensive about Jack's reaction. He had never been one for exotic adventurous travel, and Kate feared that life in the bush would not suit him. Her fears and worries were unfounded. He had fallen in love with the wildness of Kenya, just like she had. She could not have made the research project a success without him. His calm manner and ease of handling people got them out of several precarious situations. It was the least she could do for him, to be supportive if he returned to major league baseball. Besides, seeing their old friends would be nice. Maybe they could fill in the emptiness she felt.

Kate clicked the remote key to unlock the Jeep and was surprised to find it already unlocked. She was almost certain that she locked it last night. With all the crazy events of the day, she had probably forgotten. She opened the door and reached in to retrieve the photos from the console. Instead, she grabbed a handful of soft fur. She jumped back, knocking off her hat and banging her head on the doorjamb. The shadow of a live oak tree darkened the inside of the Jeep. Kate had to push the front seat back for a closer look. She wasn't sure how long she stood there—a second or two—then a barrage of feelings: anger, fear, then hatred flooded in, and brought back her breath.

Kate knew the dog was dead, even though she could see no sign of injury. How was she going to tell Rosa Linda? First Jesús and now Luna. There was no doubt in Kate's mind that the incidents were related. What message was the killer giving by leaving his victims for others to find? Kate bitterly wished for the chance to meet the evildoer face to face.

Before she broke the news to her goddaughter, she

called McCrae and told him to meet her at the bungalow.

****

"Did you hear anything last night?" McCrae asked while a young assisting officer dusted the Jeep for fingerprints.

"Max came around about nine-thirty. I was dead to the world. He knocked several times before I woke up. We visited a while and then soon after he left I was in dreamland again. A herd of buffalo could have stampeded the bungalow and I wouldn't have heard them."

"Heavy sleeper?"

"Not usually. But life's been tough lately."

"The dog's been dead awhile. I'd say a good full day, judging by the smell. We'll match the prints we took off of Jesús's body and the cross from the cemetery, but I don't hold any hope in finding much. Whoever is doing this is pretty clever. Rosa Linda has certainly stirred up a hornet's nest with her protests and accusations."

"If that were the case, why put the dog's body here for me to find it? Why not leave it at the Rodriguez home?"

"Because the person who did this knows why you're here and that you're driving Rosa Linda's Jeep. That's if Jesús Flores's murder and this incident are related. The warning is for you."

"Well, they don't know me very well."

"Yep. I was afraid of that. Let's go get some answers."

When they stepped into the kitchen, Olga was pouring herself a cup of coffee. She smiled when she saw Kate. Then her smile quickly disappeared when she saw McCrae in tow. She set her cup down on the kitchen table. "What is it?"

"Olga, we need to talk to Rosa Linda. I'm afraid we have some bad news. I just found Luna's body."

Olga looked from Kate to McCrae and back to Kate. "That's silly. I just fed her a few minutes ago." Everyone turned as the sound of nails clicking on the terra-cotta tile grew louder with each prancing step. Luna rounded the corner a little too fast and failing to get traction on the tile, slid passed the doorway and barely missed crashing into Olga's cherry wood table. "I've got to move that darn table. I've given up on trying to teach her not to run in the house," said Olga. "But I am beginning to think that this sliding thing is a new game for her."

A wave of relief washed over Kate. Luna righted herself and came into the kitchen. Kate bent over and gave the greyhound a big hug.

"Now what's this about finding Luna's body?" Olga pulled two coffee mugs from the cabinet and, without asking, filled each one, and handed them to Kate and McCrae.

Kate added a dollop of cream to her coffee, stalling, hoping McCrae would answer Olga's question. He took his coffee black, and while Kate sipped hers, he started talking.

"It seems that either someone has a sick sense of humor, or Kate's investigation is causing a bit of discomfort," McCrae said.

Olga looked at Kate for clarity.

"Holden's right," Kate said. "I found the body of a greyhound in the Jeep this morning. I thought it was Luna. Wait a minute." Kate stood up and pressed the palms of her hands on her forehead. "I saw that dog yesterday at the track. I was amazed how much she

113

resembled Luna. She was the one that died during the race yesterday. When I left, Brad Gates was about to perform an autopsy. He suspected that she had died of a seizure."

"There was no autopsy performed on that dog. Except for being somewhat stiff, she looks as if she had died in her sleep," said McCrae. "Give Brad a call. If he's not at the track, try his office. I'll be right back."

"Where are you going?" Kate said to McCrae.

"All registered greyhounds have an ID number tattooed in their ear. I'll check the number, if it has one. If this dog died at the track yesterday, we'll find out soon enough."

Olga wrote down a few numbers on a note pad. "Try his house first." She handed Kate the slip of paper. "He's usually not at the track this early. I don't like what's going on here, Katie."

Bradford Gates answered the phone on the first ring. "Animal clinic. This is Dr. Gates."

"Brad, this is Kate Caraway. Did you do the autopsy on that greyhound yesterday?"

There was a too-long pause on the other end of the line. "Why do you ask?"

"Because a dead greyhound that looks a lot like the one that died yesterday in your office is in the back seat of Rosa Linda's Jeep."

"Did you check the ID number?"

"Holden McCrae is checking right now."

"I got called away soon after you left, and when I returned the dog was gone. I figured the handler had taken it. It really teed me off, but I had no real authority to perform the procedure without Fordyce's permission. Let me look in my record book for the number. Hold on."

Kate looked at Olga. "He says he never got around to doing the autopsy. Someone had removed the dog while Brad was called away."

McCrae walked in. "Number 2772."

"Kate?" Brad was back on the phone. "The dog's number was 2772." Kate nodded affirmatively.

"Tell him we'll be right there," said McCrae.

****

On the way over, they picked each other's brains, but putting two and two together got no closer to four than a trip to the moon. Kate decided that she needed to come clean about the photos. She had no excuse for not calling McCrae the night Rosa Linda handed them over. Protecting her goddaughter was something Kate could not do, especially since she had no idea what she was protecting Rosa Linda from.

But the photos were evidence of...of what? Had Jesús taken pictures of Guy or Wayne with the dogs, that would have been a different story. If the photos proved useless, maybe McCrae would not hit the ceiling when she told him.

"I didn't tell you this earlier, but whoever left the dog took something in return," Kate said. "On Friday evening after you left, Rosa Linda handed me an envelope of photos."

"Friday, three days ago?"

"Yeah, well, I sort of forgot to tell you."

McCrae pulled his sunglasses down on the bridge of his nose and looked directly at Kate. "I'm listening."

"Some showed graphic pictures of dead greyhounds. A whole pile of them—emaciated. Some photos showed healthy dogs being loaded onto a truck, ready for transport I suppose."

"Who took the photos?"

"Jesús."

"How do you know?"

"Rosa Linda gave him the camera."

"And now the photos are gone."

McCrae turned onto Highway 12 toward Wimberley. Neither one had spoken for a couple of minutes. Kate decided to break the silence.

"I talked to Guy yesterday, and he claimed that he had not seen the blackmail note."

"Guy's one of those wealthy good ol' boys who thinks that if you have money, you can live by your own rules."

"Guy also thinks that your officers confused his housekeeper to the point where she was willing to tell them what they wanted to hear."

"Yeah, well, that's convenient for him, isn't it? I was the one who spoke to Nora, and she was pretty clear about what she heard. I didn't have to exactly coax anything out of her. She said that Jesús and Guy were in Guy's study with the door closed. Jesús was shouting about Guy being responsible for something. Then, according to Nora, they both stormed out through the garden door. She rushed to the kitchen window and saw Jesús drive off in the red ranch truck, and Guy left after him driving his Mercedes."

"If Guy was outraged enough to kill Jesús, why make a display out of it and drag him to the cemetery and tie him to a cross? By the way, what led you to arrest Guy so quickly?"

"Guy's .22 was found near the truck. He threatened to kill Jesús minutes before he died."

"Sounds a bit like a set-up. Do you really think

Guy's guilty?"

"Everything points in that direction. Did anyone else know about the photos?"

"I showed them to Guy yesterday."

"I see."

They crossed the Cypress River through downtown and then turned south. Brad's clinic was about two miles from the town square.

Chapter Eight

Kate was not sure what to expect. But when she and McCrae drove up to the Wimberley Animal Hospital, astonishment pretty much told the story. The place was enormous. This was no mere cat and dog operation. A series of whitewashed corrals with networks of interlocking paddocks ran along the quarter-mile entrance road. Several old but well maintained cinderblock buildings stretched across acres of lush, rolling hills. It was a scene straight from the Kentucky countryside. Suddenly, Kate's surprise gave way to an odd feeling. The pastures were void of horses and the parking lot was empty. For an operation this large, she expected to find several horse trailers parked in the gravel lot, with attendants scurrying across the paddocks, tending to business. Then Kate remembered Brad's mention of bankruptcy.

Sheriff McCrae rolled to a stop and parked in front of the main building. A red, faded wooden sign hung from a cross beam on a rusty metal post. Through the dark, patchy mold growing over the stenciling, Kate had to look closely to make out the proprietors' names. The one on top read Dr. John W. Gates, DVM., and underneath, Dr. Bradford D. Gates, DVM.

"I didn't know Brad had a partner. Is John his brother?" Kate asked.

"John was Brad's father. They were in business

together for a short time before John died. Let's see…that was about two years ago. This was some big operation back then. John Gates also raised quarter horses. That huge barn at the end of the drive used to house a couple of dozen prized equines."

"Brad mentioned yesterday that his business was suffering. He attributed that to an incident that occurred at River City Racetrack a few months ago."

McCrae cut the engine, and paused before opening the door. "I know." He looked across the empty fields. "Brad didn't deserve the bad publicity. That pretty much did it for him. It's been tough ever since the old man died. No one knew quarter horses like John Gates. He had quite a respected reputation. He also made a great deal of money from the horse business, something that Brad had no part of managing. When he joined his father, Brad intended to build up the small animal practice. After John died, Brad wasn't interested in the large animal business or in raising horses. He eventually sold the horses and has been hanging on by the skin of his teeth. The incident at the track was the last straw."

The scenario played out in Kate's mind: a young veterinarian trying to impress his father, a skilled vet with old-school commonsense, a much-loved doctor and successful businessman. Large shoes for a son to fill. It seemed to Kate that if the local sheriff knew the story of Brad's misfortune, the rest of the community had chewed over this gossip as well, and clients tended to avoid a sinking ship.

They walked inside to an empty reception area. "Let's go to the back," McCrae said. "Brad's probably in the office."

"You know your way around."

"When John was alive, he took care of my two horses. Those nags always had me here for one reason or another."

Kate followed McCrae down the hall. The smell of antiseptic hung thick in the air. A sense of sadness overwhelmed Kate, as she envisioned a once-bustling business where animal technicians darted in and out, and ranchers guffawed and flirted across the long counter while receptionists scanned the appointment book.

"Brad, ya back there?" McCrae called out.

"Yeah, come in, Holden."

Kate and Sheriff McCrae walked in to a neatly arranged room. Horse prints decorated the wall, and a polished leather saddle was draped over a wooden horse-frame. Four framed diplomas hung on the wall behind an old, well-polished roll-top desk. John W. Gates's name was scrolled on each diploma. Family photos, clearly taken in the fifties, hung on the wall behind the desk. It was evident to Kate that in spite of his death, Brad's father's presence in this office had not diminished.

There was no evidence of Brad's accomplishments anywhere.

"Kate, nice to see you. Take a seat, both of you."

"Looks like we got some bad business here." McCrae removed his hat and hung it on a peg near the door. He picked up a chair, turned it backwards, and straddled the seat. "Tell me what happened yesterday at the track."

Kate sat down on the sofa, the picture of the dead greyhound contorted on the examination table, still fresh in her mind.

"Like I told Kate over the phone, I had planned to perform an autopsy on the dog when I got called away.

Seems the handler went to George Callaway's office to lodge a complaint." Brad turned to Kate. "He's the racing secretary. George was concerned about the recent deaths and wanted to know what killed the dog, but he wanted to speak to Fordyce first. I agreed to wait until he put a call through. When I returned to the clinic, the dog was gone."

"Did you report it?"

"You bet I did. I called George immediately and told him the dog was missing. We both assumed that the handler had taken her. George told me he'd call Fordyce and get back with me. By the end of the day, I hadn't heard anything. Where's the dog now?"

"At the station, on ice. Forget Fordyce. This is a police matter now, and I'll order the autopsy and get you a copy of the results. I doubt we'll find anything, but just in case."

"I spoke to Guy yesterday, and he hadn't heard about the dog's death," Kate said. "When I told him, he didn't seem that concerned."

"He has other things on his mind," Brad said.

Kate detected the resentment again, slight, but there nonetheless.

"Here, you'll want this," Brad continued. "It may prove helpful. I made a copy of the dog's Bertillon Card before I left yesterday."

Kate stepped forward. "What's a Bertillon Card?"

McCrae handed her the copy.

"It's an identification card. Each dog has one," Brad said.

"I thought they were tagged by a number in the ear," Kate said.

"They are, but this card provides complete

information. Many greyhounds look pretty much alike, and unless you work closely with the dogs, it's difficult to tell them apart."

"Don't I know it," Kate said. "When I first saw the greyhound in the Jeep, I thought it was Rosa Linda's dog."

"That's why they need this card," Brad said. "Each dog has slight distinctive markings, and it's the job of the paddock judge to make sure the right dog is running in the right race. There are fifty-six identification marks that must be registered on this card. Look here." He picked up the card and pointed to the top. "Here's the name of the greyhound, its color, sex, owner, and kennel number. This dog's name was Lady Banjo, a fawn-colored female, owned by Guy Fordyce and the kennel number is forty-two. Below that are the ear tattoos. Her right ear is stamped with the date she was whelped and the chronological order in which she was tattooed in the litter. The left ear contains the four-digit litter registration number."

"These are some pretty detailed drawings." McCrae placed his reading glasses on his nose and walked over for a closer look. Rudimentary sketches, showing a front view of the dog, as well as the left and right sides, indicated specific markings. Each paw was also drawn on the card.

"Detailed, but extremely necessary," Brad said. "They indicate specific coloration and markings. For instance, the first toe on the left front foot is light-colored, the next one is dark, the third one is dark, and the fourth one is horned, hence the letters L, D, D, H under the sketch of the left foot. This card leaves no doubt to the dog's identity."

"Whoever took the dog from the track yesterday knew I was there," said Kate. "They also knew where I was staying."

"Sounds like someone doesn't want you asking questions," Brad said.

Kate sighed. "I feel like I've barely scratched the surface."

"Who knew you were at the track yesterday?" McCrae asked.

"No one who would warrant suspicion: Jack, Max, Olga, Rosa Linda and her fiancé, Daniel Martinez. In fact, I had asked Rosa Linda to come with me, but she declined. Seems she and Daniel had other plans."

"I see." McCrae lifted a small leather notebook from his shirt pocket and added to his notes.

With her last statement, Kate realized she'd thrown suspicion on Rosa Linda and Daniel. Although she knew they were up to something, she was positive it did not involve stealing the dead greyhounds. "Evidently, I was at the track long enough to be seen by the wrong people."

"Did you speak to anyone besides Brad?"

"Only Tammy," Kate said.

"Tammy?" McCrae looked up.

"Tammy is the tour guide who was on duty yesterday," Brad explained.

"She gave me the complete tour," Kate said. "I hadn't exactly hidden in Brad's office. Tammy showed me how to place a bet, then we walked around the parade ring and the kennels. Brad, tell Holden about the epilepsy."

"Right. This was the fourth dog that had died of a seizure in the past two weeks. All the dogs came from Fordyce's kennel."

"You mean his dogs were defective in some way." McCrae said. "A bad gene? Is epilepsy inherited?"

"Yes and no. Epilepsy is a term used for many brain disorders, which cause fits or convulsions. It can be inherited or it can result from an environment reaction of some sort. It can also occur for no apparent reason. Unless I looked at the bloodlines of all four dogs, I can't be sure. It could be a coincidence. But I doubt it."

"I want to talk to Wayne Brody." McCrae closed his notebook. "Thanks for the copy of the Bertillon Card, Brad. Are you scheduled at the track today in case I need more information?"

"No, not today. A new vet out of San Marcos will be there. I have an appointment with my banker. He wants me to put the business and property up for sale. I've held out as long as I can. Letting go of this place isn't going to be easy. I grew up here. This is my home." Brad stood up and walked his guests through the long, sterile hallway and into the outer office. "I never can get used to this place being so empty."

The three of them stepped out into the bright, hot sun. McCrae wished Brad luck. Kate found herself at a loss for words. To lose a business, especially one inherited from your father who had spent his entire life building, must do a number on one's self-esteem. Losing one's home to boot must make it difficult to get out of bed each day. After Kate's father died, she wanted to crawl into a dark cave and never come out. Although he had left Kate financially secure, he was her only family, and his death seemed to end so many aspects of a life that she had taken for granted. Kate could imagine what Brad was feeling, having not only to deal with the loss of his father, but with the guilt of not being able to carry on the business he'd spent decades building.

Kate's suspicions turned to Brad again. Was Brad's resentment toward Guy strong enough to drive him to revenge? He could easily have taken the dog after Kate left and dumped it in the Jeep during the night. They only had Brad's word for the epilepsy story. Could he have intentionally killed the dog? But if Brad was hell-bent on getting back at Guy for the fiasco that ruined his business, why dump the dog for Kate to find? Unless she was getting in Brad's way.

The idea of breakfast slipped away with the morning. Kate and Sheriff McCrae drove back to Wimberley and stopped for lunch. When McCrae recommended the Cypress Creek Cafe rather than Micah's, she could see his relief when she agreed. Bagels and lattes would not cut it after skipping breakfast, at least not for McCrae.

The restaurant was situated in the heart of Wimberley among a line of arts and crafts shops for which the town was well known. It was eleven-fifteen and the lunch crowd had not yet arrived. They took a seat at a table overlooking the dry creek bed that was home to Cypress Creek waters when there was some.

"The chicken-fried steak here is the best in the county," McCrae said as he put the menu back in its caddy, having easily made his decision. Kate perused the menu a little longer and decided on the soup of the day and a salad.

"So, where do you go from here, concerning Jesús murder?" Kate asked.

"My work is done, at least for now. I handed the DA enough evidence for an arrest. It's up to them to make it stick."

"Do you think Guy Fordyce is guilty?"

"It doesn't matter what I think. There was an argument and I have a witness who stated she overheard Fordyce threaten to kill Jesús. Jesús stormed out of the house and Fordyce followed. Less than an hour later, Jesús is dead and Fordyce's gun is found near the body."

"Even though I don't know him that well, considering all the stress Guy's been under lately, I can see him losing it. It happens all the time—back a desperate man in a corner, and if the stakes are high enough, someone gets killed. Guy panics and takes Jesús's body to the cemetery to hide it. He could bury it, burn it, or dump it in the bushes, but tying it to a cross is not an act of a frightened murderer. It smacks of undue justice, or revenge, even hatred—it's not the act of someone who flips out in a moment of desperation. It doesn't make sense."

The waitress came by, took their order, and returned immediately with McCrae's iced tea and Kate's coffee.

McCrae lifted three sugar packets from the bowl, tore them open, and poured them into his tea. He stirred, tasted, and added more sugar. "It sounds like you believe he's innocent."

"Things don't add up," Kate said. "I can't help but think of Garrison."

"No motive. Besides, we checked his Mercedes—clean—as well as the other vehicles on the ranch. The DA's office is still investigating. Don't forget about the blackmail note left in Guy's office."

"That's what I mean. Guy claims he never saw it. If he did, why throw it in his own trash can and then go after Jesús and kill him? Doesn't that strike you as strange?"

"If you believe what Fordyce says, yes. But if he is guilty, he's probably lying. Maybe he didn't throw it in the trash, maybe Jesús did when they were arguing."

"Too many maybes. What are you going to do about the greyhound? Do you think the two crimes are related?"

"I'll speak with Brody. See if I can find out what's going on. If someone doesn't like you asking questions, there's got to be a reason."

Kate sipped her coffee and thought about the occurrences of the past two days. The more information she gathered, the less she knew. She was not ready to express her suspicions concerning Brad Gates. She needed more time to think that one through before she talked about it with McCrae.

The waitress placed a platter of chicken-fried steak, along with a bowl of cream gravy in front of McCrae. He poured a ladle-full over the steak, scooped up another and covered his French fries.

"If I ate like that, all the jogging in the world wouldn't keep the fat from my thighs," Kate said.

"You sound like my wife. Women worry too much about their weight. By the way, how's my baseball connection?"

Kate laughed. "He's still in Chicago. Comp tickets are on hold for now."

"Do you want to come to the ranch with me and talk to Brody after lunch?"

"Thanks for the offer, but I need to talk to Rosa Linda. She was anxious for me to look into the alleged dog abuse, and then all of a sudden she has made herself scarce. I'd like to know if you find out anything from Brody." She wrote down the numbers of the bungalow

127

and the cellphone on a napkin and handed it to him.

McCrae picked up a bottle of ketchup, and added a large dollop on top of the gravy. Kate sipped her tomato bisque and tried not to watch.

Chapter Nine

McCrae's phone buzzed. "Gotta go." He threw a twenty on the table. "I'll call you. Be careful." Before leaving the restaurant, Kate decided to phone Rosa Linda before the busy young lady could slip away. The phone call was not necessary. The door flew opened and Rosa Linda stormed in red-faced and fuming.

"I saw Sheriff McCrae's car in the parking lot. Mom said that you were with him. I really need to talk to you right now. I hope—" Her lower lip started to tremble and she sucked in air to try to regain some composure.

"Sweetheart, what's happened?" In spite Rosa Linda's hotheaded determination and desire to claim her independence, at times like this Kate was quickly reminded of how young Rosa Linda was.

"Daniel came to the house to pick me up this morning. Dad lost his temper and threatened to cancel the wedding. Daniel tried to talk to him, but Dad wouldn't listen. Then Daniel got angry and left." Tears rolled down her face.

Kate put a loving arm around Rosa Linda. "Your father's pigheaded and you know when he gets angry he says things that he doesn't mean."

"But this time was different. He shouted and called Daniel a liar, and then said Daniel wasn't welcome in our house again. I don't know what Dad is talking about."

So much for staying calm and listening to Daniel's

side of the story, Kate thought. She wondered if there was another reason for Max's explosion.

"Let's go for a walk and you can tell me what happened," Kate said.

They crossed the street and walked past the town square toward a shady area where even during a drought some water trickled over the limestone riverbed of the lower branch of Cypress Creek. Giant cypress trees formed a canopy over the bank and as they walked down to a picnic table, the temperature seemed to drop ten degrees.

Kate lifted Rosa Linda's baseball cap off her head. "Start by telling me the real reason why you and Daniel went to Laredo yesterday. It's the middle of the week. Don't you have classes to attend?"

Rosa Linda reached down and picked up a gayfeather that was growing in a tuft of stubborn grass.

"I can't tell you. Not right now—soon, but not now. We left after my last class yesterday, and I don't have classes on Tuesdays."

Rosa Linda ran her finger along the long, purple plume. Kate noticed that familiar crease in the middle of Rosa Linda's brow and remembered seeing it for the first time when her goddaughter was a toddler. Instead of outgrowing her stubbornness, Rosa Linda's tenacity had solidified. And Kate suddenly knew the reason why Max and his daughter bickered—they were too much alike.

Kate tried another approach. "Your father talked to me last night. He's very concerned about you. He knows Daniel is not in school this semester, and I assume that you know this as well."

Rosa Linda took a deep breath and sat up a little straighter. "I'm old enough to live my own life, and I trust Daniel. Dad needs to mind his own business."

"But you are not too old to care what your father thinks and to want his approval. Otherwise we wouldn't be sitting here and your face wouldn't be puffy and streaked with tears."

Rosa Linda shot Kate a defiant look then apparently realized her godmother was not easily intimidated. "I'm sorry. You're right. I was childish, but I get so mad when Dad starts shouting. I lose my patience. I wish I could be more like Mom. She is so calm and reasonable."

"Your mother's had more practice with your father. What did Max say when you and Daniel came in? When I spoke with Max last night, he seemed willing to hear Daniel's side of the story. I'd like to know what's going on, too, Rosa Linda. One man is dead and a prominent rancher has been arrested for his murder. Not to mention someone trying to frighten me by dumping a dead dog in the Jeep. I'm wondering if there really is a case of greyhound abuse going on here? You and Daniel are elusive, and I seem to be on a wild-goose chase."

Rosa Linda threw the flower on the ground and grabbed Kate's wrist. "Oh, Kate, believe me."

"Then try to remember exactly what Jesús told you. I need something to go on."

"Jesús called me a few days ago and said that he saw Wayne using live lures to train some of the dogs. There is a quarter-mile training track behind the kennel. It's equipped with a mechanical pole, and Jesús was sure that Wayne had tied a live rabbit to the pole. The rabbit was pretty well mangled by the time Wayne had finished the training."

"Wayne denies he uses the lures. He claimed Jesús concocted the story to stir up trouble."

"Well, he would say that, wouldn't he? Jesús even confronted Wayne, and Wayne told him to mind his own business. Then a couple of days later, Thursday, the day I called you, Jesús saw the dogs crammed into the kennel and became really upset. That's when he called me."

"Things aren't always what they seem."

"Damn it, Kate. Jesús knew what he saw."

"I don't doubt that. I'm playing devil's advocate. They could have been another group of sick dogs. Guy said that several had died of parvo, and Brad Gates was concerned because four of Guy's dogs had died at the track from symptoms resembling epilepsy. But something else must have happened Friday morning right before Jesús was to meet us. He went to see Guy in his office. They evidently had an argument over money. Then Jesús was murdered, and Holden McCrae finds a blackmail note in Guy's office."

Kate felt a light tickling across her arm. A string of sugar ants had cut a trail up the side of the concrete picnic table, across the top and over her arm to a sprinkling of fried-chicken crumbs left from someone's picnic. Kate brushed off the insects, leaving them to their feast and stood up. "We're back where we started. We need solid proof, not speculation. Do you know anything about training greyhounds? How often they're run? How long it takes to train a young dog? That sort of thing."

"Very little, but I know somebody who does." For the first time since Rosa Linda walked into the restaurant, she seemed to perk up. "Let's go. I want you to meet her."

Kate knew that if she pushed Rosa Linda for more information about her and Daniel's overnight forays, she would get nowhere. For now, she let that subject rest.

****

Molly Gibson was unloading the back of a Suburban when Kate and Rosa Linda drove up and parked. Molly set a bag of dog food in the wheelbarrow and shaded her eyes with her hand. When she recognized Rosa Linda, a warm smile spread across her face. "Just in time. I can always use an extra hand."

Rosa Linda walked over, gave Molly a peck on the cheek, and turned to Kate. "Kate, this is Molly Gibson. She was my seventh-grade science teacher at St. Francis, and now she runs the greyhound adoption program. Molly, this is my godmother, Kate Caraway."

Molly reached over and shook Kate's hand. "I've heard a lot about you. I was wondering when Rosa Linda was going to bring you around."

"You've been on a heck of a shopping trip." Kate looked inside the Suburban. Boxes of Pedialyte, bags of dry dog food, and cases of the canned variety fill the entire back. "It looks like you're feeding every dog in Hayes County."

"No, only my weekly trip to the grocery store— Petco that is. It's hard for me sometimes to believe these skinny greyhounds eat so much."

"Rosa Linda told me about your adoption program on the way over. It's nice to know that someone is taking care of these dogs after they're no longer a financial asset. How many dogs do you have?"

"Last count, twenty-seven."

Two lanky teenage boys came ambling out of a building behind the kennel and started unloading the rest of the truck. "This is Lance and Travis. They come out a few days each week and help me with the dogs as part of their requirement for their Ag class. Boys, this is Mrs.

Caraway."

Lance flashed a bright smile. "Ma'am."

Travis kept his eyes lowered and his hands in his pockets. He mumbled a barely audible hello. *Shy boy*, Kate smiled and thought of people who were more comfortable with animals than they were with humans and guessed that Travis was one of those people.

"You boys be sweet and handle the rest of the unloading and make sure you lock up when you are finished," Molly said. "Ladies, let's go inside for a glass of iced tea."

Molly's kitchen was quaint, but unpretentious. Natural light flooded the room from a skylight and bay windows that ran along the west wall. An old butcher's table sat in the center of the room. Dozens of cookbooks and an impressive collection of teapots filled the recessed shelving that made up an entire wall. A pot of chili sat bubbling on the stove, filling the room with a spicy, sweet aroma, which made Kate question her vegetarianism.

Suddenly a rumble from the back of the house captured Kate's attention. Three greyhounds bounced into the room to check things out. After sniffing shoes and licking knees, they approved the arrival of the visitors and settled down. Two of the dogs curled up on a large hook rug and one hopped up on a cushion along the bay window. Kate and Rosa Linda took a seat on the stools around the island, and Molly brought over three glasses of iced tea.

"I hope you don't mind my royal family," Molly said. "They've taken over the house, but they're gracious enough to let me live here as long as I feed them and scratch their ears occasionally."

"They're beautiful," Kate said.

"Spoiled rotten." Rosa Linda snapped her fingers and Gracie, the dog on the cushion, leapt down and strolled over to the table. "This little girl, especially."

"Was she a racer?" Kate asked.

"Yes, indeed. She earned a bundle during the first two years she raced." Molly reached down and stroked the dog's ears. "But then, she started losing and could no longer earn her keep. Gracie's owner planned to send her to a second-class track in Louisiana where the conditions are pretty gruesome. And if she continued to lose, which was inevitable, her future would have become bleak. The owner was stingy, and I actually had to purchase her for twice her value. Freda and Lupe's owner was more compassionate and called me as soon as their winnings started to diminish. I could have the dogs if I came and collected them." Molly sipped her iced tea, lost in the past for a moment.

"You have a breathtaking view from this window," Kate said.

"That wasn't always the case." Molly laughed. "Sometimes I look around and am amazed at the changes that have occurred in my life in the past year. Before I built this place, the screen-less windows in my old trailer were covered with cardboard and taped down to keep out the wind and dust. We had to step out onto the back porch to see our land. When my Lou died last year, the crazy man left me a bundle. I was mad as hell."

"Molly didn't know about the money," Rosa Linda explained.

"Seems my husband had put every extra dollar in the stock market," Molly grinned. "He simply forgot to tell me about it. We toiled over this ranch for years. Many times, I wanted to sell it and move into a better home. But despite the hard work and headaches, we loved the solitude of country life. So we held our single-wide trailer together with bailing wire and a lot of hope. Then about a week after the funeral, I woke up one morning and took a good look around. I picked up the phone and called a general contractor. That afternoon, the trailer was gone, and the cinder blocks on which it sat were bulldozed away. I moved in with my sister, and hired a ranch hand to manage the cattle. Four months later, I had a new ranch house with this panoramic view of the Hill Country right where the trailer had been. When I heard that Rosa Linda planned to organize an Adopt-A-Greyhound program, I offered to build the facility on my property and run the operation."

"That was six months ago, and now we have twenty-seven greyhounds living in roomy pens waiting for permanent homes," Rosa Linda said. "The dogs came from all over the country, not just Texas. With Brad's help, the dogs remained healthy."

"And once Rosa Linda gets this wedding over and done with, she can get my web page up and running. I'll be able to spread the word more easily," Molly said.

"That a wonderful story," Kate said. "I'm sure Lou would have been pleased."

"How's the dog that Brad brought in on Saturday?" Rosa Linda asked.

"She's still in a lot of pain," Molly said. "This morning, I coaxed her to stand for a bit. I think her hip will be fine, but it's too soon to tell if there'll be permanent damage to the leg."

"What happened?" Kate said.

"An accident at the track. Personally, I think she was

too young to run."

"Will she be adoptable?" Rosa Linda asked, trying to keep Gracie from crawling up onto the stool.

"Maybe, but if she's lame, it will take someone with the willingness and patience to care for a crippled dog. I'm picky when it comes to placing the dogs. Greyhounds are naturally loving and mild tempered, but many have spent the first few years of their lives in cages at racetracks. It takes a few weeks after they arrive for their true nature to emerge. Learning to trust comes easier for some dogs than others. That one, I'm afraid, is too traumatized to get a feel for right now. Gracie, get down." Molly laughed. "She thinks she's a lap dog."

"What if you can't find her a home?" Kate asked.

Molly took a long swallow of her tea. "First we have to see how well she recovers. How are those wedding plans coming along?" Molly asked, directing the conversation to a more pleasant topic.

"Don't ask," Rosa Linda said, and changed the subject again. "We're still trying to figure out what's going on at the Fordyce Ranch. Kate had some questions about the dogs. I know that you will be able to help."

"Shoot. I'll do my best."

"I guess you know that Jesús Flores spoke to Rosa Linda about allegations of abuse concerning Fordyce's greyhounds. But he was murdered before he could give us any details. According to Jesús, the conditions at the Fordyce kennel were pretty bad, even though we have no evidence of that. Jesús also claimed that the new trainer was using live lures. Is that a common practice?"

"Unfortunately, yes. The racing association banned the use of live lures, but it's hard to regulate what occurs on someone's private property. Also the horror stories you hear about greyhounds left to starve in their cages usually involves fly-by-night operations, such as running dogs at class C tracks. That's not the case with the Fordyce dogs. Guy runs them at class A tracks. Up until Rosa Linda and I started this program, Guy didn't give much consideration to his dogs that failed to win. They were often sent down to lower-grade tracks. I finally convinced him to allow me to have those dogs."

"I don't think Wayne cares one way or another," Rosa Linda said.

"Well, according to Guy, Wayne has been a godsend, with all of the trouble they've had," Kate said.

"They've certainly had their share. I guess you heard about the death of his daughter. She was one of my students years ago. After she died, it was one thing after another. Meredith slipped into a world of her own. Guy Junior's been getting into trouble at school. Then last week I heard someone left a gate open and several head of cattle wondered into an area of the ranch that had not been cleared. They got to feeding on oleander bushes and died. Those leaves are toxic, brings on a heart attack just like that." Molly snapped her fingers. "Then Guy's right-hand man, Diego Gomez, died, Meredith was attacked, and now this."

"When was the last time you received any of Guy's dogs?" Kate asked.

"It's been a couple of months," Molly said as she refilled their glasses. "His dogs must be winning."

"If we are to find out what's going on, we need to see for ourselves." Rosa Linda stood up and reached for a tin sitting on the shelf of cookbooks. As soon as she picked up the can, all three dogs were instantly at her feet, tails thumping. "Sit." She doled out three biscuits and the canine clan left crumbs over the tile floor. "I know a back way to the kennel. The orchard hides anyone who walks in from that direction. I say we pay the Fordyce ranch another visit—this time when no one is around."

"I'm not hearing this." Molly laughed as she held her hands over her ears. "If you two want to spy, go ahead. I want to maintain a working relationship with Guy. I'd hate to have him not trust me."

"We're not getting anywhere talking to people," Kate said.

"Let's go tonight," Rosa Linda said. "There's not a lot of work going on at the ranch after dark."

"It's a good thing Jack is in Chicago," Kate said.

Molly's hands went back up to cover her ears.

"We'll make plans after we leave here," Rosa Linda said. "How about showing Kate the kennel?"

"Now that's something I can do. The boys should be finished unloading by now."

Kate followed Molly around her facilities. Each roomy kennel housed two greyhounds, complete with comfortable beds, food and water bowls, and a plethora of chew toys. The dogs seemed content and happy, lounging in the shade of their shelter. Molly had installed mist fans to circulate cool air. A necessity when the humidity and the temperature competed for the highest number. Lance and Travis were exercising a group of dogs in the exercise yard. Kate couldn't tell who was having more fun, the dogs or the boys.

****

Kate and Rosa Linda left Molly's place around six. On the way back, they talked about the best way to deal with Max and his bullheaded nature. Kate offered suggestions and Rosa Linda listened, her facial expressions vacillating between defiance and understanding. The young woman was too smart to deny the importance of starting her marriage off on the right foot. At the same time, however, there was that inherited stubbornness of wanting to do things her own way. This, along with all the unanswered questions, made Kate uncomfortable. What were Daniel and Rosa Linda up to that Rosa Linda refused to talk about? And why had Daniel lied to Max and Olga about being registered in school this semester? Kate hoped that whatever the situation, it had nothing to do with the trouble on the Fordyce ranch.

Kate was glad that Rosa Linda had planned to spend time with Olga making arrangements for the wedding— a wedding that Kate had begun to doubt was a good idea. On the other hand, Kate trusted Olga's good sense, and if her old friend was not worried, Kate decided that she would let the Rodriguez family work things out themselves. After all, she was there to investigate greyhound abuse, not settle a domestic dispute.

Rosa Linda dropped Kate off at the bungalow and promised to return later. Grateful to have some time to herself, Kate called Jack to see if he had any news. Living in Chicago might be exactly what she needed. She'd be with old friends and have some time to reflect on what had happened in Kenya. For the past five days, Kate had been pushing the thoughts from her mind. What was happening in camp? Had she created such upheaval that caused her colleagues to spend more time cleaning up her mess than taking care of the animals and conducting research? If the research didn't move forward with substantial results, the grant money would eventually dry up and the project that she spent so much time creating would cease to exist. Maybe she could work here in the US, writing grants and lecturing until she could return.

It was too soon to call the camp and get an update. She did not want to endanger her friends in Kenya. They put their own lives on the line when they smuggled her and Jack out of the reserve in the back of a feed truck, and on to Nairobi, where they were able to catch a flight to Cairo and then into New York.

The call went to voice mail and that probably meant that the interview went well for Jack. Kate left a message and then tried not to obsess on her uncertain future. She was to meet Rosa Linda in about two hours, just after dusk. Afraid she would doze off if she spent the time reading, Kate took the luxury of turning on the TV. The Cubs were playing the Astros, and except for Roger Franks sitting in the dugout, Kate did not recognize one single player on the team.

Chapter Ten

What do you mean you're not going?" Kate looked at the hand-drawn map Rosa Linda held out. She had indicated where Kate should park, and how to find her way to the kennel.

"Kate, please don't be upset. Daniel called, and something has happened. I can't explain now."

"Let me guess, your other project? I'm sure you two aren't going to pick out China for your wedding." As soon as she said it, Kate regretted the sarcasm. She was not usually curt with her goddaughter, but Kate hated secrets, especially now.

Instead of arguing with her godmother, Rosa Linda pointed to the map. "If you drive to this south entrance to the ranch, you can pull off the road and park here, across from the ranch. This is an entrance to someone else's property, but they never use this gate. You can hide the Jeep behind this clump of cedars. Once you cross the fence onto the Fordyce ranch, walk along the fence line for about twenty yards and you'll notice the ravine. From there you can almost make it to the kennel without being seen." Rosa Linda paused, glanced at Kate, and continued. "It's an intermittent creek that has been dry for months. There are shrubs and mesquites growing along the bank. You'll be well hidden and won't have to worry about using your flashlight. The creek snakes through pasture land for about two hundred yards and then you'll see the grove of pecan trees to the left."

"And you know these minute details because…"

"A great place to drink beer."

"What?"

"High school beer parties." Rosa Linda hesitated a moment and said, "Be careful." She gave Kate a tentative hug.

There were a million things Kate wanted to say to Rosa Linda. Lecture her on…on what, being young and idealistic? Kate heard that speech too many times when she was Rosa Linda's age. The words would only fall on deaf ears. Kate wanted to trust this young woman. After all, she'd held her when the priest poured the Holy water over her tiny head during the Baptism. But Kate had not been around for the past several years. Had Rosa Linda changed? Had her strong-willed determination led her in the wrong direction? Kate recalled when Rosa Linda ran away to join Green Peace and save the whales. She was nine years old.

Max found her walking down Highway 12 and managed to get her in the car only after promising her that she could start her own fundraising campaign to earn money to send to the organization. She raised an impressive sum in less than a week. Kate wondered if Rosa Linda ever discovered that most of the money came from Max. Now she was twenty years old, and as dedicated as ever, but to what cause, Kate was not sure. She hoped that whatever it was, Max would be there again, if necessary, to bail out his only daughter.

"You're not off the hook, you know? You'll have to deal with me later," Kate said as she folded the map and stuck it in her jeans pocket.

Rosa Linda smiled and drove away.

Thunderheads were forming in the vast distance, north of the Highland Lakes where the Colorado River's flow is slowed by a series of dams. The powerful river skirted Wimberley, but the entire area is part of one huge watershed. Rain in the northern part of the Hill Country often meant flow in the creeks of Hays County. The pungent fragrance of rain permeated the air. But as Kate watched the clouds, she saw the promise of a late summer storm drift across the sky. Wind gusts from the west rolled the water-laden clouds across the Balcones Escarpment toward the east. The last rays of sunlight, reaching up from the horizon met the clouds, filtering streaks of pink, orange, and violet across the western sky, leaving a breathtaking sunset in their wake.

Kate grabbed her flashlight and crossed the gravel road to the Fordyce Ranch. She pushed down the bottom strand of barbed wire with her foot and crawled through the fence and into the cedar break. The brush was thick and in places almost too dense to maneuver through so she had to move slowly. Needles and the dark blue berries that had fallen from cedar trees cushioned the ground. Kate scanned the property and noticed a few more cedar breaks strategically growing in certain areas. Recently, ranchers had stopped eradicating the scrubby water-thirsty trees, leaving a few stands for wildlife that depended upon them.

From what Kate had seen of Guy Fordyce's ranch, he had successfully put this practice to work. Under normal circumstances, she would pick his brain and compare notes to learn more. Anyone who was into environmental causes had her attention. Why was she having a difficult time making up her mind about Guy Fordyce? It would be so easy to condemn him with only

Rosa Linda's word on the matter of greyhound abuse. Maybe he was telling the truth. Maybe he didn't know what was going on with the training of his dogs. No matter how she analyzed the situation, there was only one conclusion she could make. The dogs were his, and he was ultimately responsible. If there were abused greyhounds on this ranch, Kate planned to find them tonight.

Despite the scratches welting up on Kate's arms, she was grateful for the thick cover. She had not quite reached the ravine and two pickups had already driven down this back road.

Kate had no trouble following Rosa Linda's map and soon emerged from the break near the creek bed. The rocky bank would make the going tough, but if she watched her footing, she should be on the ranch in less than twenty minutes. The clouds now hung heavy on the horizon, blocking out the last remnants of the sunset. Sheets of rain fell in the far distance.

Less than fifty yards from the facilities, she saw the lights from the ranch house and other buildings flickering through the tree branches that undulated in the wind. As she approached the kennel, she worried about alerting the dogs. If they started barking, Wayne, or worse yet, Garrison with his shotgun, would surely investigate the commotion.

The ravine meandered to the right, away from the kennel, and according to the map, this was where Kate needed to leave her shelter and trek across the open field to the back of the pens. She crawled out and surveyed the situation. The dog facility was a hundred yards or so away, but the night had finally set in. Blue-black replaced the sunset hues, and although patches of light

145

sky could still be seen through drifting clouds, Kate felt certain that she would not be noticed.

Stepping over mounds of recently plowed earth, Kate made her way across the field. The soil was soft and loose, and despite her high-ankle hiking boots, Kate felt dirt spilling over the tops.

The air was warm and heavy. The smell of rain grew stronger.

She stopped about twenty-five yards away from the kennel, and listened. The place appeared deserted. Now that she was closer, Kate noticed the exercise track to the left of the kennel—an oval surrounded by a six-foot-tall chain-link fence.

All was quiet.

Suddenly Kate felt awkward. What did she expect to find here, sneaking around on private property, alone and in the dark? She began to feel that this entire venture was useless. Why wasn't Rosa Linda here?

A slight breeze drifted passed. *Good*, Kate thought. Hopefully, the dogs would not pick up her scent. In the distance, she could see the lights in the house and wondered how the Fordyces were spending their evening. Having a murder charge hanging over the head of the house could not possibly provide for cozy dinner conversation. Kate could not picture Meredith Fordyce and Garrison Fordyce living under the same roof. The former, refined and stoic, playing her cards close to her chest—and the latter, verbose and obnoxious, trying to live in his brother's shadow. About the only thing they had in common was the desire, or need, to handle life's misfortunes with some sort of sedative.

Standing out here in the darkness, doubting her decision to come alone was getting Kate nowhere. She walked toward the kennel. Maybe a look among Wayne's things might prove useful. There were no windows in his tack-room office, and if she could get inside, a sweep around with the flashlight should go unnoticed. In order not to disturb the dogs, she retraced her steps and skirted the area a few yards away. Then she walked behind the kennel, toward the office. She reached the back of the building, waited, and listened.

Nothing.

As she walked around to the front, she stayed close to the building. The bunkhouse was located past the barn about fifty yards away, and she had a clear view of the front door of the Fordyce house. Kate continued on only noticing a row of trashcans seconds before she bumped into one. She grabbed it before it toppled over and caused the domino of other cans lined up along the wall. The can was plastic and made little noise when she righted it, but she stopped just the same to make sure no one heard her.

Suddenly Kate's breath caught in her throat. The sound of raspy, intermittent breathing was so close it made the hair rise on the back of her neck. She pressed her back tight to the wall and listened. Slowly she looked back from where she had come. She saw no one. Then the breathing stopped. It could not have come from one of the dogs. They were too far away, and the breathing seemed only inches away. Maybe she had imagined it. All she heard now was the pounding of her own blood rushing through her head. In her near collision with the trashcan, Kate had dropped her flashlight. She squatted down, and groped around for it. Then she heard the sound again.

Closer this time.

Someone was struggling to breathe. There was no

mistaking it. She looked around on the ground, forcing her eyes to focus in the darkness, and found the flashlight. The breathing was now accompanied by a faint whine. Someone was hurt and lying close enough for Kate to touch.

Kate wanted to bolt and get the hell out of there—instead, she kept still and listened. The desperate sound came from the trashcan right next to her. She leaned closer and waited. She heard it again. Moving to the front of the can, she placed herself between it and the house in order to block the light from her flashlight. She lifted the trashcan lid and snapped the button of the flashlight. An eye stared upward, liquid and blind with shock—the pupil dilated to pinpoint size. A clump of blood had matted the hair over the eye, and Kate was dumbstruck to see that the ear hung from a strip of skin. The tiny body, barely breathing, lay on top of several others. This one appeared to be the only one still alive. The smell of blood and death was revolting. The rabbits had been discarded only a few hours ago. Live lures. Jesús was right.

In the silence of the night, she heard a car door slam and seconds later an explosion of lights illuminated the front of the kennel, causing the greyhounds to burst into an earsplitting ruckus. Kate replaced the lid, and dropped to her knees. Hidden behind the kennel, she could not see who was there. She considered creeping back into the orchard for better cover, but curiosity got the best of her and she scurried back along the kennel to the training track. A pickup had backed up to the pens and someone was unlocking one of the cages.

Kate peered around the corner. This scene was too familiar. The pictures that Jesús had taken—they were taken here. Someone was removing several dogs from their cages and shoving them into portable kennels in the bed of the pickup. Two dogs were forced into each carrier, and from where Kate stood, it looked as if eight dogs were being taken away. When the guy turned around, Kate recognized Wayne Brody's skimpy, blond ponytail.

She stepped back in the shadows to figure this out. Was Wayne stealing Guy's dogs? With all of the statistics on the Bertillon Cards, how could he manage to sell stolen dogs to another owner? Surely, Guy would have noticed if several of his dogs had disappeared, even if he was no longer active in their training. None of this made sense. Kate heard the engine start up and took a last look.

Then she saw it. She fell back against the wall and slid down until she sat in the dirt—her legs too shaky to hold her. As the pickup pulled away and drove under the light pole, there was no mistaking it. The red and white "Succeed" bumper sticker on the left bumper reflected brightly as Wayne drove away.

She was not sure how long she sat there. The kennel lights were off, and the dogs had quieted down. Kate's concern about getting back to the Jeep safely had suddenly taken on a deeper urgency. There was no doubt now that the incident on the interstate was no accident. Someone from Fordyce ranch had followed her to Austin when she drove Jack to the airport, then back to the city, and then to the track. Was it Garrison? Did he see her at the restaurant and follow her? But he was in no shape to drive, much less maneuver the truck with such precision to run her off the highway, dash across the median, and speed away in the opposite direction. If this were a ranch vehicle, anyone could have been driving it that morning, including Wayne. The thought sent a shiver up her spin.

Kate thought back on what had occurred since she started her investigation. Within a few hours of her arrival, Garrison warned her about trespassing and Wayne lied about his training practices. Then another, more foreboding thought occurred to her. Although Guy had been arrested that morning, he could have arranged the entire incident. She needed answers—now.

She stuffed down her fear as best she could, and pressed the button to illuminate her watch. It was nine-twenty. Most of the rain clouds had passed and a wide sprinkling of stars shone. Under a bright night sky, Kate worried about being seen on the way back.

But all was quiet once again.

Kate could not ignore the opportunity handed to her. Going through Wayne's things would not take long. And who else would come into that shabby excuse for an office. Fear or no fear, she remembered her vow to leave the ranch with questions answered.

Kate crept back to Wayne's office and was relieved to find the door unlocked. She stepped inside, closed the door behind her, and flicked on her flashlight. An overhanging lightbulb was the only source of light in the room. She pulled the chain and a dim glow, barely bright enough to read from, fanned across the center of the room, leaving the corners cloaked in ominous shadows.

From somewhere outside, Kate heard the haunting hoot of a barn owl. The sound, for some reason, struck her as peaceful. Under the beam of the flashlight, the grime covering Wayne's desk looked filthier than when she was here before. She scanned his calendar. It was soiled with coffee and food stains, making Wayne's scribbles difficult to read. Nonetheless, Kate was able to decipher the latest entries: Monday, August sixth, *contact Gulf State Track about sending dogs to Corpus Christi*; Saturday, August eleventh, *Bar BQ at Lake Travis;* Monday, August thirteenth, *Gates to check dogs*. Kate checked the rest of the calendar, but saw nothing out of the ordinary. Then she noticed that in the upper right-hand corner, under notes, Wayne had written the following calculations: *65 lb. ave. at .40 = 26 X 75 = 1,950*, and below that formula, *65 lb. at .40 = 26 X 82 = 2,132*. Each calculation had an asterisk after it. Kate looked across the calendar again and spotted two dates also marked with asterisks: one on Tuesday the seventh and the other marked on Tuesday the twenty-first, today's date. Kate peeled off a yellow Post-It note and copied the dates and calculations. If they proved to be statistics concerning the dogs, Brad should be able to explain them to her.

She slid open the top left drawer of a two-drawer file cabinet that made up the base of Wayne's desk. She was surprised to find them unlocked as well. Apparently, he had nothing to hide, but a search through the files could not hurt. Kate perched the flashlight on a metal bookcase behind her, providing more light in which to read the labels. The drawer contained several dozen files, each alphabetically labeled with the name of a greyhound— Abigail Runabout, Angel Light-the-Way, Attila the Red, and so on. After reading a few of the dog's profiles, Kate shut the top drawer and pulled open the one below. Here she found files of information on several racetracks across the country, again, filed alphabetically according to state and then sub-filed according to track-class within each state. These records indicated that Guy had greyhounds strewn across the southeast—the state of Florida alone kenneled thirty-five Fordyce dogs distributed among four racetracks. Kate rifled through these files and the files of seven other states, concluding that Guy raced most of his dogs at Class A tracks, and only a handful at Class Bs, as Molly had indicated.

She closed the bottom cabinet and was about to open the top-right drawer, when she heard footsteps crunching on the gravel outside. Kate grabbed her flashlight, extinguished the overhead bulb, and cautiously stepped back into the corner. She ducked behind a row of saddles draped over a wooden stand, and snapped off her light as the door opened. Although her heart was beating loud enough to wake the dead, she focused on keeping her breathing shallow and calm. Well hidden, she felt certain that she could not be seen, but her hiding place also prevented her from seeing who had entered, and she dared not risk a peek.

The visitor turned on the light, and, as quickly as he walked in, turned around and left. Maybe it was Wayne. Maybe he had forgotten something. But Kate had not heard his truck. After a few minutes, she left the safety of her hiding place and ventured back into the office part of the room. She left the overhead light off and used only her flashlight this time. On a yellow Post-It-note, stuck in the middle of the calendar, was a short message.

I'll call tomorrow!

Judging by the fanciful handwriting, Kate was certain a woman had written it. Meredith Fordyce? What connection did she have with her husband's dog trainer? Obviously, it was something that she had wanted to keep from Guy if it meant that she must sneak in here after dark. Was tonight's foray with the dogs connected to the note? Kate took another glance at the calendar. Written in tomorrow's slot were the initials MF with a question mark behind them. Evidently, Wayne was on hold for whatever was to take place tomorrow. She looked at the Wednesday following Tuesday the seventh and found that the day was blank. Kate scanned the rest of the calendar one more time, but found no other patterns other than the two Tuesdays marked with the asterisks. No other MF initials were written anywhere.

Kate needed to stay put a little while longer to make sure the coast was clear. She took the opportunity of the extra time to search the other drawers. They were stuffed with files of receipts: vet bills, food purchases, travel expenses, along with other of miscellaneous purchases. Kate surmised that Diego Gomez must have set up the filing system, since the manila folders appeared well worn. Except for the barbecue date and possible rendezvous with Meredith, there was not much that carried Wayne Brody's personal stamp. Kate hoped for an address book, or a collection of personal papers, something that would give her a lead to illegal activities concerning the dogs or clues to Jesús's murder.

Maybe she was searching the wrong office. Maybe Garrison was the person she should investigate. Kate wished Jack were here so that she could run her theories by him. Suddenly that old feeling of loneliness overcame her again. She took stock of her situation and shuddered—hiding in a tack-room on the ranch of a suspected killer. It was time to go.

Kate left the room, peered around the side of the kennel, and seeing no one, made a dash across the field. No lights came on. No footsteps crunched the gravel. No one followed her, she was fairly certain. As soon as she reached the ravine, Kate sat down to catch her breath and empty the dirt from her boots before the trek back to the Jeep. Although the sky was clear, the smell of rain was stronger than it had been all evening. Then she heard it. The once-dry creek bed was now alive with rushing water. One flick of the flashlight told her that retracing her steps through the cover of the crack in the ground would be impossible. The storm in the distance had been much closer and more severe to have had produced such runoff. The water was at least three feet deep, but judging by its swiftness, it had not yet reached its peak.

Attempting to wade through the rushing current was suicidal. Anyone who had lived through a rainy spring in the Hill Country knew the dangers of swift moving water. Too many people had underestimated its force—either children playing in a gully or motorists driving across a low-water crossing—only to be swept away, their bodies found days or weeks later.

Kate would have to make her way across the pasture without the protection of cover. Anyone looking across the field could easily see her. Remembering Garrison and his shotgun, Kate hunkered down and crouched her way along, staying as low to the ground as possible. Tomorrow she would have to spend extra time stretching before her morning run. Duck-walking half a mile was hell on anyone's legs and back, even for someone who stayed in shape.

The sound of the rushing water grew to a roar—the current rising faster with each passing second. No longer able to maintain the posture, Kate stood up to make a run for it. As she did so, something soft and feathery whizzed across her right temple. Thinking she had disturbed a brush quail or a burrowing owl, Kate ignored it and continued to sprint across the field. She managed only a few yards when a hot, searing pain shot through her right arm—the jolt knocked her off her feet. She hit the ground, slamming her head against a rock. Flashes of light streaked across her vision. Kate tried to right herself, but couldn't move. To her horror, she heard another swish and thud, this time, inches from her face. As her vision cleared, she saw a shaft with a feathered tip embedded in the earth. Someone had shot her with an arrow, piercing her arm above the elbow.

Now she heard her attacker running toward her—footsteps trudging through the field. Kate had only a few seconds before another arrow found its target. She had no choice. In desperation, she jerked her arm around and rolled over onto her back. Pain shot through her entire body. Keeping her skewered arm close to her chest, she rolled again and flung herself into the ravine. As soon as she hit the water, the current slammed her under and swept her downstream. Tumbling uncontrollably like driftwood in an angry river, the current dragged her over the creek bottom, beating and scraping her body on the jagged rocks.

Kicking hard against the rushing water, she raised her head and gulped a quick breath of air only to have the current roll her over and push her deeper below the surface. With her left hand, she grabbed for anything that would hold her—a rock, tree root, but everything gave way in her grasp and she continued to sweep farther away.

Too far below the surface to raise her head, Kate's lungs burned, fighting against the uncontrollable need to inhale. Unable to hold her breath any longer, Kate envisioned water rushing down her throat and shocking her lungs into a cold paralysis. How long would it take her to drown? Instantly, no more than a few seconds, long enough to watch her life flash before her. Please, God, Kate pleaded, she could do without the slide show, just let it be quick. Her head made contact with another rock, striking hard and forcing her mouth open. She began swallowing water. Four or five seconds more and it would be over. Then something changed. The rocks along the bottom of the creek bed seemed to disappear. She felt the ropy, gnarl of tree roots instead.

The cedar break. She was approaching the road and soon the water would pass through the culvert. Kate knew that she would not make it through the narrow tunnel alive. Her lungs screamed for air. With one final attempt, she grabbed hold of a long cedar root growing along the side of the creek bank and hung on. Miraculously, it held. She wedged her foot under the tangled growth and anchored herself against the current. Inching her way upward, she thrust her head above water and gulped for air. But debris in the current slapped her in the face, and leaves and twigs filled her mouth choking her. Dizziness overcame her ability to think—exhaustion prevented her from pulling herself higher.

She must not give in. Fighting unconsciousness, Kate inched her way up a little farther, and at last was able to take a clear breath. Her right arm hung loosely by her side, the back of the shaft had broken off in the tumble through the current, but the arrow was lodged in her arm. Numb from cold water and exhaustion, she lay on the bank as the water swept over her, and then, as quickly as it had arrived, the flow subsided and the current slowed. If she could hang on a few moments longer, survival looked promising. As thoughts of hope entered her mind, Kate feared that her pursuer might not have given up the chase. *Perfect, Kate Caraway, just perfect. You screwed up again*, she chided herself as the lights went out.

Chapter Eleven

Jack arrived at the bungalow around eleven. Surprised to found the place dark, he called Kate on the cellphone. Receiving no answer, he phoned the ranch house. Max answered on the first ring.

"Rosa Linda?" Max shouted.

"Max, it's Jack. I just got back. Is Kate there?"

"I wish she were."

"What's going on?"

"Hopefully nothing, but I think you need to come over."

When Jack walked into the kitchen, the looks on Max and Olga's faces confirmed his fears. "What's happened?" Jack said. "Where's Kate?"

"We're not sure," Max said. "We thought you were coming in tomorrow morning."

"I managed to catch a flight this evening. I knew Kate was eager to find out about my interview. Why do I have a bad feeling about things?"

"You tell him," Max said to Olga.

"Katie wanted to search Guy's dog kennels tonight."

Max handed Jack a beer. "Sit down. This will take a while."

"She was supposed to be back around ten," Olga continued. "We had a heck of a storm blow through tonight. That may be what's delaying her."

"Wait," Jack said. "Kate went to the Fordyce ranch

158

tonight alone?" He slammed his beer bottle on the counter. "Why in the hell did she go alone?"

Olga glanced over at her husband who looked as if he were about to bust a gut. "Oh, *Dios mìo*. Rosa Linda was supposed to go with her, but she—oh, Jack. I'm afraid my daughter has done a bad thing." Olga grabbed a wad of tissues from the box on the counter and began crying.

"What have I been telling you, Olga?" Max shouted.

Jack put his arm around her. "Max, calm down. Olga, tell me what happened."

"Rosa Linda and I were supposed to make the final arrangements for the wedding after dinner tonight."

"A wedding which will never happen!" Max said.

"Let her talk, Max."

"I knew something was up," Olga continued. "She was fidgety. Her mind was clearly not on the wedding. She agreed to every suggestion I made and then said she had to go to meet Daniel. As she was walking out, I confronted her about what was going on. She told me that she and Kate had planned to go to the ranch tonight to search the kennels together, but that something had come up. She refused to say what, only that I shouldn't worry. She said she gave Kate a map to the back entrance of the ranch on Red Corral Road and said she should be back around ten, then she left before I could find out more. I called Kate, but she didn't answer. I was on my way to look for her when the storm blew in."

"I drove in from Austin a little while ago," Max said. "I was about to drive out to Guy's ranch when you called."

Jack downed his rest of his beer. "Let's go."

"You two go. I'll stay here in case either one calls,"

Olga said.

****

"Guy's ranch starts at this fence line," Max said. "I hate snooping around like this. I have a good mind to call Guy and get him out here."

"You know him better than any of us, Max, but let's have a look around before we do that," Jack said. "Kate may be on her way now. I'd hate to have her arrested for trespassing so shortly after what happened in Kenya." Jack tried to make light of the situation, but the memory of those two days before they left was too much to bear, and the sudden realization that his wife might be in trouble again changed his concern to fear.

Max neared the back gate when they spotted Rosa Linda's Jeep. He pulled in behind it, and Jack was out of the truck before it stopped rolling. Max caught up with him and soon they were shoving their way through the cedar break and up to the edge of the ravine. Max shone his flashlight illuminating the few inches of water that remained after the current washed through. A thick pile of brush had bottlenecked where the culvert ran under the road. "Creek's been running heavy tonight." Max chuckled in an attempt to dispel Jack's fear. "You know, I'll bet Kate didn't find anything and, unwilling to come back empty-handed, she probably walked right up to Guy's front door and confronted him."

"Let's hope you're right," Jack said. "I think Kate feels the same way you do about Guy's innocence. But when it comes to animal abuse, she can easily lose her head. She'd dog the Pope to his grave if she believed he had mistreated an animal."

"I'll call Guy and see if she's been there," Max said.

"No, let's surprise him."

They started back to the truck when Max shone the flashlight across the creek bank. On the other side, tangled in a heap of brush, Jack spotted Kate lying face down in the mud.

****

Kate drifted in and out of consciousness trying to grasp onto her husband's voice.

"Let me think," Jack said. "About two years ago, Kate was held at knife-point by the angry brother of a well-known poacher whom she managed to get arrested. And when we were in Uganda last February, while I was negotiating with a local merchant to buy gas for our truck, Kate was kidnapped, but only for a couple of hours. Once the kidnapper found out who he had captured, he let her go, not so much out of respect or kindness, but out of fear." Jack took a sip of his coffee. "This is the first time, however, a weapon has managed to actually break the skin."

Holden McCrae laughed—an annoying sound. *Shut the hell up*, Kate's brain shouted, but the words never reached her mouth. Then more voices, more irritating conversation. Kate wished that they would all leave. Except for Jack. *Oh, God. Jack, are you hurt?* Kate cried out in silence.

"I think she's coming to."

Kate recognized Olga's melodic voice and felt Jack's fingers gently brush the hair off her forehead. Now, more than anything she wanted to wake up, to see her husband and reassure herself that she was not having another vivid nightmare. Heavy eyelids hung like drapes over her vision. Her mouth was too dry to utter a word.

"Sweetheart, can you hear me?" Jack asked.

Kate smiled and tried to reach for his hand, but her

arm would not cooperate. Seeing the distress on her face, Jack picked up her hand, gave it a squeeze and kissed her on the cheek. "Kate, it's me. Do you remember what happened?"

"Jack?" Kate opened her eyes. *Have I done it again, put you in danger?* "Are you—" Maybe if she could think straight, she could figure out a way to stay in Kenya, at least until things quieted down. But thinking straight was impossible; staying awake was impossible. Kate gave up and fell back asleep.

"That sedative was pretty strong. I think we should let her sleep." Jack was grateful that Max and Olga were here, despite their own problems.

"Call me when she wakes up," McCrae said. He turned to look at Max and Olga. The strain on their faces was not merely on account of Kate's mishap. "We'll check at Daniel's apartment first and then contact some of Rosa Linda's friends and see if we can find them. I'm sure once we do, we'll be able to piece this together." He grabbed his hat and started to leave, then turned around. "Oh, I haven't told you. The murder charges against Guy were dropped. I'm back to square one."

"How did that happen?" Jack asked.

"You tell me. A good lawyer, friends in high places—the word I got was that the case was too flimsy, and oh, yeah, something about discovering an alibi."

"When I find Rosa Linda," Max said, "I'm going to lock her in her room. How many times did I tell her not to get involved?"

Olga went over and began massaging her husband's shoulders. "You know you can't do that."

"I know what you're going to say, that she's an adult and that she can make her own decisions. But if she's going to live in my house, she's going to live by my rules. And after what happened last night, I think she might need some reminding...of...of what those rules are."

"I'm sure she's okay," Jack said. His reassurance did little to dissipate Olga's concern.

"I can't understand," Olga said. "She always lets us know where she is. Even when she goes away for the weekend with Daniel."

"I plan to put a stop to that," Max said.

"You two go home and wait for your daughter. There's not much you can do here. Call me if you find out anything," Jack said.

****

When Kate finally awoke, it was to the sound of steady breathing and Jack's hair tickling her arm. A bright sun shone through the blinds, causing her head to feel as if it were splitting open. As soon as her vision cleared she saw that her husband, sitting in a chair next to her, and had dozed off with his head on the bed and his hand covering hers. His touch, warm and safe.

Kate cleared her throat. "Jack."

Startled, he jumped and knocked over a hospital tray.

"I feel like I've been hit by a truck."

"Not a truck, but tumbling rocks." He held up a glass. "Water?"

"Please. A landslide or a stoning?" Kate's throat burned.

Jack put the straw up to her lips. "Glad to see you've retained your sense of humor. You have a concussion and a major body piercing in your right arm. Other than that, you came out pretty well. Take it easy and when

163

you're ready, you can tell me what happened. They have you doped up on some powerful stuff."

Kate felt like her lungs would ignite with each breath, and the pounding behind her eyes was worse than any migraine she had ever had. The water helped, and the desire to return to the land of the living grew with each sip. "The last thing I remember is—" She swallowed. "—looking through Wayne Brody's files in his office. Did I get caught?"

"We're not sure what happened."

"I dreamed we were back in Kenya in the middle of all of that trouble."

Jack laughed. "Yes, I know. You talked quite a lot about those last few days."

Tears welled up in Kate's eyes, congesting her sinuses and making her headache worse. "When I heard your voice, I got really scared. I thought that I had gotten us into more trouble. Then, I heard you laugh, and…well, I went back to sleep." She swallowed away the tears and held tight onto Jack's hand. Then bits and pieces of last night flashed in her mind, and she jerked her head up to stare at her right arm.

"An arrow— Who?" Trying hard to grab hold of a fleeting memory, she laid her head back down on the pillow, and her feelings of melancholy gave way to anger.

"The best we can figure is that someone shot you while you were trying to make your way back to the Jeep. You must have fallen into the creek and then were carried by the current. Max and I found you on the creek bank."

"You and Max—How did you know where to look? Oh, Rosa Linda—when I didn't return."

"Not quite, sweetheart. We don't know where Rosa Linda is. We were hoping you might be able to point us in the right direction."

"Did I hear McCrae's voice? Was he here?"

"For a while, but you were in no shape to answer questions. He'll be back later."

The memory of last night returned and Kate told Jack of the plan to search Guy's kennel and Rosa Linda's sudden decision not to accompany her. Too much talk wore her out, and Jack convinced her to rest while he called McCrae. Consumed with worry and guilt about her goddaughter, Kate knew that she would not be able to go back to sleep. But as soon as Jack made the call, she drifted off again.

The next time Kate awoke, it was to the smell of hospital food. Despite the indigestible thoughts the food conjured up in her mind, hunger pangs tugged at her stomach.

"I'll be your slave forever if you wheel that tray out into the hall and send out for a cheese and garlic pizza."

"Add jalapenos to it, make it a large, and we'll have a party," said McCrae. Kate turned and noticed the sheriff standing by the window.

"Good sign," Jack said. "As long as she has her appetite, I know it's only a matter of minutes before she's ready to tackle another adversary." Jack was perched on the side of Kate's bed. "Holden walked in about five minutes ago. I've filled him in on what you told me. Remember anything else?"

Kate's grogginess disappeared with the decrease of drug that dripped through her IV. Her headache also started to dissipate, and using her left arm, she rose up as Jack reached behind her and propped up her pillows.

"I'm serious about the pizza. You want more info, then you need to get me food."

"You'll have to settle for fast-food pizza. That's all we have in Wimberley, all that's deliverable anyway," said McCrae.

"As long as it is hot and greasy," Kate said.

Jack made the call, and McCrae pulled his notebook out of his shirt pocket. "Rosa Linda gave you no indication as to where she was going?"

"Like I told Jack, she was supposed to go with me to check out the kennel, but changed her mind at the last minute." Kate reached for her glass of water to put out the fire in her throat. "She said something had come up that she and Daniel needed to take care of. Getting Rosa Linda to talk once she's made up her mind to keep a secret is like pulling ticks off a cougar. I suggest calling Molly Gibson."

"You still think this has something to do with the greyhounds?" McCrae asked. "That there's a connection?"

"And Jesús's murder," Kate answered, sounding more defensive than she meant to. "Jesús makes allegations concerning dog abuse and is murdered. I'm run off the highway. A dead dog is found in Rosa Linda's Jeep, and I'm shot on the Fordyce ranch—" Kate laid her head back on the pillow and stared up at the white plaster on the ceiling. "Oh, Lord."

Jack reached over. "What is it? Are you feeling bad again?"

"No, I remembered something else." Kate sighed. "When that pickup tried to run me off the highway—" She stopped, recalling that she had not had a chance to tell Jack about that incident.

"I know," Jack said. "Holden told me all about it last night while you were asleep."

"Speaking of connections," Kate continued. "As Wayne drove away from the kennel last night, I got a good look at the truck. It was the same one that tried to squash me like a bug on the way to the racetrack."

"How can you be sure?" McCrae asked.

"The 'Succeed' bumper sticker on the left, rear bumper. It's the same pickup, all right. I suppose you spoke to Guy this morning and told him about last night. What did he say? Is he planning to file charges against me for being on his ranch?"

"Man, when she recovers, she really recovers," McCrae said to Jack. Then he looked back at Kate. "The plot thickens. Yes, I went to see Guy this morning. Seems he and Meredith are celebrating their good fortune. After the murder charges were dropped yesterday afternoon, the Fordyce family left on a vacation. Their maid doesn't know where. They left in a hurry. The school secretary said that Guy called about four o'clock and asked for a few day's worth of lessons for Guy Jr. No Guy, no Meredith, no Rosa Linda, no Daniel."

"How about Wayne and Garrison? Were you able to talk to them about the dead dog in the Jeep or about last night?"

"Wayne wasn't there. The ranch foreman hadn't seen him since yesterday afternoon. Garrison has an ironclad alibi for last night. He was playing poker with the ranch hands in the bunkhouse from seven-thirty to way past midnight. All four corroborated his story. Seems that Garrison has a standing invitation to Tuesday night's weekly card game, since he loses his shirt every time. As far as yesterday afternoon, Garrison claims that he spent the day with a girlfriend. We're checking out his story now."

"Whoever shot you had to be experienced in using a bow," Jack said. "It's not like firing a gun, which any idiot can do. Shooting an arrow with enough precision to hit a moving target, especially at night, is a honed skill."

"According to what I know, it could be one of three Fordyces," Kate said, "father, son, or brother."

****

Kate winced, gritted her teeth, and tried not to complain. After a great deal of persuading, making promises she did not intend to keep, and finally resorting to out-and-out threats, her doctor reluctantly released her from the hospital.

While the bargaining was going on, Jack sat back and listened with a grin on his face. This doctor did not have a chance in hell of winning this argument. Talking folks into giving her what she wanted was one of Kate's most creative talents. It got her out of trouble, into trouble, and it was one of the many reasons Jack loved her. Two hours later, they were back at the bungalow.

"Your head feels like an ill-formed cantaloupe. Are you sure you can handle this?" Jack poured another dollop of shampoo in the palm of his hand and lathered up Kate's hair. "I think the third time is the charm. The water is finally clear of mud."

Jack washed Kate's hair while she lay in the bathtub keeping her right arm floating on a plastic pillow. Together, they tried to solve the human jigsaw puzzle that had consumed Kate's life for the past five days.

"You're very good at that," Kate said as Jack rinsed her hair. "I'd like to soak in this tub forever, but we have work to do. Help me dry off, and let's get started."

With her hair wrapped in a towel, and her body in a bathrobe, Kate sat on the bed while Jack took out a legal pad and made himself comfortable at the table.

"Make a facts column," Kate instructed her husband. "We'll start with that. Fact one: Jesús was murdered. Two: we have photos of dead greyhounds."

"Fact three," Jack added. "You had an accident on the highway on the way to the track."

"Right. But let's make that fact four. Fact three was seeing Garrison in the restaurant right before the accident."

"Fact five: someone put a dead greyhound in the Jeep for you to find."

"Fact six: I saw Wayne taking dogs away from Guy's kennel, and fact seven: I'm shot with an arrow while leaving Guy's ranch. Oh, and fact eight: Rosa Linda and Daniel are up to something and they've disappeared."

"Right," Jack said. "Except, for now, that's uncertain. I agree that they are not leveling with you, but we don't know for sure, so let's put that piece of information under…"

"Speculations," Kate added.

"Good. That's spec one," Jack said. "Spec two: Wayne's up to no good."

"Spec three: Guy's up to no good," Kate said. "And while I was in Wayne's office, Meredith Fordyce came in, at least I think it was her. She left a note on his desk telling him she'll call tomorrow."

"Okay. Spec four: Meredith's up to no good."

"A few more facts: the Fordyces have suddenly left and I found a barrel of dismembered rabbits near the training track. Guy's dogs have been getting sick. Remember? He claimed that some of the young ones became ill with parvo, and Brad said that four had recently died while racing. He suspected epilepsy."

"I'll place that under speculations," Jack said. "We're some team, huh?"

"Speaking of team, let this list gel for a moment while you comb out my hair, otherwise I'm going to look like Einstein if my hair dries under this towel."

"I'm great at washing, but I can't make any guarantees about my ability to style hair."

"Anyone whose preferred style is a ponytail isn't too particular. Go easy on the lumps. So, have you found us a place to live? If not, I'd check out the Hancock Tower. If it was good enough for Sosa."

"Pitching coaches don't make as much as home-run hitters. You'll have to settle for an efficiency. How did you know I got the job?"

"I heard you telling Max and Olga while I was drifting in and out in the hospital."

"Are you okay with this?"

"Hey, you keep washing my hair, and I'll follow you anywhere."

The knock on the door caused them both to jump. Jack opened it and Olga walked in, eyes red-rimmed and a look of panic frozen on her face. Kate's good mood evaporated instantly. She had never seen her dear friend look so upset.

Olga looked as if she were about to topple over. Jack caught her by her elbow and seated her in the chair. She took a deep breath. "Rosa Linda and Daniel have been arrested in Laredo."

"What happened?" Jack and Kate asked.

"We don't know. Rosa Linda called about an hour ago. She would not tell me what—happened." Olga faltered. "All she said was that she and Daniel were involved in some kind of demonstration and were arrested. She said that Daniel called a lawyer that he knew in San Antonio and was able to get bail posted for both of them. She said that—"

Olga could no longer hold back the tears. Jack brought her a box of tissue from the bathroom. He held her while she cried.

"I'm sorry. Rosa Linda said that she was not coming home. She was moving in with Daniel and dropping out of school. What's happening, Katie? I don't understand. She's gotten herself into trouble and will not allow us to help. She didn't even call us when she was arrested."

"She's embarrassed and angry, and scared to come home," Jack said. "Give her time. Where is she now?"

"She won't tell me, but the phone number that registered was from Laredo. Max is tracing it. Rosa Linda said that she only called so that we wouldn't worry, but she was adamant about not coming home. Yesterday, we made wedding plans and today she's left me. I guess Max was right about Daniel. But I still can't believe that he is a bad person. I don't know what to think."

"What was the demonstration over?" Jack asked.

"Rosa Linda wouldn't say."

"Should be easy to find out," Jack said. "If the demonstration led to an arrest, it'll be in the online news, the local news at least. I'll do a search and if necessary, call a Laredo news station and see what I can find out."

"I'm going back to the house. I left my phone there. I want it in case she calls again. I wanted you to know. I knew you were worried."

"We'll do what we can here, Olga," Kate said. "Let us know if anything new develops, and don't worry. Jack's right. As soon as she calms downs, she'll call again. At least we know she's okay."

After Olga left, Jack stepped out onto the porch to make some phone calls while Kate read over their list. She felt certain that Rosa Linda's brief account of their escapades was not quite the truth. Kate recalled Daniel's passionate speech on the day of the brunch, and then suddenly it all made sense.

Jack walked in interrupting Kate's ruminations. "Well, there was no demonstration or protest in Laredo last night."

"I'm not surprised. I know why Rosa Linda and Daniel were arrested."

Chapter Twelve

Later that evening, too anxious to sit and wait for further news, Kate and Jack walked over to the Rodriguez home. Maria brought them into Max's study where Olga was waiting for her husband to get off the phone. The short walk to the house had taken its toll on Kate. She had been out of the hospital less than six hours and although prescription Advil had dulled her headache, her arm throbbed from the twenty-one stitches holding it together.

Olga noticed Kate's discomfort and insisted she sit down. "How are you doing? You should still be in bed."

"And miss all the fun."

"You're not as tough as you think you are. If that arrow had hit a bone or severed a blood vessel, you might not have made it."

"Well it didn't. I was lucky." Kate repositioned herself in the chair.

"They're staying at the Rio Bravo Motel," Max said as he hung up the phone. "I got the number off caller ID and did a reverse search. I spoke to the desk clerk and he assured me that they haven't checked out." Max paced in front of his desk. "Rosa Linda's of age, and there's not much I can do. I called cellphones and their motel room several times, and they're either out or not answering." Max continued on for several minutes, letting off stream. They all knew the details, but they let Max rehash them over and over, as if one more time and it would make sense to him.

"Tell them what you found out, Jack," Kate said.

"There was no protest in Laredo last night," Jack said.

"I'm not surprised. She's been lying to us for some time." Max's healthy tan had turned ashen overnight. He walked over to Olga, picked up her hand, and sat down next to her on the sofa. For a moment, his anger diminished as he took comfort in his wife's quiet nature.

"I don't understand," Olga said.

Kate had never seen Olga look so frightened and helpless. Seeing her two closest friends on the verge of collapse was more than Kate could handle, especially since she felt somewhat responsible. But she was not yet ready to reveal her suspicions.

"I can't sit here." Max rose and walked over to his desk. "I'm going to Laredo."

"You're not going alone," Jack said.

"I don't plan to. You're coming with me. If we leave right away, we'll be in Laredo before dark." Max turned to Kate. "Do you mind if I borrow your husband for a couple of days?"

"I insist. Bring him back in one piece." Kate winked a thank-you to Jack.

"Max, are you sure you should do this?" Olga said. "Maybe you should wait."

"It'll be okay. I promise to wait and skin our daughter alive while you're here to help," Max said as he walked out to pack his bags.

"Make sure he behaves," Olga said as she gave Jack a hug.

****

Kate and Olga sat in the airy kitchen and talked while the sun disappeared behind the western hills. Kate faked hunger as an excuse to give her friend something to do. While Olga puttered around throwing together a salad and toasting some homemade bread, Kate went over the events of the past few days. She summarized the list that she and Jack had made, and encouraged Olga's suggestions as to how these events might be related. Kate was careful with the facts regarding Jesús's murder. She was sure his death was connected to what was going on in Laredo. However, she chose to keep her speculations to herself until they heard from Max and Jack. No need to add another obstacle to the problems of a murdered ranch hand and disappearing dogs.

Sensing tension in the air, Luna sulked in and curled up on the rug next to Kate, resting her pointed snout on Kate's foot. Kate and Olga finished dinner and some color had returned to Olga's complexion. Kate could only imagine what Olga was going through. Being a godmother and loving Rosa Linda like a daughter was hard enough. As they sat there in silence, watching the final flicker of sunlight slip away, Kate reflected over a pivotal conversation she and Jack had had over twenty years ago.

When talk of a permanent relationship came up, the subject of children had been, at first, avoided. Kate knew from a very young age that she would not have kids. If Jack wanted them, she was certain that she would not be able to consent to his wishes. He was the one who tentatively brought up the subject. Having children anytime soon would not be a good idea since his baseball career kept him on the road. Kate agreed. The subject had not been discussed since, except to share with one another the joy they felt with their chosen lifestyle.

As the hours slipped away, Kate knew that finding her assailant and Jesús's murderer would become increasingly difficult. She had decided to call McCrae and find out if he had learned anything new, when Luna suddenly jumped up and ran to the front door. Before Kate and Olga could reach the foyer, Rosa Linda stormed in and headed for the stairs. When she saw her mother, Rosa Linda said, "Mom, I know Dad's not here. I checked before I came in and his truck's gone. I don't want to talk to him yet." Then she settled down, walked over to her mother, and held her briefly. "It's okay, Mom. Everything will be fine. Daniel's got an attorney and he's taking care of everything. I've only come back to get some clothes and pick up Luna." She turned for the stairs.

"Your father may not be here right now, young lady, but that doesn't mean that you don't have to answer to me. You can't waltz in here like that, speak your piece, and walk out."

Her tone shocked both Kate and Rosa Linda. Mother and daughter had always treated one another like sisters. Kate had never heard Olga use a stern voice with her daughter. The reprimand only caused Rosa Linda to pause for a few seconds.

"No, Mom. When things settle down, we'll talk. I don't want to be here when Dad returns."

Olga looked over at Kate and she understood that Max's trip to Laredo was not to be mentioned right now. Rosa Linda ran upstairs and Olga let out a big sigh.

"I'll go up and talk to her, if you think it's a good idea," Kate said.

"Good luck," Olga replied. "I doubt I can talk any

sense into her. I was so worried and now that she's here, I'm madder than hell. She didn't even notice your arm wrapped up. She didn't even ask about last night."

"Well, maybe it's time I told her."

Kate went after Rosa Linda, angry for Olga more than for herself. After the last few hours, Kate now seriously believed that the entire greyhound abuse situation was one big hoax. One bum arm or not, Kate was not letting Rosa Linda out of the house without some answers. When Kate stepped into Rosa Linda's room, she was flinging clothes into two suitcases that lay open on the bed.

Kate pushed the suitcases away, sat down in the middle of the melee, and said, "You can slow down. Your dad will not be back for a few hours." Rosa Linda stopped and seemed to see Kate for the first time since she came in.

"How did you—oh, my God. Kate, what happened?"

"Abused greyhounds? Spying at the Fordyce ranch? Remember?"

Rosa Linda sat down and dropped her head in her hands. "I'm so sorry about last night, Kate. Are you all right?"

"Rosa Linda, I've been shot with an arrow, and I almost drowned. No, I'm not all right."

Tears started rolling down Rosa Linda's face. "I don't know what to say."

"You can start by telling me how the greyhounds are connected with the fact that you and Daniel have been smuggling illegals."

Rosa Linda jerked her head up. Kate's intimidation tactic only managed to bring Rosa Linda's anger back to

177

the surface.

She stuffed the last of her clothes in the suitcases and zipped them shut. "I don't know how you found out. Daniel and I had planned to tell you, eventually."

"Rosa Linda, I don't think you realize what danger you and Daniel are in."

"Danger! What danger *we* are in, seriously? Do you think these Mexicans cross the border to instant sanctuary? They give everything they have to *coyotes* who bring them here only to betray them once they cross the fence, or river, or wherever. They're often beaten and robbed inside our borders. They're left with nothing. They deserve a chance. You, of all people, should understand. But it doesn't matter now."

Rosa Linda grabbed her bags and ran downstairs. Kate followed, the pounding of each step painfully jarring every sore place on her body. Rosa Linda darted into the kitchen and grabbed Luna's leash off the hook by the pantry.

As she started for the front door, Olga tried one last effort to stall her daughter. "Rosa Linda, your father will surely call off the wedding if you and Daniel don't come back and discuss this with us. I'm sure we can—"

Rosa Linda snapped her head around and looked at Kate and then at Olga. "That won't be necessary. Daniel and I were married in Laredo this afternoon." She opened the door and ran down the front steps. Luna loped after her. Before Olga could catch her breath, they were gone.

****

Kate went to the refrigerator and pulled out two Carta Blancas. She handed one to Olga. "Here, I think you need this."

"I like 'em really cold. Take the rest and ice them

down in the sink. It's gonna be a long night," Olga said.

"One's good for now—something to take the edge off while I let the other shoe drop," Kate said.

"Excuse me?"

"Okay, maybe two beers then." Kate took two glasses from the cabinet, and set one down in front of Olga.

Olga ignored the beer glass and took a long swig from her bottle. "Spit it out."

"It hit me while Jack was on the phone last night speaking to one of the news stations in Laredo. Rosa Linda and Daniel have been spending a lot of time in border towns. They're either smuggling drugs—"

"Katie!" Olga shouted.

"Hold on. Or they're smuggling something else."

"What're you getting at?"

"Olga, Rosa Linda and Daniel are smuggling or involved in smuggling illegals across the border. Think about it: Daniel's background, Jesús trying to get the rest of his family across, Rosa Linda's evasions about where they went on the weekends. I confronted her, and it's true."

"Max and I have often talked to her about our families migrating to this country when we were young, how difficult it was for them to start again in a new country. To tell you the truth, I'm not surprised. She's one headstrong girl. At least we know what this is all about."

Kate on the other hand, was not yet ready to pat herself on the back for solving one of the mysteries. Right now time was an important factor. She needed Olga's help if this investigation was to move forward. Besides, Kate wanted to keep Olga busy while they awaited further news about her daughter and new son-in-law. Kate's thoughts were interrupted with a rap on the table.

"Okay, what's up? I was making a joke about not having to pay for a big wedding and when it came time for you to laugh, I look over and see a morbid face," Olga said. "So, what is it now?"

"Olga, do you think that Jesús's death had something to do with the people that Rosa Linda and Daniel helped carry across the border?"

"Lord, I hope not."

"Jesús was here on a work visa and was trying, without much success, to get his family across. His initial concern may have been the greyhounds, but when he called Rosa Linda at the last minute, sounding panicked—maybe it was not about the dogs. Maybe it was about something else. I keep having a problem with the motive for his murder."

"Yes, I see what you mean." Olga pulled her braid over her shoulder and began tightening the end.

"If the murder was committed because of the dogs, then Guy's the main suspect. After all they were his dogs," Kate said. "If he had neglected their well-being, even if he was unaware of any abuse, the blame would come back to him. But is that a strong enough motive?"

"I thought that also. I can't see Guy killing anyone. And I can't believe that Jesús was killed because he saw Wayne Brody using live lures to train those dogs. It doesn't add up."

"Something is still going on with the dogs though, something serious. Someone wants me dead. I don't think it was because I was caught snooping around the kennel last night. After all, someone from Guy's ranch tried to kill me on the highway the day before."

Things became more muddled as Kate tried to unravel the tangled mess. She was not looking at the situation from the correct angle. Her paradigms were too narrow and subjective. Solving this was simply a matter of taking the pieces and rearranging them. But the important piece still eluded her. Why had Jesús called the morning he was murdered?

The doorbell rang. A few seconds later, Maria escorted McCrae to the kitchen. "I decided to drop by instead of calling. Hope you don't mind, Olga."

"Come in, Holden. I'd offer you a beer, but I know you're on duty," Olga said.

"Just don't ask me twice. At times like these, I'm easily tempted. One minute I'm searching for a murder suspect and the next, I'm scouting the county for lost dogs."

Kate and Olga looked at one another.

"Guy's greyhounds?" Kate said.

"Not the Fordyce dogs. I got a call from Molly Gibson. Seems some of her wards have escaped. The lock on one of the cages was not secured and four adventurous hounds decided to explore the countryside. I doubt she'll find them. She never does."

"This has happened before?" Kate said.

"A few times. Molly has so many high-school students working with her that every once in a while they get careless and don't completely fasten the locks."

"And she never finds the lost dogs?"

"No."

"Doesn't that seem absurd to you?"

Kate regretted the edge in her voice, but McCrae shrugged and turned to Olga. "Anyway, any word on your daughter, Olga?"

"Oh, I guess you can say that we've heard from her. In less than twenty-four hours, she managed to get herself arrested for smuggling illegals across the border, and while waiting for her lawyer, she got married."

"Well, at least her arrest is her husband's problem now. What does he have to say about her being in jail?"

Kate and Olga looked at one another and burst out laughing. It was an uncontrollable, contagious laughter, and McCrae could not help but join in, although he was not sure why he was laughing.

"Daniel was arrested too," Olga said, through more fits of laughter. She doubled over and gasped to catch her breath. Then the hiccupping started, and the situation became funnier.

"I'll bet you gals laugh at funerals too," McCrae said. "If you ladies can get a hold of yourselves, I'll fill you in on Kate's situation."

Kate and Olga wiped their eyes.

"I'm afraid we don't have much to go on. Now that you're feeling better, let's talk in more detail about what happened last night."

Since Kate returned from the hospital, more bits and pieces of the prior evening's events had emerged. She added them to the list she and Jack made, but was unable to draw any conclusion. Now she hoped that McCrae would supply some missing facts.

"Olga and I were discussing the two attempts on my life and how they're related—*if* they're related—to Guy's alleged dog problems," Kate said.

"Don't forget about the little present someone placed in the Jeep." McCrae said.

"Have you talked to Wayne Brody about the attack

made on me last night?"

"He claims that he was taking several dogs to the track in Corpus Christi and delivering others that had been sold to an owner/trainer near Lockhart. He didn't return until early this morning."

"But why sneak off at night?" Olga said.

"I asked him that," McCrae said. "He said he often transports the dogs at night because of the heat."

"I'm sorry, Sheriff, but I can't believe that Wayne wasn't up to something," Kate said. "Call it intuition, or an overactive imagination, but what was going on last night was not without suspicion. Something about the dogs did not seem right."

"Wayne had the bill of sale and transfer papers to prove it. He might also have an alibi. You were shot around ten o'clock. Wayne swears that a ranch hand saw him leave the ranch around nine-thirty. I'll question everyone and find out if what Wayne's says is true. Anything else?"

The events were clear in Kate's mind. She related them again, this time remembering the photos. "Those photos Jesús took."

"The ones Rosa Linda stole from his pickup? Those you conveniently forgot to tell me about until three days later? The ones someone stole from the Jeep and replaced with the dead greyhound? Vaguely," McCrae said.

"I would call you a smartass, but since you let me off the hook, I'll be nice. Anyway, when I saw Wayne load those dogs into the pickup, all of a sudden I knew that Jesús had seen the same thing. And for some reason, he was compelled to snap photos of the incident and give those photos to Rosa Linda."

"Jesús must have known that Wayne was doing something shady," Olga said.

"I know for a fact that he was doing something shady," Kate retorted. "I saw a barrel of mutilated rabbits. Jesús was right. Wayne uses live lures, and he lied about it."

"Still, no serious crime there," McCrae said.

"Okay then! So, *that's* not a crime in your book." Kate slammed her fist on the table. "Then let's not forget about me getting shot."

"Take it easy." McCrae said.

"Any information on that crime?" Kate said.

"Typical wooden shaft. About eighteen inches long. There's only one sporting goods store in Austin that carries that type, but according to the sales manager, most archers purchase their arrows from merchandise catalogs or online, and most archers use steel arrows rather than wooden ones."

"Guy's son is an archer. And so are Guy and Garrison. Did you find out what time Guy and his family left the ranch?" Kate said.

"Their maid said they left around six that evening." McCrae checked his notes.

"That leaves Garrison, then," Kate said. "But Guy alluded to the fact that Garrison's archery skills are questionable. Whoever shot me was an experienced archer. Even though the first arrow missed, it flew just a few inches away from my head. Did Garrison leave any time during the poker game?"

"With an endless supply of food and beer, according to the ranch hands, Garrison stayed put until the bitter end." McCrae said. "He always does."

"Do you think Wayne and Garrison could have been

working together?" Olga said.

"When I talked to Garrison, I got the distinct impression that he doesn't think much of Guy's new greyhound trainer," McCrae said.

"Guy doesn't share Garrison's opinion of Wayne. Evidently, he arrived just when Guy needed him," Kate said. "Wayne's not happy about training the dogs, but I think he's hoping for a promotion and wants to stay on Guy's good side. Did you find out anything about Guy suddenly packing up the family and leaving?"

"Not much. Garrison turned as red as a fat tick when I questioned him. I'm sure he doesn't know where Guy is. And if I wager to guess, he's been left out of the loop, although he'd never admit it. He said if I were wrongly arrested for murder, that I'd get the hell out of town for a while, too."

"Maybe he's playing dumb. He threatened Rosa Linda and me when he found us on the ranch waiting for Jesús that day he was murdered. He may have an alibi, but I still don't trust him. Seems he's protective of his older brother. Do you think he could be covering for Guy? Guy could have come back to the ranch. And I was almost certain the note left on Wayne's desk was from Meredith. It was written in a florid handwriting, not the handwriting you would expect from a ranch hand."

"When we searched Wayne's office, we didn't find any note," said McCrae.

Kate glanced at the clock above Olga's stove and was surprised to see that it was only eight-thirty. She felt as if she had been up for days. The throbbing in her arm was doing a good job of keeping pace with the throbbing in her head. Kate wasn't sure which felt worse. She just wished they'd throb to the same beat. There was nothing more to hash over, and McCrae finally left.

Olga suggested that Kate stay at the ranch house rather than go back to the bungalow. But Kate declined the offer. She wanted time to think, and despite her fatigue, she knew that she wouldn't be able to sleep. The tension of the last few days seemed to swing back and forth like a pendulum. Rosa Linda was safe, albeit the problems she faced. Discovering what was behind Rosa Linda's secrets removed a heavy cloud of uncertainty. Olga walked Kate back to the bungalow and handed her a basket packed with food so Kate would not have to cook. As Olga turned to leave, she informed Kate that in the bottom of the basket was an Antonio Banderas video.

"*Desperado*?" Kate peeked inside. "I'm not sure if I'm ready for an overdose of gunplay."

"You have been gone a long time. No, this one is a bit less violent—more like a swashbuckler. I'm sure it hasn't made it all the way to the African bush yet. It's called the *The Mask of Zorro*."

"Sounds perfect."

"Oh, and also in the basket is my .38."

Chapter Thirteen

When Kate got back to the bungalow, she looked up Gibson's kennel online, and dialed the number. Molly answered on the first ring. From the strain in her voice, Kate knew that Molly was not as casual about the disappearance of her dogs as McCrae made it sound.

"Molly, this is Kate Caraway. I hope I'm not calling too late."

"Oh, Kate," Molly said, "not at all. I'm happy you called. But I don't mind saying I hoped you were someone calling about my greyhounds."

"I spoke to Holden McCrae. He told me four of your rescue dogs are missing."

"Actually, three from the shelter and Gracie. I'm worried sick."

"Oh, Molly, I'm so sorry."

"I left her out last night. She was in the yard and had rolled around in Lord knows what. I didn't have time to bathe her, so I put her in one of the kennels. It's not like her to run away. I've been driving around and she's nowhere in sight. Oh, my. Please forgive me. Here I am bemoaning about my troubles. I heard about your accident last night. Are you still in the hospital?"

"I was released this morning. A few stitches and some lumps on my hard head aren't enough to cause me to suffer hospital food any longer than I have to. Would you like a visit? I'll update you on life at the Rodriguez ranch, and maybe we can drive around and look for your dogs."

"I'd like that. But I have someone out searching for them now. Are you able to drive?"

"Automatic transmission and power steering—no problem. See you in about fifteen minutes."

Kate started to lock the door to the bungalow when she remembered Olga's .38. Kate knew how to fire a gun—a skill she had been forced to learn while in Kenya—but preferred not to have them around. *Two close calls is enough*, Kate reminded herself, *don't be a fool*. She went back inside, removed the .38 from its case, checked the safety, and stuck the gun in her purse.

Kate checked the Jeep for dead dogs. Finding none, she climbed in, hit the door lock, and drove toward Molly's place. Driving along country roads in the dark called for another kind of caution. Instead of watching out for crazy drivers, where certain sections of the roads were cut through dense wilderness, one watched for deer. At forty miles-per-hour, a collision with a whitetail would total a car. Kate remembered the advice in a defensive-driving course.

"Accelerate if a deer darts out in front of your car. You want the animal to fly over the hood," said the instructor. "You don't want two hundred pounds of muscle and antler to careen through your windshield and spear you to the seat."

Kate wondered what would happen if she hit a deer and did not kill it? What if it laid suffering on the side of the road? What would she do then? Maybe having a gun wasn't such a bad idea.

Kate's mind drifted back to Kenya, and without warning, the acrid smell of gunpowder returned, and along with it the look of hate on the man's face and the sight of blood gushing from his leg.

Not now. She couldn't think about that now.

Defensive driving—she would concentrate on watching for deer.

"Except for pigs," the driving instructor said. "Swerve for swine. Remember that. Never hit a pig. Their low center of gravity will flip even an eighteen-wheeler."

Flashes of the wounded man running for cover invaded her thoughts once more.

She wondered if he had bled to death—if, for the first time in her life, she'd actually killed someone. She and Jack weren't allowed to stick around long enough to find out.

Why now? Why was this surfacing now? Kate tried to focus on her driving, but the incident of a few days ago replayed in her mind with a vividness she could not ignore.

Then she remembered that she had been thinking of the driving instructor's advice that day in Kenya, where the unpaved roads were no more than animal trails and the once-paved highways were riddled with potholes where the pavement had washed away decades ago.

Swerve for warthogs. Swerve for bushpigs. Swerve for elephant calves.

The ugly memory was too clear in her mind. Kate did not want to think about the event that precipitated her attack, an event that would forever sicken her with pain and suffering. Since she had left Kenya, she had buried the details, locked them away in the denial part of her brain, but here on this dark road in Central Texas, the memory surfaced like an image burned sharp on her retinas.

Kate had been alone, making the eight-hour drive from Nairobi back to camp, a drive she rarely made herself. Jack had been unable to accompany her to the city, and they desperately needed medical supplies. Safari camps dotted the nature reserves, bringing in thousands of tourists each year. On one drive through the Maasi Mara, Kate noticed eighteen tour vans parked in a circle like covered wagons on the prairie. But instead of keeping the predators out, they had one surrounded. In the center was a cheetah sleeping in a clump of grass. It was a common sight, one that even the cheetah tolerated.

However, even with all the tourist traffic in East Africa, a white woman driving alone in the bush was still an odd sight. Whenever Kate traveled alone, she made sure she took a rifle.

She had just driven onto the reserve when she heard a sound that resounded through her nervous system like electricity. The elephant calf had run in front of her Jeep. She swerved just in time, missing it, but the calf, less than a week old, was terror-stricken. It ran in circles, waving its tiny trunk in the air—its eyes wide open—frozen with fright. Kate looked from where the calf had come and saw the bloody massacre. An elephant cow had been machine-gunned down and the other twin calf was wailing and rubbing its trunk over the body of its dead mother, willing her to stand. Kate looked back at the first calf—it had been caught in the machine gun fire and was bleeding from the right, rear flank. Kate approached the scene only a few minutes after the slaughter. The poachers had not yet sliced the ivory from the mother's head.

Kate looked in the distance and saw the swirling

dust from the poacher's truck, and without thinking, she gunned the engine and took off after them. She was no match for a truckload of killers with automatic weapons. But all logic was lost after seeing the massacre. The only thought in Kate's mind was revenge. These were reserve elephants—elephants that had been part of her research. They had numbers. They had names. They were the hope for the future.

She was driving a four-wheel drive Jeep and gaining on the heavy truck was easy. To give herself an advantage, she left the road, plowed through the bushes, and drove up onto a ridge. She got ahead of the poachers and stopped. Familiar with this route, she knew that the truck would have to slow down in order to traverse the ruts and washed out sections of road that lay ahead. But to Kate's surprise the truck did not slow, and in flying over the rutted road it slammed down hard and stalled. The driver lost sight of Kate, and got out to look under the truck.

There was no doubt in Kate's mind. She caught him in the rifle's sight. She would kill him. All reason disappeared. Afterward, she would have to return and shoot the calves as well. They were too young to survive on their own, and her research facility could not afford to raise any more orphans. She remembered the calm that wafted over her. There was no right or wrong. There was no guilt or fear. There was no future, no consequences. Only revenge.

She aimed the rifle at the driver's back and fired. The bullet struck the windshield, and the poachers scattered. There were four of them. They took cover behind the truck. Kate fired again. This time she hit the gas tank, and the truck went up in flames. The back had been covered with a tarp, and as the tarp burned away, she saw the result of a day's work. The cow was not the first elephant they had shot that day. Kate saw at least half a dozen ivory tusks toasting in the fire.

She reloaded and fired again. The four men ran across into the bush. Kate was sure that they were not aware that their attacker was one small white woman with a rifle. The idea gave her a morbid sense of satisfaction. Kate fired once more, hitting the driver in the leg. Then her amoral, vigilante world came to a screeching halt, and she catapulted back to reality. She threw the rifle in the back of the Jeep and drove back to camp—

Suddenly Kate was jolted out of her deep reflection by two headlights beaming into her rearview mirror. She chastised herself for letting her guard down and driving on automatic pilot. Her hands were clammy and her heart raced. She looked down the road, and for an instant was uncertain where she was.

Then her concern turned to fear. The car behind her seemed to come out of nowhere. What was she doing driving alone at night on an unfamiliar road? There had already been two attempts made on her life and she was foolish enough to think that the killer would not try again. The headlights glared back into her eyes and she flipped the night vision setting on the mirror. Expecting to see a white Dodge Ram, she was somewhat relived to find a dark-colored sedan behind her. Trying to get her bearings, Kate looked for familiar sites. She had visited Molly only once and that was during the day. Molly lived about five miles from the Rodriguez Ranch off Highway 12. The place was easy to find: one left turn onto Spoke Hill Road and Molly's small ranch was two miles down on the right. The highway curved around a sharp bend and crossed the Blanco River Bridge. Now she knew for certain that she had missed her turn, for she did not cross the river on her first trip.

The two-lane highway was too narrow to attempt a U-turn, so Kate started looking for a driveway or ranch entrance in which to turn around. The driver behind her was trailing too close. Kate tapped her brakes and the driver slowed. Then she saw a ranch entrance to the left and turned on her blinker. Kate tapped her brakes again, cut a sharp turn off the road, and stopped. She waited for the driver to past. Instead, he slowed as if to stop. Kate made sure she had locked the doors and reached into her purse. As she turned to get a look at the driver, the car sped up and continued down Highway 12. She breathed a sigh of relief.

Kate put the Jeep in reverse, backed out, and pulled back onto the highway. As best she could figure, she had driven about a mile past Spoke Hill Road. She looked in her rear view mirror and saw the rear brake lights of the sedan. The car was turning around as well. Kate accelerated. Her fear had turned to anger, and she was determined to put some distance between herself and whoever was following her so she could make the turn into Molly's place without being seen. She took the curve going sixty and prayed that the local white-tail deer were smart enough to avoid Highway 12. Spoke Hill Road suddenly came into view. Kate slammed on her brakes and turned off the highway. In her mirror, she saw the sedan pass by. She continued, but the winding route prevented her from seeing if the car had turned back around as well. Now she was sure she was being followed, but she did not recognize the driver or the car.

It had to be someone from the Fordyce Ranch. Someone who had watched her leave the bungalow tonight.

Had the same person been watching her the night he put the dead greyhound in the Jeep? Had he been watching her the entire time she was snooping around the kennel and Wayne's office? Was he the one who had stepped from the orchard, took aim with his bow, and let fly the arrow that had wedged into her arm?

Get a grip, Kate told herself. *You can't afford to let your mind wander.*

Her headlights flashed across the Gibson's Greyhound Adoption Kennel sign. Kate turned into the driveway and drove about twenty yards. She stopped and waited. Less than a minute later, the car slowed down and drove by Molly's place, but kept going. Kate's impulsive nature told her to follow the car and get the plate number, but that same impulsive nature was the reason she had twenty-one stitches in her arm. The car appeared to be an older model Honda or maybe a Toyota: reddish or purple, four doors, other than that, she could make out nothing more. She chastised herself for letting her guard down. She did not want Jack to come back to town and find her missing again, tangled under another twisted root in some ditch too remote for anyone to find her body.

Molly was in the exercise yard carrying a small greyhound back to its kennel when Kate parked the Jeep. "I saw you drive up and stop," Molly said. "Is everything okay?"

"Just paranoid." Besides the obvious injuries, every muscle in Kate's body seemed to remind her of her float down the creek the night before. She eased herself out of the Jeep, and after her recent decision not to be so dense about her own safety, she grabbed her purse.

"Is that the injured dog you were concerned about?"

"Yes. She's not as skittish, but she still can't walk. Would you like to see her?"

"I'd love to."

"Come in. You can help me bed her down for the night."

Kate watched as Molly gently lowered the dog onto a bed made from bubbly foam rubber covered with a soft layer of lamb's wool. The greyhound whimpered as Molly positioned the dog on her good hip. Kate sat down next to them. Molly was whispering a soft melody intermingled with shushes.

The greyhound could not have weighed more than fifty pounds. The color of a butter bean, the soft, whitish hair covered her entire body except for the black on her snout and a black starburst in the middle of her chest. Dark eyes stared up at Kate and she noticed streams of wet in the corners of each one. She was obviously in pain, and Kate's heart broke. She would give anything to make the dog's pain go away.

Kate held out her hand, palm up, offering her fingers for a sniff. The greyhound pulled back. Kate waited a few seconds and moved her hand closer. This time the dog smelled Kate's fingers and gave them a lick. Her tongue was warm, and Kate feared she might have a fever.

"I hope she makes it," Kate said.

"I'm sure she'll recover, but whether she'll be a normal, healthy dog...well, that remains to be seen. Whoever adopts her, *if* someone adopts her, will have to spend a lot of time and money on rehab." Molly folded a towel and used it to prop up the dog's right front leg, the one injured in the race. The greyhound laid her head down and closed her eyes.

"Brad has her on antibiotics and steroids. Mind if we sit here awhile?" Molly said. "I'm glad she's comfortable with you."

Kate did not want to ask what would happen to the dog if Molly could not find her a home. Years ago, Kate and Jack owned two dogs when they lived in Chicago. One was a Jack Russell mix they got from a neighbor whose dog had had puppies, and the other was a shorthaired, third world type dog that they had rescued from the pound.

Both had lived almost fifteen years, and not a day had gone by that Kate did not ache for another dog. But her and Jack's current lifestyle had prevented them from starting another canine family.

She tried to reach over and pat the dog's head, but Kate's sore body resisted.

"Are you sure you should be out running around so soon?"

"I wonder about that myself. Can you recommend a good massage therapist?"

"In Wimberley, Texas? Are you kidding? Throw a stone and you'll hit one. I can recommend several. What kind do you need? A Rolfer, one who specializes in Swedish style, or a deep-muscle masseur? We even have a woman who will read your muscles and tell your future in the process. Wimberley has come of age—new age that is."

"How does that sit with the good old boys?" Kate asked. "Holden McCrae mentioned the new espresso shop in town." Kate changed positions and moved closer to the greyhound to stroke her neck. The dog blinked a few times and fell back to sleep.

"Yeah, well, what can I say? Our clean air attracts healthy people. Wimberley has changed over the past few years, but most of us feel the change is for the better. We've become known as an art community. But I know that you're not here to talk about Wimberley's economy."

"Molly, I'm not sure where to turn. I'm no further along than when we last visited. Except that I must be stepping on someone's toes hard enough for them to want me dead. Right before I was shot, I saw Wayne loading up a truck full of greyhounds. Initially, I thought he was stealing them, but McCrae said that Wayne Brody had receipts and papers for their sale."

"Let's talk about this. How about some coffee? I have decaf, but I always drink the real stuff," Molly said. "Sleep is the last thing on my mind. I can't begin to relax with Gracie missing."

"I don't sleep well, so it doesn't matter. Bring on the good stuff."

Molly locked the kennel and they walked back to house.

Kate settled herself along the window seat. Molly's kitchen smelled of fresh-baked bread. The aroma alone was enough to quell some of Kate's worrying. Molly took a package of coffee beans from the freezer. She ground them and had the coffee brewing in no time. "Why do you think Wayne is stealing the dogs?"

"Something didn't seem right to me. I don't buy the heat thing as the reason for transporting the dogs at night."

"That doesn't make sense to me, either. What does Guy say about that?" Molly sat a cup of steaming coffee in front of Kate. "Cream and sugar?"

"Just cream, thanks. Guy's not around. He decided to make himself scarce after the charges against him were dropped. Right now, I need to find out who shot me. Wayne was seen leaving the ranch before I was shot. Garrison has a darn good alibi too."

"Not many people know how to use a bow and arrow."

"Exactly, but of the three Fordyces who do, father and son were nowhere near the ranch and Garrison was playing poker with ranch hands. The reason I called was to ask about *your* missing dogs. McCrae said that this had happened before."

The forlorn look returned to Molly's face. Kate had almost wished that she had not brought up the subject.

"My dogs are like my family. I know their stay here is only temporary, but while they're in my care...well, let's just say, I love 'em all. But some dogs, especially greyhounds, if given the opportunity, will bolt. But I can't understand Gracie. She would never run off. Even if she followed the others, she wouldn't go far. She's too much of a chicken."

"What do you think happened?"

"One of the kids could have left the cages unlocked. Although, I am constantly lecturing them on making sure the locks on the cages are secure, every once in a while someone gets careless."

"But none of the dogs are ever found? Doesn't that seem strange? Seems like some would at least be spotted. How many have you lost?"

"That seems odd to me too. I've put ads in the paper, but never received even one call. This has happened about four times in the past year. About fourteen dogs total."

"And none of them stayed around or wandered back? I used to have a dog that would dig out of her backyard, and as soon as she tunneled her way to freedom, she became too frightened to leave. I'd hear her whimpering on the front porch, curled up in a ball on the doormat, shivering with fear."

"All have disappeared. I guess it's a greyhound thing. You know, born to run."

"Could the dogs have been stolen?"

"I considered that, but the locks were never broken or tampered with."

"Do you remember which students worked on the days the dogs got loose?"

"You think someone could have deliberately left the cages unlocked? That idea had crossed my mind, especially now, with the fourth escape. But I trust all of my kids, and I hate to think that they would do it deliberately. I taught the parents of most of these students, and I screen their applications thoroughly."

"Do you keep records of who was on duty and when?"

"I keep a notebook mainly for the Ag teacher to record the number of hours each student works. I e-mail him with the totals every week."

"How about the dates the dogs disappeared?"

"I have that too."

"Well, while we're wired on this coffee, what do you say we have a look at your notebook?"

Molly disappeared into her office where her roommates must have been staying. As soon as Kate heard the door open, the noise of claws clicking their way across the hardwood floor sounded like a stampede coming from a nail salon. Molly called from the office, "You dogs be good dogs. Kate, shout at them to sit, otherwise they'll jump all over you."

Kate's normal reaction to a bunch of high-jumping, attention-seeking canines was a welcome one, but with every muscle and bone in her body feeling as if they had been sent through a meat grinder, the idea of a hundred plus pounds of greyhounds pounding her body was not pleasant. "Sit!" Both butts hit the floor at once. "You guys *are* good."

Molly walked in with a spiral notebook in her hand. "They sure are. I'll give them a biscuit, and we'll have a look here." The dogs calmly followed Molly to the cupboard where she took out the Italian cookie can. She pulled out two candy-bar size charbroiled biscuits, and the dogs immediately sat down again. Each waited patiently for their treat and then retreated. Freda went into the sunroom and Lupe took her prize and crept under the kitchen table. "You know, you don't realize how important something is until you lose it. Today when I went to the kennel and saw Gracie was gone, I realized how attached I've become to that little girl. I don't know what I'll do if I don't find her."

Freda and Lupe happily crunched their hard biscuits as Molly handed Kate a note pad. "So, let's see if we can figure this out." She opened her spiral notebook. "The first escape happened last November, on the eighteenth; the second, on February fifteenth; another, on May seventeenth; and then last night, August twentieth."

"That's about every three months, and around the middle of each month. Who worked on those days?"

"Students work in pairs. It's too much for one student to handle alone," Molly explained. "Lance

Billings and Travis Landon worked yesterday. In fact, you met them when you were here. On November eighteenth, Bob Jennings and Travis Landon; on February fifteenth, it was Lance Billings and Travis Landon again; on May seventeenth, it was Jenny Rajek and—uh oh—" Molly's mood darkened. She looked at Kate.

"Let me guess: Travis Landon."

"I can't believe Travis would steal my dogs. He was working again today after school and when I told him what had happened he seemed devastated. He assured me that he had locked up before he left last night."

"Did you speak to him before he left?"

"Yes, the kids usually finish up between eight and nine. I always have them knock on the kitchen door before they leave. Lance was already in the car. They arrived together. Travis knocked, and said they were leaving."

"Did he say anything else? Or act differently in anyway?"

"Travis? He is the shiest boy I know. I'm sad to say he's one of those kids who most people don't notice. I've always felt sorry for him. He has had a rough life. His father left when Travis was in the second grade, and not long after that his mother gave up trying to raise three kids alone. She vacillated between dead-end jobs and drinking binges. Travis eventually became financially responsible for the family. I give him as many hours as possible. "

"If it is Travis who's selling the dogs, wouldn't he have a difficult time without their Bertillon Cards?"

"The regular person doesn't know Bertillon Cards. Travis stealing my dogs—damn." Freda crept up to

Molly, and placed her head on Molly's foot. She reached down and scratched the dog's ears. "I thought Travis loved these dogs. He finished his work early tonight and the other student, Jenny Rajek, closed up for him. He wanted to drive around the area and see if he could locate the dogs. Had I known he needed money, I would have helped."

"What kind of car does Travis drive?"

"A maroon Honda."

"With four doors?"

"I believe so. Why?"

"Just wondering."

Chapter Fourteen

It was late when Kate left Molly's place. In her pocket was a list that contained Travis Landon's phone number, along with the numbers of all the students who worked with him. They'd all be at school tomorrow, but Lance Billings and Jenny Rajek were scheduled to work at Molly's after school. Kate decided to try to catch Travis as soon as the four o'clock bell rang and then she'd head back to Molly's to speak with the two kids who had worked with Travis most recently.

This time she made sure that she gave her full attention to her drive back to the ranch. Molly insisted that Kate call as soon as she arrived. Kate pulled into the driveway of the bungalow as the cellphone rang. She parked, fumbled in her purse, and yanked out the phone.

"Hey, where have you been? I've been calling all evening. I certainly didn't expect you to be running around, but then I should know better." Jack sounded tired and Kate wished that she could talk to him in person rather than over the phone.

"I'm fine, Jack. I've just returned from Molly Gibson's kennel. How's Max? Have you prevented him from scalping his daughter and—

"Son-in-law? Yes, we know. I've been playing mediator between Max and Daniel. Max can't talk to the boy without losing his temper. Daniel told me everything. I guess you spoke to Rosa Linda when she returned to get Luna."

"She was in and out in a flash. What will happen to them?"

"We won't know until the morning. I've convinced Max to call it a night. We've checked into the same motel where Rosa Linda and Daniel are staying. Not my idea. My room number is 407. I hope we'll be back tomorrow evening."

"I love you. Please get some rest."

"Don't worry. After the day I had, sleep will be no problem. I love you, too."

"Jack, what happened to those two elephant calves? I should have gone back for them."

"Are you sure you're ready to talk about this?"

"No...no, I'm not sure. Just a little at a time, maybe."

"You were in shock. Michael went back after them as soon as you arrived. I don't know any more than that. We left in such a hurry. You know that with your permits, you were legally justified in shooting those poachers?"

"Yes, but legalities in Kenya tend to fluctuate. And—"

"That's the first time you ever shot a person. I know, sweetheart. Whenever you're ready, I'll call the camp for an update."

"Thanks. Take care of yourself."

"You should talk. See you tomorrow."

Kate took a thorough look around before she got out of the Jeep and walked to the door. She should have taken up Olga's offer to stay with her, but it was too late now. If Olga weren't asleep, she'd surely be in bed worrying about her daughter.

Kate unlocked the door, flipped on the light switch, and stepped inside. As she closed the door, she noticed a white envelope on the floor. She locked the door behind her, laid her purse down on the bed, and picked up the envelope. It would not be from Olga. If she needed to talk to Kate, she'd simply leave a phone message. Kate opened the envelope and inside were four twenty-dollar bills with a printed note, "Please give to Molly Gibson." It was not signed, but Kate knew it was from Travis. It had to be. He had been following her since she left the bungalow and had probably delivered the envelope while she was at Molly's. "Shiest boy I ever knew," Kate remembered Molly's words. *Damn.* Kate now planned to be at the high school first thing in the morning. She would not wait until the end of the day.

****

Despite the late-night coffee, Kate slept well and was awake at five-thirty. In no condition to jog, she tried a few stretching exercises which seemed to make matters worse. She made herself a note to get the name and number of a massage therapist from Molly. Once they started talking about the missing greyhounds, Kate had forgotten about the massage.

She put on the coffee, took two Advil, and filled the bathtub with hot water. While she soaked, Kate contemplated how to approach Travis Landon. Why had he wanted to give Molly eighty dollars? Had he stolen the money and later felt guilty? Or was it to make up for the lost dogs: four twenties, four dogs? Travis was not a talker. She would have to handle him with kid gloves, play on the guilt that was obviously eating at him. If she only had proof that it was Travis, or at least a convincing lie that would make him believe she did. She could tell him that she saw him drive away from the bungalow, but she had no idea what time he had come by. She had been at Molly's between nine and ten-thirty. If Travis delivered the money after nine, he'd know that she was lying. Kate could tell him that Molly suspected him of stealing her dogs, but Kate would not accuse him without talking to Molly about this latest development. Molly had a soft place in her heart for the boy. However Kate decided to handle her meeting with Travis, she'd have to be careful.

By six, except for her arm, much of Kate's soreness had subsided. She was confident now that she'd make it through the day. She left the steamy bathroom and took her second cup of coffee and slice of Olga's Mexican cornbread out to the porch. Finally, the morning air had a slight, crisp coolness about it. The humidity was lower, and it was almost pleasant. The weather channel showed the first cool front dipping down from the Texas Panhandle, and Kate felt a spike of energy. The phone rang, and it was Olga.

"I knew you'd be up. How's the cornbread?"

"Am I so transparent?"

"No, just predictable."

"I'm going to have to change that, or I'll surely end up dead."

"That's not funny."

"You sound better." Kate had never known Olga to be down for long.

"Max called last night about midnight. Rosa Linda had just come in, but Jack prevented my hotheaded husband from storming outside to confront her. Max refused to sleep until she arrived. Your husband's a godsend. I'd follow him to Chicago any day."

"Oh, shut up."

It was good to hear Olga laughing.

"Everything will be fine," Kate told her.

"I know. We'll have a rough road ahead, but we'll make it. Any thoughts about today?"

"Yeah, I'm about to make a visit to the high school, and then I'll be by to pick you up. We'll spend the rest of the morning at the Fordyce ranch—in broad daylight. Surely, no one will try to kill me under a bright Texas sun with my best friend in tow."

"Ah, *Dios mìo*! Between you and my daughter, I'll go to an early grave."

****

Kate pulled up in a parking lot that resembled a practice ring for a bumper car tournament. She cautiously maneuvered her way out of the student parking section in search of safer territory. To the left of the building's main entrance, visitor parking appeared free of infallible teenagers unconcerned with having to pay their own car insurance.

She located a spot where she could not only see the students enter their parking lot, but in case Travis was riding to school with a buddy, she could see each student go into the building. Quickly her vantage point became useless, as the entire student body began to arrive at the same time. Now Kate doubted that she could spot her quarry, having seen him once, and with his face partially hidden under the bill of his cap.

The students crossed the parking lot in mass, like a flood of Abercrombie and Fitch models, boys wearing baggy pants and long T-shirts and girls in tight jeans and skimpy tops. Then she saw the maroon Honda pull in. Kate hurried over to meet Travis at his car. She walked up as he was gathering his books from the back seat. When he turned around and saw her standing there, he almost dropped his backpack.

"Travis, we need to talk. You remember me?"

"Ma'am, I mean, Mrs. Caraway. I'll be late for class." He attempted to walk past her, but Kate stepped in front of him.

"This won't take long. I know it was you who put the envelope under my door."

"I don't know what you're talking about." He was looking over her shoulder toward the school.

"And I know that it was you who followed me last night."

"I was out looking for Mrs. Gibson's dogs." Now he was staring at the ground, stomping pebbles with the heel of his boot. Like that day she first met him, he refused to look her in the eye.

"Whatever you did with Mrs. Gibson's greyhounds, you need to tell me. Paying for their disappearance will not relieve Molly's pain and worry. She's heartbroken over losing Gracie." Kate provoked the reaction she wanted.

He looked up, shock in his eyes. "Gracie? I didn't know she was one that got loose." He bit his lower lip. "But I didn't steal Mrs. Gibson's dogs. I swear."

"Is that why you put eighty dollars in the envelope for me to give Molly? Is that how much you received for selling the dogs? Who paid you, Travis?"

His lower lip started to tremble, and a tear welled up in the corner of his eye.

"I didn't steal or sell any dogs."

"But you made it possible for someone else to, right?"

"Please don't tell Mrs. Gibson, please. She's a nice lady and—and I don't want to lose my job."

"Who was paying you to do this, Travis?" Kate repeated.

"I don't know." He gained control of himself, and his voice strengthened.

Kate knew he was lying.

"I—I got a phone call one day, telling me that if I wanted to—to make some money to leave one of the cages unlocked. I thought it was a joke."

"But you did as you were told and the money appeared. Amazing." Kate could have kicked herself as soon as she let the sarcasm slip. Travis's jaw tightened.

"I have to go to class. I don't care what you do with the money. If you tell Mrs. Gibson, I'll deny it. I'll deny that we ever spoke this morning." He brushed passed her and ran into the building.

At least her hunch was right. Travis was responsible for the missing dogs, and, evidently, his guilt had gotten the better of him. But who would buy stolen greyhounds? Owners would need their Bertillon Cards, and these dogs were past their racing prime. Were they used for breeding purposes? *Not likely*, Kate thought. A greyhound with good genes would not be put up for adoption. Someone wanting a pet could buy a greyhound from an adoption agency. She added to her note to call Brad Gates, and find out if he knew of any other reason why someone would steal washed-up greyhounds. Finding the missing dogs at this point might prove impossible. Kate dreaded breaking the news to Molly.

****

Olga was ready and waiting when Kate arrived. "Any luck at the high school?" she asked.

209

"One step forward, two steps back. I'll explain in a minute. I need to make a quick call." Kate went into the kitchen and dialed Brad at his clinic, but got his voice mail. She left a message and then called the track.

"Dr. Gates."

"Hey, I just left a message at your clinic. This is Kate Caraway."

"Find any more canine corpses in your Jeep?"

"No, thank God. But I do need some information."

"It's yours if I have it."

"Why would someone steal a bunch of retired greyhounds? Their ownership can easily be traced, right?"

"Why does anyone need a reason to steal anything? Sorry, you're right. What do you mean by washed-up?"

"Those dogs that were put up for adoption."

"If the dogs were somewhat successful, bringing in an adequate amount of money, they might be useful at lower-grade tracks where officials don't always go by the books."

"Lower-grade tracks? Like the one in Corpus Christi."

"Lower. Corpus is a class-B track. You won't find the best dogs racing there, but the officials are usually trustworthy. It would probably have to be a class-D track."

"Where is the closest D track?"

"There are none in Texas. The closest one is in Florida. What's going on? New developments?"

"Maybe. Molly Gibson has had several dogs stolen during the past few months, and we're trying to figure out why."

"Do you think it has anything to do with the Flores

murder?"

"Who knows? Everything seems to lead back to the Fordyce ranch, our only common denominator."

"If I think of anything, I'll call. Hey, I heard that your husband is rejoining the Cubs as pitching coach."

"If you ask me for baseball tickets, I'll scream."

****

"Let's take my Explorer," Olga said. "We're less likely to get our tires shot out. If they see Rosa Linda's Jeep, the bad guys might recognize you and get antsy."

"There are several people living on that ranch. I've been focusing on the family and the dog trainer. There must be a dozen ranch hands," Kate said. "And there's that foreman in charge of the cattle. He was pretty hot the first day I arrived to talk to Wayne. He was angry at his ranch hands about losing some of the herd. He looked mad enough to rip off their heads. Maybe he had some dealings with Jesús. Maybe I need to widen my net."

"You mean Glen Dickson? I remember Max telling me that Guy had lost several head of cattle when they wandered into a pasture that hadn't been cleared."

"That's right. That's what he was shouting about. Molly Gibson said the cattle had eaten oleander."

"It's one of the only native plants that I refuse to have in my garden. When Rosa Linda was little, she used to sample everything she could get her hands on. Cows are known to eat it, too. All they have to do is nibble a few leaves and bam—heart attack."

When Kate and Olga arrived at the Fordyce Ranch, all seemed quiet. Olga used the main entrance and drove up to the house. Their plan was to speak with the Fordyce's maid first to find out if she had heard from the family.

"I know Nora fairly well. She and Maria are friends, and on Nora's day off, Maria often visits. I might be able to get more information out of her than Holden did. Many of the Hispanic workers, even if they are here legally, are reluctant to speak to the police."

They rang the bell and waited several minutes before Nora answered. She opened the door reluctantly and peered out as if afraid of what she might find.

"*Buenos dìas*, Mrs. Rodriguez. Mr. and Mrs. Fordyce, they are not here."

"*Buenos dìas*, Nora. I know, but Mrs. Caraway and I have come to speak with you."

"Mr. Fordyce and his lawyer say that I am not to speak about it."

The stricken look on Nora's face told Kate that Guy's maid had probably been reprimanded for her loose tongue when speaking with the sheriff. Kate was glad that Olga came along, otherwise a visit with Nora to get information would have been a waste of time.

"Nora, we aren't here to ask questions about the case. I'd like to speak with Mrs. Fordyce. It's very important. Do you know where they are?"

"No, I am sorry. The family, they left suddenly."

They stood in the foyer. The silence hung thick like a cold sheet of ice. The place felt like a museum rather than a home. Kate instinctively hugged her arms around her body and looked around wishing for some form of life to walk down the long hall. She noticed the door to Guy's office was closed. Chances were he left nothing around to indicate where they had gone, but if she could have a quick look, she might find a hotel listing, name of a travel agent, or something that would give her a clue as to where the Fordyces had gone, or how long they planned to be away. Kate stepped away from Olga and Nora, and pretended to study the iron sculpture near Guy's office door. When she was behind Nora, Kate pointed toward the kitchen, and Olga picked up the clue.

"I know that you are worried about them, Nora. Do you mind if we visit a while? We can talk, and maybe I can convince you to give me that famous recipe for your pork tamales."

Nora blushed. "*Si*, I will make some coffee."

Half-an-hour and a cup of coffee later left them with no more information than when they arrived, but it gave Kate a good excuse to visit the bathroom. Nora pointed down the hall from the kitchen, and Kate excused herself. Luckily, the bathroom was next to Guy's office. She opened the bathroom door, turned on the light and vent, closed the door, then hurried to the office. "Damn." Kate muttered. The door was locked. She went back to the bathroom to turn off the light and vent and noticed another door toward the back. Kate walked over and tried it. It opened with a slight click, and the next moment, Kate was standing inside Guy's office. With no time to waste, she hurried over to Guy's desk. The man was meticulous. Nothing out of place. The desk surface was swept clean. The desk drawers were locked—a fruitless endeavor.

Kate turned to leave when, from the corner of her eye, she saw the green light on Guy's computer. Kate tapped the space bar and the screen lite up. His email had been minimized. She only had a few minutes before Nora became suspicious, and before her conscience talked her into doing the moral thing. Without hesitation, Kate opened the email. There were at least a dozen messages, all left that morning. The first was from Guy's banker, a

Mrs. Simmons reminding him about a CD coming due. Then a man named Bert called about the stalled campaign. Finally, John Davenport wanted to know how everything went at Santa Rita Center, and if he could help in any other way, please give him a call.

Kate walked back into the bathroom, switched off the light, and opened the door. She stepped out, and came nose to chest with Garrison. She feared he had been standing at the bathroom door listening. If that were the case, he was weirder than she had imagined.

"I can't seem to get rid of you, can I?"

"Maybe next time your aim will be better."

Garrison threw his head back and chortled. "Honey, I prefer my shotgun. Don't say I didn't warn you about trespassing. But it wasn't me who shot you. I have an alibi."

"How convenient. I'm glad I ran into you, Garrison. Saved me the trouble of having to ferret you out of your weasel hole. You're next on my list of people to pester. I need answers to a lot of questions."

"Why should I give you the time of day?"

"Because when people try to kill me, I get pissed. You, Guy, and Guy Junior are the only ones I know of who are skilled archers. And I don't buy that alibi shit. I plan to speak to every hand on this ranch and find a hole in your story large enough to thread your slimy body through. You made a big mistake when you threatened me."

"You screw with me all you want. But leave my brother and his family alone. They've been through hell and back, and if Guy wants to hide out for a while, it's none of your goddamn business."

He turned on his heel and walked into the den. As

Kate made her way back to the kitchen, she heard the tinkling of ice cubes. Kate glanced at her watch. It was a little early for a cocktail, but judging by the smell of Garrison's breath, this was definitely not his first drink of the day.

Olga and Nora stood in the doorway of the kitchen. Olga said her goodbyes. Nora, more flustered than before, saw them to the door.

Once outside, Olga said, "I like having you around, Katie, when Max is not here. I never get lonely. You two are very much alike."

"Oh, you heard."

"So did Nora. Losing your cool with your number-one suspect won't get you very far."

"I'm beginning to wonder about my number-one suspect. If he's drunk every day by noon, I doubt he could use a bow and arrow, much less hit his target."

Chapter Fifteen

Kate and Olga left the Fordyce home and walked to the bunkhouse, hoping to find Glen Dickson and the ranch hands had who played poker that night with Garrison.

"You're right, Olga. I shouldn't have lost my temper with Garrison. That was a mistake, but something about that man rubs me the wrong way. Alibi or not, he stays on the top of my suspect list."

"Whatever you say," Olga said.

"It has to be someone from the ranch. Jesús was killed and his body removed only minutes before Rosa Linda and I found his pickup. We ran into Garrison moments after it happened. Was there enough time for him to shoot Jesús, remove his body, and drive away without being seen?"

"Good question."

"You're no help."

"My job is to listen. Keep talking."

"Garrison could have followed me the morning I left Angie's Bar and Grill. And he was at the ranch the night I was shot."

"He was playing poker with the boys."

"He could have stepped out for some air, and saw me nosing around. He could have grabbed his bow and arrow, followed me to the ravine, and shot me as I ran toward the road."

"But why kill you?"

"He thinks I know something. What bothers me is his drinking. Every time I've seen him he's been drunk, or almost. Two of those times were in the morning. The two attempts on my life called for someone's quick maneuvering and skilled dexterity. That wouldn't be Garrison if he was hitting the bottle."

"Garrison's drinking is no secret."

"Hey," Kate stopped. "I thought of something. Maybe the two Fordyce brothers are in this together. Lack of evidence or not, maybe Guy did kill Jesús. Maybe Guy had not left the ranch by six that evening as Nora had claimed."

"They left all right."

"How do you know?"

"While you were having it out with Garrison, I managed to get a bit of information out of Nora. She was the one who went into Wayne's office and left the note on his desk."

"Nora?"

"Meredith called her and told her to deliver the message to Wayne."

"What did the message mean?"

"Nora doesn't know."

"How could she not know?"

"Katie, Nora is hired help. She knows better than to ask questions."

"Maybe we should go back—"

"You will not find out any more from her."

"I need to return to square one and find out what frightened Jesús the morning he died."

"And why he was blackmailing Guy."

"I'm keeping you with me today. You're a good

influence."

"I'm at your service. No more wedding to plan. You know, that's beginning to sound pretty good."

"Don't get too comfortable with that idea. As soon as this blows over, an all-out Texas-style reception might be just the thing."

"Right, everyone in the entire county will be there except the bride's father."

"First things first. Let's go talk to some cowboys."

****

Glen Dickson was in a much better mood than the first time Kate had seen him, chastising his men after the poisoning of Guy's cattle. He stood at the corral with his foot resting on the fence, talking on the cellphone. "You bet. I'll handle it. You relax and enjoy yourself. Right. I'll tell him. I'm glad you called, boss. We were beginning to worry."

Kate and Olga turned and looked at one another.

The phone beeped off and he turned around. He smiled when he saw Olga.

"Mrs. Rodriguez, what brings you out here today? Where's that cranky, old man of yours?"

"Hi, Glen. He went to Laredo to put out some fires our daughter started. I don't think you've met my friend, Kate Caraway."

If he had suspicions about Kate, he did not show them. Minus his cowboy hat, Kate noticed his blue eyes—clear and delicate—reflecting the blue from his crisp, denim shirt. Kate had no idea how old he was. Years of sun and wind could play tricks on one's age. Glen Dickson could be forty. He could be sixty.

"You were out here a few days ago looking for Wayne Brody. I'm afraid I was rude." He stuck out his hand and Kate accepted it. His palm felt dry and callused. "I was having a pretty bad day. Please accept my apology."

"I understand," said Kate. "No offense taken."

"What can I do for you ladies?"

"I'll get right to the point, Glen. We'd like to talk to a few of your guys. Those who played poker with Garrison night before last."

"Oh, yes. Sorry about your accident Mrs. Caraway."

Kate held her tongue. She wondered how much he knew about her "accident".

"The sheriff's already been here," Dickson said. "Spent most of yesterday morning speaking with the hands. We're really busy around here, ladies. I don't know what more you can find out."

"We won't take much time," Olga said. "We were hoping to catch them on their lunch break."

"Suit yourself. There were four guys playing poker with Garrison, Jim Riggs, Red Dryden, PJ Boggs, and Willie Brown. They're driving up right now. I'll send them over. If you'll excuse me, I'm on my way to town."

Kate looked past the corral as four men filed out of a ranch pickup and moseyed their way toward the bunkhouse. Dust and grime covered every square inch of clothing, from the top of their hats, over their sweaty, cotton shirts and leather chaps and down to their well-worn boots. Except for the short, stocky man who walked with a limp, the others looked no older than twenty. Dickson stopped them on the way and spoke a few words to the older man who nodded and looked towards Kate and Olga.

"Do you know any of these guys, Olga?"

"Nope, we'll have to turn on the charm."

"I don't think it'll take much. They look pretty forlorn." As the four approached, Kate noticed Dickson driving away in the white Dodge Ram—a "Succeed" bumper sticker on the back flashed red, white, and blue in the glare of the sun.

"Howdy. Glen said that you wanted to talk with us." An old man whose bowed legs were wide enough apart to ride a horse through walked up.

"My name is Olga Rodriguez and this is Kate Caraway."

"Yes ma'am, I know." He looked over at Kate. "You're the lady who got shot here Tuesday night. Glad you're up and about."

"Thanks, Mr…"

"Name's Willie Brown and these are my boys. We work the south pasture. I don't know what more we can tell you that we haven't already told the sheriff. We was all playing poker like we do every Tuesday night."

The three guys stood behind him with their hats in their hands. One young man looked too young to have finished high school. He probably hadn't. It was clear that Willie Brown planned to do the talking for his boys. Kate had hoped to speak to them separately, but she did not see how that was possible. She was sure Brown would not allow it. He seemed a little defensive, and he displayed a protective nature toward the others. In fact, he was old enough to be their grandfather.

Kate was not sure how much he knew. Was it a well-known fact among the hands that Kate had been trespassing when she was shot? McCrae had probably not mentioned that Kate was an uninvited guest. But gossip spreads quickly in a small town, and it was likely they'd heard various and sundry rumors. Surely,

Garrison's tongue had been wagging since that night.

How close were these guys to Garrison? Was he someone they looked up to because he was Guy's brother, or was Garrison merely their poker dupe, always available with full pockets and poor poker skills?

If she started out by sounding accusatory concerning Garrison's presence that night, she was sure they'd clam up. Who would point the finger at their employer's brother? The four men standing here were gracious and mannerly, men whose lives centered around ranch work. Except for Willie Brown, the others appeared nervous and uncomfortable. Kate wondered if their unease stemmed from two ladies asking questions, or from the recent incidents on the ranch.

"We heard about your poker parties." Olga laughed. "My husband has them all the time. He and his buddies used to meet in my kitchen, until I banned them from the house. Too much cigar smoke and loud carryings-on. I moved them out to our patio, and then eventually out to the far corner of the garden."

The men laughed and muttered words of understanding.

"Yeah, them parties can get pretty wild," said Willie Brown. He removed his hat and scratched his head, sending flakes of dandruff through the air.

"What time do you usually play?" Kate asked.

"We get rolling around seven-thirty and wrap it up by midnight. We used to go on to all hours of the morning, but…well, I'm not as young as I used to be and this work is pretty hard, and them boys need to be ready to go early in the morning."

"Did any of you happen to leave the game for a few minutes?" Kate noticed Willie Brown's posture stiffen.

She was sure that her question came as no surprise. "I mean, you could have seen someone around the ranch that night, someone who you didn't know. But I'm sure if you had, you would have told Sheriff McCrae."

"We all stayed put ma'am, except for PJ. He had to leave early."

Kate looked over at the other three men. The youngest one lifted one finger to indicate that he was PJ.

"Like I told the Sheriff, it was PJ's turn to take the nightshift and sleep in the barn. We had a mare that was about ready to foal. This was her third one and she'd had hard times in the past. PJ didn't see anything that night, did you, son?"

"No, sir."

"PJ, I hope they gave you a decent mattress in that barn," Olga said.

"Yes, ma'am." PJ blushed. He had hopped up on the fence and sat with his hands folded between his knees, looking down at the ground. Using the sleeve of his shirt, he wiped the sweat off his face, smearing the grime around in swirls.

"Did you hear anything?" Olga asked again.

"No ma'am. I sleep like a log. My head hits the pillow and I'm zonked."

Kate wondered how useful a zonked young man would be if the horse went into labor. "About what time did you leave for your watch, PJ?" Kate said.

Willie Brown gave PJ a slight frown and answered for him. "Sometime after nine-fifteen," he said.

Kate suspected that PJ, given a chance, liked to exercise his tongue. This interview was going nowhere. "Thick as thieves," is how Dickson described this small group of men in charge of the south pasture and a pregnant mare.

Refusing to be intimidated by a bowlegged cowhand with dandruff, Kate turned to PJ. "Who did you relieve?"

Again, Willie Brown answered. "Stubby Platt."

"Is he around?" Kate asked.

"Not today. He's got the day off. He's gone to San Angelo to visit his mother."

"How about the morning Jesús Flores was killed?" Kate asked. All four men straightened up. The guy, who was undoubtedly Red Dryden, put his hat back on to indicate that he had heard enough. "Isn't the south pasture near where Jesús's truck was found?" Kate continued in a voice as demure as she could conjure up.

"We don't know nothing about that ma'am. We barely knew Jesús," Willie Brown said. "He didn't work with us. Besides, that pasture covers three hundred and fifty acres. A volcano could erupt on one side, and we wouldn't know it."

Kate could hardly believe that. Nonetheless, if these guys knew anything it was clear that they were not parting with one iota of information. Kate kept her eyes on PJ during most of the conversation, and she noticed him sneaking glances in her direction. His statement about sleeping like a log, sounded somewhat rehearsed. He must have been the ranch hand who saw Wayne leave around nine-thirty. Had he also seen Kate? The barn is near the kennel, and if he walked out of the game early, he could have seen her, or the person who shot her. In fact, throw Nora into the picture, and the place was virtually a Grand Central Station. Kate changed her line of questioning.

"How's the mare?"

"She had the colt last night," said Willie Brown. "I

was on duty when the little bugger slid out like a snail on ice. Third time's a charm, I guess. Well, if that's it, we're gonna grab a bite and get back to work."

Kate needed to get PJ alone. She was certain that the young man had more to say. But getting PJ away from Willie Brown was not possible right now. Maybe she could arrange something with Glen Dickson. But at this point, Kate was not sure who on this ranch she could trust. If Glen Dickson had something to hide, he would certainly make sure that PJ held his tongue.

The four men left, with PJ dragging behind. Right before they walked into the bunkhouse, he turned around and glanced at Kate, looking lost and soulful. Was he having second thoughts about keeping his mouth shut? Kate couldn't imagine what life was like for PJ. Did he even have a life beyond the ranch? He was so young. If he had dropped out of school in order to work, he would not have the time to hang out with other teenagers, date, or play sports. Kate's maternal instincts did not usually extend beyond exploited and abused animals. PJ, however, tugged at her heart. Perhaps his resemblance to a helpless fawn was the reason she warmed to the boy.

"What do you think?" Kate asked Olga.

"I think young PJ knows something. And I think Willie Brown knows he knows."

"Sounded that way to me, too. Do you know a John Davenport?"

"A local rancher, chairman of the Holistic Ranch Commission. I think he used to be a doctor, retired now. Why?"

"He sent an email to Guy's. Something about if Guy needed any more help to give him a call."

"You got into Guy's email? Never mind. I should

know better than ask. Max has received several calls lately from Davenport. He keeps all the ranchers updated on legislation concerning the Commission."

"Let's see if we can find Wayne Brody while we're here. And then give Davenport a call. Maybe we can get an idea of where Guy took off to and why," Kate said.

"How do we get that information from Davenport?"

"I've no idea. You'll think of something, I'm sure. 'Decent mattress in the barn.' You're such a mom, Olga."

"Yeah, well, I raised a rebel daughter and a hotheaded husband. One learns all sorts of tricks in order to get reluctant children to talk."

"Give me a bunch of bull-elephants vying for a female any day. At least in that situation there are few surprises. The big guy gets the girl and the losers furl and unfurl their trunks like party noisemakers, gnashing their tusks, and having a pachyderm fit."

"How dare you come back here empty handed?" Kate and Olga turned around to see Wayne walking up behind them. "Two women call for two six packs." He tipped the brim of his grungy baseball cap.

"Sorry, Wayne. I come bearing no gifts this time. Olga and I—"

"I know. I just ran into Garrison. He was fuming. You know, Mrs. Caraway, he doesn't much care for you."

I wonder why, Kate thought, but decided not to mince words with Wayne Brody right now. If he were indeed innocent of any wrongdoing concerning Jesús, then maybe he'd have some information worth sharing. He was not innocent, however, in his dealings with the greyhounds, and Kate doubted that she could trust him.

Why was he transporting sick, undernourished greyhounds as well as healthy ones? Why did he lie about using live lures for training the racers?

"We're all concerned about Guy and his family, as well as what is going on here at the ranch," Olga said. "One man was already killed, and Kate came very close to becoming the second victim. If you can give us any information that would be helpful, something that might have crossed your mind after you talked to Sheriff McCrae yesterday."

Olga worked her magic again. Wayne looked at his watch and glanced around. "There have been weird things going on here. I find myself looking over my shoulder a lot lately. Listen. Meet me at Jake's in a few minutes. We can't talk here."

Chapter Sixteen

Overwhelmed with confusion, Kate was uncertain which lead, if you could call any of the information that she had gathered a lead, to pursue first. But one thing she was certain of, she could not handle another greasy grilled-cheese sandwich at Jake's Tavern. She and Olga stopped at Micah's espresso shop. They bought bagels and coffee-to-go, and on the way to meet Wayne, Kate and Olga discussed their strategy.

"What's up with Wayne? First, he lied to me about using live lures, and now he wants to talk. Something must have frightened him. I can't figure him out. Do you know much about him, Olga?"

"All I know is that he's not from around here. Being the new guy on the ranch, he might be unsure of where his alliance lies."

"Guy trusts him, though. He told me Wayne has been a big help. He even assisted Victoria in training her greyhound."

"That might be why he and Garrison don't get along," Olga said. "I don't think Guy takes his younger brother seriously. Otherwise he'd give him something meaningful to do."

"I wonder if anyone would notice if we walked into Jake's wearing allergy masks?" Kate said as she swallowed her last bite of bagel.

"Allergy mask?"

"Cigarette smoke."

"I guess that means that I'll have to wash my hair tonight."

By the time they arrived at the tavern, the only game plan, which Olga suggested, was to convince Wayne that they were on his side.

The strategy was not necessary.

With another cool front dipping down from the Panhandle, the day's temperature stayed below ninety and a stiff breeze blew in from the north. This time the door to Jake's stood wide open, the ceiling fans wafting out the hot, stale air. Hazy smoke drifted through the door, causing the tavern to appear as if it were on fire. As they walked inside Olga said, "Surely this place has no smoke alarms, otherwise they'd never stop beeping."

Through the haze, they saw Wayne sitting at a booth, away from the crowd at the bar. There were two beer cans on the table. He was using one for an ashtray. He didn't bother to stand when the two women approached his table. Kate brushed off the seat and slid into the booth with Olga alongside her.

"Beer? It's happy hour all day on Thursdays. Hey, Bev," Wayne shouted. "Bring these two gals a beer."

Bev was already walking over to their table with a tray holding two cans of coke, two glasses of ice, and a plate of meat loaf smothered in reddish, brown gravy. "I never forget a customer's drink. And you, ma'am," Bev said to Olga. "I figured you don't want beer neither, right?"

Olga smiled and gratefully accepted the coke.

"Y'all hungry?" said Bev. "Mr. Manners here already ordered." Bev set the plate in front of Wayne. Some of the gravy sloshed off the side and on to the table.

"The cokes will be fine. Thanks," Kate said.

Kate waited until Bev was out of earshot. "We need your help, Wayne."

"Well, I don't know what the hell you were doing on the ranch on Tuesday night. McCrae grilled me pretty good. At first I was pissed as hell." A coy smile spread across his face. "No offense, but you're one nosy woman, you know that? But I got to thinking that I might need your help too. Things have gotten real strange at the ranch." He unscrewed the top off the bottle of Tabasco and splattered the sauce over the gravy. "With Flores getting himself killed and you getting shot, and now Guy's taken off, well...I swear I'm not mixed up with any of this. I mean, I don't have nothing to hide, but I've been too close when those two incidents occurred. I don't feel that I'm off the hook."

"McCrae considers you a suspect?" Olga said.

"Everyone at the ranch is a suspect. Everyone is looking at everyone else, wondering who the killer is. I had no reason to kill Jesús, nor you, for that matter." He picked up a slice of thin white bread. With his knife, he swirled the hot sauce into the gravy turning it a sickish orange color and smeared the glob over the bread. He took a bite, washed it down with a gulp of beer, then continued. "But that drunken brother of Guy's keeps making comments about me being an outsider and causing trouble. Guy and I have a good working relationship, but—you know—blood's thicker than water."

"Garrison's giving you trouble?" Kate said.

"He wants me out of there. I don't trust the asshole. I'm not saying that he's guilty of anything either. What I'm saying is that he's nervous and might point the finger at me. The guy's bad news. He slinks around, popping up all over the place like he's some kind of watchman."

"I know what you mean," Kate said.

"Not only that, someone was in my office that night you were shot. I had suspected someone of coming in and rooting around in my stuff several times before, going through the files. It smacks of Garrison's slime-ball tricks. Anyway, I set a little trap and someone tripped it."

Kate nudged Olga under the table. "Trap?"

"Yeah. I started leaving the bottom right hand drawer of my filing cabinet open about an inch and when I came in the day after your attack, it was closed.

"You don't lock the room?" Olga asked.

"It wouldn't matter. Several people have keys. There's a lot of equipment the guys need to get to."

Kate couldn't remember if the file drawer had been opened the night she was in the tack room. Then Kate was struck with the idea that she might have been set up. As best she could figure, she was shot around ten. But there was no way she could trust Wayne. He had lied to her about the lures. And if Guy was telling the truth, Wayne had lied to him also. There did, however, seem to be a change in Wayne? His cockiness was now replaced with genuine fear.

"Why should I trust you, Wayne? You lied about using live lures. I saw the discarded rabbits in the barrel."

"So sue me. But I'm not lying now. It took me a while to put things together. I left the ranch around nine-thirty, and I saw PJ heading for the barn. I told McCrae I was sure PJ saw me. But what McCrae doesn't know is that Garrison was not playing poker the entire time. I saw him outside the bunkhouse."

"The ranch hands said that he didn't leave the game," Kate said.

"Well, we're talking Garrison here. We're talking the brother of the boss. A little extra cash might keep the boys quiet. A little extra cash might cause them to tell lies. I mean, Garrison has it in for me. He knows I'm smarter than he is, and he feels threatened. If I were you, I'd talk to PJ. He's young. He might still have a conscience. If he saw me, maybe he also saw Garrison."

"Why didn't you tell McCrae about this?"

"McCrae was already convinced that Garrison was telling the truth. The cards are stacked against me."

Kate recalled PJ's behavior earlier, and thought Wayne might be right. Maybe Garrison did leave the game. Maybe PJ did see him. But no one's talking. Kate wondered why.

Wayne finished his lunch and a third beer. "I need to get back to work." He threw a few dollars on the table. "And yeah, I use live lures, and so did Gomez. If Guy wants winners, then those dogs need to have a taste for blood. I'm training the dogs on private property, and I ain't breaking no laws. Let me do my job. You go after Garrison."

Kate wanted to scream every filthy word that she could think of. Instead, she swallowed her anger. Wayne rose to leave. "One more question," she said. "Any idea why Jesús was trying to blackmail Guy?"

"Yeah, I got an idea. Jesús was desperate to get his family here."

"But wouldn't blackmailing his employer be like cutting his own throat?"

"When someone's desperate, they don't think. And Jesús was desperate."

231

****

It was after one when Kate and Olga left Jake's Tavern. They split up their forces for the afternoon, and agreed to meet early in the evening.

Olga wanted to wait for further word from Max, and while doing so she would think of some viable excuse for contacting John Davidson in hopes of discovering where Guy was.

Kate planned to arrive at Molly's before Lance and Jenny showed up for work, but it was still early. After running around all morning, Kate's back muscles protested. Her head finally stopped hurting, except when she combed her hair.

But as soon as the Advil wore off, her muscles tightened up for another dose of punishment from her tumble through the rapids. She called Molly to get the name of a masseuse, and to let her know that she'd be at the kennel later.

Kate did not want to tell Molly over the phone what she had learned about Travis Landon. Instead, she wanted to give Molly some hope, even if only a shred.

"There's Sensation Relaxation. They have a masseuse that gives a deep muscle massage that will relax you so much all you can do afterward is cry," Molly said. "You know, something about releasing all that negativity. Then there's a place called Heavenly Touch where they'll pamper you with a lengthy treatment of massage, pedicures, manicures, along with soft music and scented candles. With the full treatment, you even get your own ceramic angel when you leave."

"I'll keep my unreleased negativity, for now, and take the angel. But I have to arrange for the full treatment another day. I'd like to be at your place before Lance and

Jenny arrive so we can talk. Does the angel place take new clients at the last minute?"

"Don't worry, I'll call Carolyn, and she'll get you in no matter what. She has, as we speak, two greyhounds adopted from my organization."

"Any word on your missing dogs?"

"Nothing. I've looked everywhere. I took Freda and Lupe with me today, and we drove every road around. I don't think Gracie's ever spent the night outside. I can't image what she's going through."

"I know it must be hard. I still don't know what happened to your dogs, but I can be fairly sure you will not have to worry about losing any more. I'll explain when I get there."

****

Heavenly Touch, located one block from Cyprus Creek under a grove of live oaks, had once been a Victorian home. Its newly painted cream-colored shutters accented its mild yellow exterior. When she walked in, Kate felt as if she had entered the house of someone's grandmother. Warm and fuzzy decor covered the walls, surrounded the windows, and moved across the doorways. Victorian settees, made comfortable with time, were arranged around the waiting room. Mixed with a sweet scent of vanilla, Kate's olfactory senses detected the aroma of fresh baked pastries. Brahms's "Lullaby" played softly, and Kate immediately wanted to curl up on a settee.

Gliding through a doorway covered with white lace curtains was a motherly looking woman in her late forties. Her dyed, blonde hair, French braided with a pink, satin ribbon, matched her pink nail polish, her pink smock, and the paint that trimmed the room. Her makeup was perfect and her smile warm and welcoming.

"You must be Kate. Molly called. I'm Carolyn Meeks."

"Hello, Carolyn. Do I smell muffins baking?"

"Banana nut. They'll be cool enough to eat by the time your massage is over. Oh, honey, what happened to your arm, you poor baby." Then Carolyn scanned the purplish, blue bruises that marred Kate's skin, and assumed the worst. "Honey, you're not in any kind of trouble are you?" She lowered her voice to barely above a whisper. "Cause, right next door, there's a great counselor. She specializes in...you know...relationships."

Kate knew exactly what Carolyn meant and rather than take offense, Kate felt sure that the proprietor's concern was genuine.

"No, it's nothing like that. Actually I had a nasty fall—a lateral fall for about a hundred yards." Kate was not sure she had convinced Carolyn that she was not dealing with a victim of domestic violence, but despite Carolyn's nurturing nature, she was professional enough to accept Kate's explanation and kind enough to pretend that she believed her.

"Oh, honey, forgive me for being nosy. Melissa's gonna take good care of you—don't worry one little bit. When you leave here, you'll be a new woman."

A young woman who bore a striking resemblance to Carolyn escorted Kate to a small room. It was difficult to tell the woman's age under the dim light. She could have been Carolyn's sister or her daughter.

"Hi, I'm Melissa."

Kate stuck out her hand, but Melissa presented her with a hug instead. "Get comfortable, I'll be back in a couple of minutes, and we'll get started."

Five minutes later, Kate was on the table, drifting off into another world. She was conscious enough to roll over onto her back whenever Melissa asked her to do so, but for what it was worth, Kate could have died and gone to heaven. Kate had told Melissa the reason for the bruises, and she kneaded each muscle with slow, gentle movements. It was as if Melissa could feel the sorest places, and took the utmost care to massage the pain away.

The next thing Kate remembered was someone calling her name. The lights in the room had brightened enough for Kate to see her surroundings.

"How do you feel, Mrs. Caraway? It's fine with me if you stay here all day. We could even abandon this room and use the others, but I'm afraid your light snoring might put everyone to sleep." Melissa had set a glass of water on the side table and asked Kate if she needed help getting up.

"How long was I out? Was I really snoring?"

"Not long. And your secret is safe with me. I gathered that some of that tension has disappeared."

"Will you come home with me?" Kate stretched and her neck popped with pleasure. "I feel like Rip Van Winkle."

"I'm here Monday through Friday, all day." Melissa left her card on the table and stepped out so Kate could get dressed. Kate made a promise to herself that as long as she was in Wimberley, she'd get back here as often as possible.

After Kate paid the receptionist a fee that was ridiculously low for having had a celestial experience, Carolyn came out to say goodbye. "How did my daughter treat you?"

"Melissa has a true gift, and a new client."

Carolyn pinned a small, pink angel to Kate's T-shirt and handed her a brown paper sack. "Two muffins, one for you and one for Molly. Tell her that Gabby and Raph are fat and happy." She pointed to two framed photos on the reception desk. The greyhounds were curled up on a sofa. The picture was taken at Christmas. Each dog had a red and green ribbon tied around its neck and a golden bow stuck to the tops of its sleek head.

"Gabby and Raph, as in Angels Gabriel and Raphael, right?"

"Yes, ma'am, they are my guardians." Carolyn laughed. "When they're not napping, that is."

Feeling years younger and almost too relaxed to walk, Kate drove to Molly's house. Olga insisted that Kate take the Explorer because it had a full tank of gas. Kate didn't say anything, but she knew that Olga was still concerned for Kate's safety. If someone had been following Kate, the Explorer might afford her some protection.

Molly was in the exercise yard when Kate drove up. The afternoon maintained the coolness of the morning, making it a gorgeous day. Five greyhounds were chasing a Frisbee, dashing about and leaping through the air with speed and grace. Kate walked over and stood by the fence to watch. The dogs reminded Kate of figure skaters, defying gravity with ease and dexterity. Their joy over the game was evident in their yapping and nudging one another. Two greyhounds grabbed hold of their prize simultaneously and trotted back, tugging on the Frisbee and playfully growling as they went. When Kate saw Molly, it was obvious that the dogs weren't the only ones enjoying the game.

Molly looked around, smiled, and waved at Kate.

"I see Freda and Lupe have removed themselves from the air-conditioned house to play outside," Kate said. Freda broke away from the pack and ran to the fence when she saw Kate.

"Only because it's a bit cooler today. I think Freda likes you."

"It's the muffin." Kate held up the sack.

"Looks like Carolyn took good care of you."

"It was her daughter Melissa. I feel years younger."

"Well, let's get this over with. What did you find out about Travis?" Molly let herself out of the yard and locked the gate behind her. The game of Frisbee, without the tosser, now became a game of tug-of-war. With no one around to give orders, the yapping and growling rose to a louder level and Kate and Molly walked over to the patio where they could hear one another.

Kate handed Molly the envelope. "I found this when I got back to the bungalow last night. Someone shoved it under the door."

Molly opened the envelope and read the note. Kate related the conversation she had with Travis earlier in the day.

"I'm not sure what he did with the dogs," Kate continued. "I called Brad Gates to get his opinion and he was in a quandary as well. Do you have any ideas, Molly?" It pained Kate deeply to see Molly taking the news so hard. No doubt, she felt betrayed. How could Travis have been so untrustworthy and disloyal to someone who obviously cared for him?

"I'm not sure, either," Molly said with hesitation.

Kate suspected that Molly did have an idea, but

perhaps out of protection for the boy, despite his actions, Molly was not yet ready to voice her concern.

"When is his next shift? Maybe you can speak to him. He thinks a lot of you and how he stands in your eyes."

"Travis called this afternoon. He left a message on my machine. He quit."

"What about his Ag class?"

"I called his Ag teacher. Travis wasn't in class this afternoon. Seems he skipped."

"Oh, God. I'm afraid I'm to blame. I must have pushed him too hard. You'd think after forty years, I'd learn to develop some poise and tactfulness?" For the first time Kate had to admit that, like Molly, she had a soft spot for Travis as well. Maybe it was his shyness or his poor home life. What would his family do without his income?

"Kate, listen to me. This was not your fault. If Travis was doing something illegal, and I believe he was, then it couldn't be overlooked. He is a troubled young man."

"What will he do now?"

"I don't know. I tried calling his house several times this afternoon, but got no answer. I'm going to put the dogs up, and then I'm going over to his house. We need to get to the bottom of this. Do you mind staying here? Jenny and Lance should arrive shortly, and be my guest, ask them as many questions as you want. They might be more willing to talk if I'm not here. I'll be right back."

Molly went inside the house and Kate sat under the trees feeling like Pontius Pilate. Maybe Travis did have a bad home life. Maybe he was a troubled young man, but if Kate were the straw that broke Travis, she would never forgive herself. Molly came back a couple of minutes later with a tall glass of ice tea. She handed Kate a note. "There's more tea in the fridge. Make yourself at home. Here's a note for you to give to the kids. I've explained that we have a serious situation here, and that they should trust you and answer your questions. You handle the rest as you see fit. And stop kicking yourself. If I'm not back by the time you leave, call me later."

Jenny arrived first. Kate was surprised when she saw the teenager climb down from the cab of the monster truck she was driving. Jenny appeared to weigh less than the greyhounds she attended. She was dressed in long overalls over a skimpy tie-dyed tank top. Her long strawberry blonde hair was tipped on the ends with a bright green color, the remnants of a bold statement no longer important.

As Jenny strolled toward the kennel, Kate walked over, introduced herself, and gave Jenny Molly's note.

"This must be about Travis Landon. There are rumors going around that he skipped town. Did he get in trouble?"

"We're not sure, Jenny. We're trying to find out. You worked with Travis on Tuesday. How did he seem to you? Did he say anything that indicated that he was nervous or worried?"

Jenny's tiny face brightened. "Travis never talks much. I always tease him about being so quiet. I'm not mean to him. You know, friendly teasing. He just smiles and keeps on working. In fact, I like working with Travis because he does all the work. I mean, I'm not a slacker. I do my share, but Travis makes it easier."

Kate guessed Jenny had a crush on Travis. He was a handsome boy with an innocent face that cried out for attention.

"Did you and Travis leave at the same time?"

"Yes, we always walk out together. It gets pretty dark here at night and Travis makes sure I get in my truck okay. He tells me to lock my doors. That's all he ever says." A slight crease appeared in the middle of Jenny's forehead. "I hope he's okay."

Thumping loud speakers caused Kate and Jenny to turn. Lance drove up in a black mustang and parked behind Jenny's truck. "Talk about a slacker. I hate working with Lance. He's such a jock. He's always late, but Travis covers for him."

"Thanks for your help, Jenny. We're here to help Travis too. If you hear of anything, please let Mrs. Gibson know." Kate let Jenny start on her chores. She wanted to talk to Lance alone.

"Hi, Lance."

"Hey."

Lance was stockier than she had remembered—almost as tall as Travis, but with broader shoulders. Under his grimy maroon Texas A&M baseball cap, Kate could see short-cropped blond hair at the neckline. Spreading across the sides of his face from ear to cheek were bleached sideburns so light they were almost invisible until one stood close.

Kate had a strong feeling that Lance had been expecting her. She did not think Molly's note was necessary. Either Lance would talk or he wouldn't. Kate suspected the latter. She was right. Lance stuck his hands firmly in the front pockets of his jeans, and pursed his lips. Despite his size, he looked like a stubborn two-year old. All he had to do was to stick out his lower lip.

Kate was not sure if his defiance was for his own wellbeing or for that of his friend. He did not strike Kate as the type of young man who would sacrifice his own skin to help a buddy.

With the intention of making him uncomfortable, Kate smiled and said nothing. Lance glanced over to where Jenny was tending to the dogs. No help there. Then he looked back at Kate. "I saw you this morning at school talking to Travis."

"He could be in trouble. We're worried about him. Do you know where he is?"

"Are you with the cops? 'Cause if you're not, I don't have to talk to you."

"That's true. No, I'm not with the cops, but I am helping Molly. I know that you're aware that several of her dogs are missing, not only those from Tuesday evening. Molly has lost many over the past few months. Sheriff McCrae is involved now. You were working with Travis on Tuesday."

Lance removed his hands from his pockets and folded his arms as if to protect himself from Kate's questions.

"Do you know where he is?" Kate repeated her question. "He must be really upset if whatever trouble he's in caused him to skip school."

"I don't know anything. I heard he left school after lunch."

"Aren't you worried about him, Lance? I hear you two are good friends."

"Not good friends. Travis doesn't have time to hang out. He's always working some sort of job."

"Is Travis a good enough friend to keep quiet about you if you were in trouble?"

Surprised by the question, Lance responded, "Me in trouble? You can't pin nothing on me."

"You worked with Travis on two of the nights the dogs disappeared. Did you go home after work on Tuesday night?"

"I don't know. I guess."

"Think, did you go home on Tuesday night? You can tell me or you can tell Sheriff McCrae. It would be easy enough to check and find out if you went home."

"Well, you do that. I got work to do." He walked over to the kennel and joined Jenny.

Kate felt certain that Lance's unwillingness to talk about Travis was for Lance's own protection. She took the cellphone from the Explorer and made herself comfortable at the patio table. She had a good view of the kids. Jenny was giving Lance a hard time. She pointed to the cages, spewed out some instructions, and stood in the exercise yard with her hands on her hips. It was clear who was in charge today. Lance muttered complaints, but it was evident that he would rather follow Jenny's instructions than initiate any chores himself, or be subjected to more of Kate's questions. Occasionally, he'd glance over at Kate to see if she was still watching. She was.

This was a good time to follow up on her threat. She had not spoken to McCrae since yesterday. She dialed his number.

"This is Kate Caraway. May I speak to the Sheriff?"

"If I knew where the heck he was, I'd let you. That man takes off and never tells me where he's going."

Kate was amused by the dispatcher's response. What else would one expect from a county sheriff? Kate got the impression that McCrae's habit of sporadic checking-in did not suit his dispatcher well. She left a message for McCrae to contact her at Molly Gibson's house. She would be at the kennel for about an hour.

Kate took out her facts list to add the latest information concerning Travis, when she saw Jenny unlock the cage of the injured greyhound. The dog had been on Kate's mind since yesterday. Jenny walked inside, and, within a few minutes, she came out carrying the dog and gently set it down on the ground. It stood on shaky legs. Jenny coaxed it to take a few steps. The greyhound tried and then slid down onto her rump. Jenny gently lifted the patient and held her up so that she could relieve herself. Every movement seemed painful, and Kate's heart broke watching. She hated, more than anything, to see animals suffer. She wanted desperately to do something, but the young greyhound was safe with Jenny, and the dog's recovery would have to be left to a greater power.

Kate called Olga. She had just hung up the phone after speaking with Max. Rosa Linda was not making things easy. She and Daniel were not willing to cooperate with their attorneys. They were planning to use the incident as a means to bring about awareness of their cause. Kate wasn't surprised. Olga reported that they would not return tonight. Max would call again in the morning. Jack sent his love with a message that he'd call Kate later.

"I need to cook," Olga said after giving Kate an update. "Would you mind picking up a pork roast or a flank steak at Bennet's Market on the square? They're open until seven on Thursdays, so you don't have to rush over now."

"No problem. Give me specifics. I usually don't buy meat."

"Do you have something to write with?" Olga said.

Kate pulled a note pad from her purse. "Shoot."

"Look for a pork roast, about five pounds, it should run about $7.99 per pound. If he's out of pork roast, look for a skirt steak about the same size. I'll marinate it and make fajitas. But don't let Bennet talk you into a steak that's more than $5.99 a pound."

"Okay, got it. It's on my list. See you this evening."

"Wait, I remembered that John Davenport used to be a psychiatrist before he retired and took up ranching."

"Then maybe his connection with Guy was on a more personal level," Kate said. "His message asked how things went at Santa Rita Center and if he could be of more help."

"You're right."

"How do you know?"

"I called him today. I told him that he had been referred to me by Guy Fordyce, and that I had this friend who had just come back from Africa and was suffering from post-traumatic stress and was severely depressed."

"Gee, thanks."

"Hey, you left this one up to me, and besides, what are friends for?"

"I'm not severely depressed."

"Okay, post-traumatic stress, then. Shut up and listen. He said that he was not practicing any more, but he did recommend a rehab clinic. It's a bit pricey, though. It's located in a remote area near Fort Davis."

"And?"

"And it's called the Santa Rita Center."

"Meredith's in rehab, then? Good work, Olga."

"No shit."

As Kate hung up, McCrae's squad car slowed to a stop behind the Explorer.

"I got your message, anything new?"

"Travis Landon."

"I know Travis. I've brought his mother home many times when she was in no shape to drive. He never says much. He just helps me get her out of the car and into the house. I guess he's too embarrassed."

"He's the one responsible for Molly's missing dogs. Seems that on the four different occasions when the dogs disappeared, Travis was the one on duty. Then last night someone shoved an envelope containing eighty dollars under the door of the bungalow. There was a note that said for me to give the money to Molly."

"Guilty conscience?"

"I confronted him this morning. Reading between the lines, it was obvious that he was responsible and that he wasn't working alone. He wouldn't tell me who paid him the money or why. Then this afternoon, he skipped school and disappeared. Molly's out looking for him now."

McCrae removed his hat, and tossed it on the patio table in frustration.

At that moment, Lance walked out of the workroom, carrying a huge sack of dog food over his shoulder. When he saw McCrae, he almost lost his footing.

While Kate had the boy's attention, she nodded in his direction. "See that kid over there? Do you know him?"

"Lance? What self-respecting baseball fan doesn't know Lance Billings? He was our little league star and now his coach is grooming him for something bigger," McCrae said.

"He worked with Travis on a couple of the nights the dogs disappeared. He may not be involved, but I think he knows, or at least has an idea of what Travis was doing. But I couldn't get much out of him."

"I'll have a talk with him before I leave. Anything else?"

"I spoke to Wayne Brody today, and he claims that he saw Garrison walking toward the kennel around nine-thirty on the night I was shot."

"Garrison had several witnesses who said he never left the game."

"I spoke to those witnesses today, too, or at least I spoke to the spokesperson. Willie Brown wouldn't let me talk to his boys."

"I got a little further than you. I talked to each of the guys separately. But I wasn't comfortable with their stories."

"They all sounded the same?"

"Word for word."

"Wayne thinks that Garrison is setting him up."

"For shooting you? I don't have to ask what Garrison's motive is, but what about Wayne's? It comes back to what Jesús found out, and we still don't have a clue. No bodies have turned up."

"Except for the rabbits. I think PJ, the young ranch hand, knows something. If he was on his way to the stable and saw Wayne leaving, chances are he saw Garrison as well. I'm going back to the Fordyce Ranch and have another visit with Wayne."

"I wouldn't do that if I were you."

"Are you telling me not to?"

"I'm telling you not to press your luck."

"I'll be careful, and I'll call you later."

"Are you always this stubborn?"

"Most of the time. Good luck with Lance. I think

we've let him stew long enough."

"Before I forget, you may want to take Spoke Hill Road to the right. As I was driving up, the county was laying down a layer of asphalt. The crew was making their way up from Ranch Road 12, heading in this direction. To the right, Spoke Hill road winds around for about three miles and meets up again with 12 west of town. It'll take a little longer, but you don't have to worry about liquid asphalt spraying your car."

"Thanks, I'll do that." As Kate drove off, she saw McCrae speaking to Lance across the fence. The Sheriff had his notebook poised, and Lance's hands were back in his front pockets. His lips were pursed once more, but this time he didn't look so defiant.

Kate looked to the left down Spoke Hill and saw the county work crew with their massive equipment spread across the road. Grateful for McCrae's warning, she turned right, and soon a spectacular view of a sprawling meadow appeared up ahead. She drove over two low-water crossings, still trickling after the rain from two nights ago, and passed two quaint bed and breakfast places tucked in among numerous species of evergreens. To the right of the road, a steep limestone escarpment covered with a completely different type of vegetation, rose sharply upward. An ancient fault line had divided this area, separating the evergreen from the deciduous. Ashe juniper, pinyon pine, and yaupon holly grew thick and green on the north side of the road while baldcypress, Texas red oak, and eastern cottonwoods were scattered across the escarpment on the south. A few leaves, splashed with a hint of yellow, and the cooler air promised an early fall. It was difficult to believe that only a week ago, Kate sat boiling under a hot, humid sun waiting for Jesús to deliver his message. A message that was still a mystery.

Just beyond another low-water crossing, Kate drove passed a weathered, wooden sign with faded white letters that read, "Driftwood Cemetery." She slowed and put the Explorer in reverse.

Less than a mile down, Cemetery Road narrowed to one lane. Huge limbs of ancient big-tooth maples lined each side of the road and intertwined above, creating a dense canopy blocking out the sun. The road dipped and rose, winding at every crest and trough. Kate slowed and turned on her headlights. In the deep shadows, it was impossible to see if another driver was coming in the opposite direction. But after a while, she relaxed, opened the sunroof, and rolled down the windows. The sound of mockingbirds mixed with the rustle of leaves, made Kate think of the drive north of Chicago along Lake Michigan.

At the first sign of fall, she and Jack would leave Chicago for a long weekend to take in the fall foliage. They would start out early in the morning, stopping in Kenosha, Wisconsin for a light breakfast, then continue on to Two Rivers, arriving at lunchtime. After a bowl of clam chowder at Peninsula Cafe, they would drive up to Ellison Bay and spend a few nights at Ray and Joan's Bed and Breakfast. Kate felt the first flutter of excitement since Jack had received the call from Gary. Being back in Illinois among their old baseball crowd might be nice. Then Kate's thoughts drifted back to camp, and she wondered how her research crew was managing without her. Too many mixed feelings, too many uncertainties.

Kate crested a steep hill, and feeling safe from anyone approaching in either direction, pulled off the road and parked to take in the view. The trees had thinned, opening up a window to the rolling hills and valleys below. Pink tahoka daisies and Texas yellow stars dotted the landscape. Lofty purple gayfeathers sprinkled the roadside. In a small meadow beyond the road, tiny golden butterflies swarmed a colony of Maximilian sunflowers. Then Kate saw a flash of metallic yellow, the sun reflecting on the hood of a car up ahead. She looked again and it had disappeared. When the car did not surface over the hill, she thankfully realized that it was driving away from her, allowing her more time to linger at this heavenly place.

She and Jack would have to return to this spot after things settled down—maybe in the early evening. She'd pack a basket of wine and cheese, along with whatever delicacies Olga had in the fridge.

In the peacefulness of the moment, Kate remembered where she was going and why. She put the picnic idea out of her mind, and climbed back into Olga's SUV. Two more miles down the road, she came upon the Driftwood Cemetery. She parked in a gravel lot in front of a small clapboard chapel, and followed the signs, leading down another valley to the graveyard. The path descended downward passing a grove of redbuds. The foliage had thinned and suddenly Kate spotted the cross, standing strong and straight among the gravestones—a sentinel for the dead.

Eerie.

Kate recalled Meredith Fordyce's attack, and turned around and looked behind her. Tending to the overgrown graves, Meredith would not have seen her attacker approaching. No one driving by would have seen the assault either. Kate wished that she had taken Olga's pistol rather than leave it in the Explorer. It was a good hike from the parking lot to the cemetery, and there were too many places for a person to hide.

Then Kate thought of Jesús. Did his killer carry his body down this same path, all the way from the parking lot? It was not impossible, if the killer was strong and healthy. In fact, an adult of average strength, even a woman, could have dragged the body down the hill the entire way. But the killer had to have been strong enough to hoist the body up onto the cross, and tie it in place—unless there were two people.

Garrison and Guy.

If Guy was being blackmailed by Jesús, then Guy might have convinced his little brother to shoot Jesús, and then together they could have brought the body here. But if their intention was to keep Jesús quiet, why not just kill him and dump his body on one of the many country roads around Wimberley? No one would find the body for weeks, maybe months. This was no ordinary killing. The killer needed to make a statement—a passionate, brutal statement.

Was the murder a warning? But to whom, and why?

No, whoever had killed Jesús and hung his body on the cross, acted out of rage. Killing him was not enough. Having someone find the body was not important. Crows could have picked it clean before it was discovered in this isolated graveyard. The killer, in a fitful rage, needed to punish his victim more than death itself. Kate was sure of this. What had Jesús done to cause such hatred?

A twig snapped, causing Kate to dive off the path and duck behind a scrawny persimmon tree. She waited and listened, keeping her breathing silent and shallow. The bushes rustled and two squirrels leapt from the ground and scurried up the closest tree, chasing one another across the branches. Feeling silly, Kate stood up, and continued down the path.

When she reached the cemetery, she found the small wrought-iron gate secured with a new lock—probably McCrae's doing. The locked gate would not keep anyone out. The fence was only two feet tall and anyone could step over.

Kate looked across the graveyard. The gravestones were old. Most were simple slabs of limestone with names and dates carved roughly with a chisel. The taller ones, some shoulder high, were decorated with statues of stone-carved cherubs resting on top. Many of the graves dated back to the early 1800s. Some were starting to lean and crumble with the shifting earth. The newly planted grass that grew over each grave had been neatly clipped. Flowers had been planted in the center, most likely recent work of the historical society.

On her way down the path, and now here at the gate, Kate looked for signs of blood. To her surprise, she did not find any. She climbed over the fence, and slowly walked toward the cross, looking for anything that might give her a lead. The idea was crazy. There were dozens of different footprints on the dirt paths and around the cross and nearby graves. McCrae's investigators had been very thorough.

The cross stood about eight feet high, the crossbeam level with the top of Kate's head. She tried to imagine how she would hoist a dead body upward and tie it down. She imagined creating a large noose and looping it round the chest and under the arms. Then she'd throw the rope over the crossbeam and pull from the back. With a great amount of tugging, she could pull the body to a standing position, but by herself it would be impossible to lift the body off the ground. A man could do it. With two people, it would be easier, even easier with a small ladder to stand on.

Kate looked around for divots in the soil under the cross. She found none. Then she noticed one of the taller gravestones right behind the cross. With one person holding the body in place, another person could have stood on the gravestone, instead of a ladder. She looked around the marker for scuff marks, and then around the other side for evidence of disturbed ground. What she found, instead, was Travis Landon.

Chapter Seventeen

Kate prayed the young boy was still alive. She reached over and felt the side of his neck for a pulse. Hope welled up inside her chest—he was still warm. She moved her fingers slightly to better cover the carotid artery, but felt nothing, and the hope of a few seconds ago vanished. It was probably better that he had died. The back of his skull was crushed to a pulpy mess. No one could survive this kind of injury and be more than a vegetable.

Too late to do anything for Travis, she raced to the parking lot, grabbed her purse from the car, and called McCrae. He had not yet left Molly's house and would be at the cemetery as soon as possible. She returned to the graveyard. Travis had been attacked only moments before her arrival. Kate did not want to follow in his footsteps. She removed the gun from her purse and snapped off the safety, only then did she scan the area for clues.

Lying on his stomach, the left side of his face to the ground and his arms stretched out in front, Kate was certain that Travis had been taken by surprise. There were no signs of a fight. His assailant struck Travis from behind and he fell face down. One hard hit could have killed him, but the damage to his skull was so severe that he had to have been struck more than once. It looked as if the killer had tried to embed Travis's head into the soft ground.

Again, a violent killing. Again, a tremendous amount of rage.

Travis had been standing on the path when he was hit, his killer only a few feet behind the boy. Kate studied the ground closely. Then she saw them.

Boot heels had ground divots two feet apart into the soil at the edge of the grass. Someone had walked up behind Travis, dug their feet into the earth for traction, and pulled back for a powerful swing. Travis trusted the person who struck him. Was it his dog-stealing partner? Did they drive here together? Travis's car was not in the parking lot. For the first time, Kate was absolutely certain that the disappearing dogs and the murders were connected. How? She still had no idea.

Kate squatted down close to Travis's body and studied the right side of his face. His eye and mouth were opened. She tried not to look at the back of his head, or at the blood that had seeped out onto the ground. The look of shock on his face was frightening enough. Then a disturbing thought crossed Kate mind. What if the first hit had not killed him? Had Travis known for a flash of a second that he was going to die? For the briefest of moments, before the second blow, was he aware of what was happening? He was so young. For a teenager, his face was clear and smooth. Kate remembered Jenny—how her eyes had brightened when she spoke of Travis. Kate felt tears run down her cheeks.

Whatever Travis had done, he did not deserve this. As she stood up to step away, her foot caught on a flat stone marker and she grabbed hold of the cross to keep from falling. It gave slightly under her weight, and the grim vision of Jesús's body strung up onto the structure gave her an ill feeling. She brushed the dirt from her jeans, and suddenly heard the snap of twigs behind her. She spun around, and grasping the gun in both hands, pointing the barrel at the intruder.

McCrae hit the ground and the two deputies behind him sprang off the trail.

"Ho there!" McCrae shouted. "Where in the goddamn hell did you get that gun?"

Kate stood speechless for a couple of seconds. "You should know not to sneak up on a person when she's in the company of a dead body." Kate lowered the gun.

"I called out to you several times. I became concerned when you didn't answer. Are you okay?"

For the first time in several hours, Kate's arm began to throb, reminding her that two days ago she had spent the night in the hospital.

"Do I look okay?" Kate's acerbic words had no effect on the sheriff.

"Actually, now that you mentioned it, you don't look so good. Where's the body?" McCrae and his two deputies stepped over the fence and walked towards Kate. "Christ. Someone wanted to make sure this boy was dead."

Then he noticed that Kate was losing her color. "I think you need to sit down." He took her by the arm and escorted her to a small stone bench under a pecan tree.

"You boys do your thing." He turned back to Kate. "If you're not careful, you're going to end up back in the hospital. What the hell made you come out here anyway?"

"I wanted to see where the killer left Jesús to be able to picture it in my mind. Travis couldn't have happened more than a few minutes ago. He rode out here with someone he trusted, and that person brutally killed him."

"Not exactly. We found Travis's car. It was driven off the parking lot into the bushes on the other side of the chapel. One of my deputies spotted it on the way down. He's going through the car now."

"So Travis met someone out here. Why? Another payoff?"

"I figure whoever Travis was working with got word of his change of heart and decided that Travis was too much of a risk to stay alive."

"I didn't see any cars on the way here. But I did see one driving off. Actually, I noticed a brief reflection from a car's hood—" Kate paused. "A yellow hood—my number one suspect."

"What?"

"Garrison Fordyce. Where does this road lead?"

"It winds through this area, connecting with the country roads leading to most the ranches." McCrae rubbed his hands across his face. "About a mile down, Cemetery Road intersects with FM 2234, and two miles later that road runs into FM 2236."

"The Fordyce Ranch."

"Right. Traveling along 12, it would take twenty minutes to get here, but if you knew the back roads, you could get here in less than five minutes. Looks like it's gonna be a long evening. You've done enough for one day. I'll send one of my men back with you."

"No, I'll be fine. I'll be at Olga's tonight. Did you find out anything more from Lance?"

"Not much. Seems that Lance ran into Travis as he was leaving school after lunch. Travis said something about going to Stanley Institute. Lance figured it was to see about another job. They hire a lot of high school students."

"Stanley Institute?"

"Pharmaceutical company located near San Marcos," said McCrae. "I was about to call the company and check if Travis had been there when I got your call. The young man must have been desperate for work. Maybe he didn't get the job. Maybe he decided to go back into the dog stealing business. Now it doesn't seem to matter."

"What confuses me is why Travis would agree to meet anyone here," Kate said. "Surely everyone in the county knows Jesús's killer brought his body here. If Travis's partner arranged for a meeting in the cemetery, wouldn't Travis get suspicious?"

"Unless he was in on the murder. Or maybe he found out who this person was and what he did, and decided to confront him in the cemetery."

"I'm certain the two murders are linked with the greyhound situation. I keep thinking of Garrison. If Jesús was threatening Guy, that would give Garrison a motive to kill Jesús."

"That would also give Guy a motive."

"And Meredith Fordyce. But what is the connection to the dogs? Wayne Brody?"

"No motive. Besides, his story checks out."

"Travis must have found out that connection. Poor Travis."

"Yeah, poor Travis."

"Sheriff," a deputy called out. "You may want to take a look in the trunk of Landon's car."

"What did you find?" McCrae called back.

"Looks like a shower curtain. It's covered in blood."

****

It was six o'clock by the time Kate headed back to Wimberley, and it was not until she drove through the town square that she remembered her promise to Olga to stop by Bennet's Market. The parking lot around the square was full. Kate pulled around to the side street, and parked in the last space near a trash dumpster, a place clearly avoided by anyone concerned with protecting the integrity of their automobile. She had an hour before Bennet's closed. After what she had seen this afternoon, Kate was not ready to walk into a meat market and peruse the display case.

"Ma'am?"

Kate spun around. At first, she didn't recognize the young man. PJ looked as if he just stepped out of a shower. Kate's nose caught a hint of ivory soap. His jeans were clean and creased and his white sleeveless T-shirt, although yellow around the neckline, was clean as well. With the dirt gone and a fresh set of clothes, he looked no older than fourteen. His arms were beginning to show some muscular development, but he was too thin to be considered healthy. Long, dark eyelashes enhanced almond-shaped eyes, giving his hollowed face an innocent look that melted Kate's heart. She wanted to take him home and feed him.

"Sorry, didn't mean to scare ya. I was across the street at the Bible Church when I saw ya drive up."

"Hello, PJ." Kate looked at the church where several people were milling around its small white porch.

"We have a Bible lesson on Thursday nights." His face lit up, as if pleased to reveal this special part of himself. "Ma'am...well, I'm not supposed to say this, but...well, Garrison didn't do nothing wrong."

"What do you mean, PJ?"

"We all said that he didn't leave the poker game, and well, that was pretty much true. Ya see—we like Garrison. He gets real drunk, and then he gets funny. And well, sometimes the guys kind of…you know…make sure that he drinks as much as he wants."

"I understand."

"It's not what you think. I think the sheriff figured we were getting Garrison drunk so we could take his money. The boys don't bet that much. We just have a good laugh. It's all in fun."

"What did you mean when you said that it 'was pretty much true,' that Garrison didn't leave the game?"

"Well, he got drunk pretty fast that night. And we was eating barbecue. Willie makes some real spicy stuff, and…well, I guess it was too much for Garrison, and he ran out behind the bunkhouse. It was pretty funny. We could hear him—being sick—ya know. And then we felt kinda bad. He'd never gotten sick before."

"I see. What time did that happen?"

"Right before I left to sit with the mare. Garrison came back in, but I heard from the guys the next day that he had to leave the game a couple of more times. I guess it was the barbecue that did it."

"I'm glad you told me, PJ."

"It's not that we lied, ma'am. We sort of felt bad about what happened. Are you gonna tell the sheriff?"

"It might be important, but you did the right thing by telling me."

Kate looked across the street. Most of the people had gone inside. A large man wearing black pants and a white short-sleeved shirt stood on the porch watching Kate and PJ. "I think your Bible lesson is about to begin."

PJ smiled and ran across the street and up the steps of the church. The man placed a meaty arm around PJ's shoulder and they went inside.

Kate walked into the Cypress Café and into the quiet, cool bar to think. The waitress came over, and Kate ordered a glass of Merlot. When she returned and sat the glass down, she raised her eyebrows and quickly walked away. Kate kept forgetting about her bruises. If she only wore makeup, she could attempt to cover them up. *What the hell*, she thought as she took her wine out to the patio and sat down at a table overlooking the creek. A few moments later, the waitress brought out a bowl of snack mix. Kate suspected that the young woman wanted another look at her battered customer. After a few sips of wine and a few peanuts, Kate's head began to clear.

Did Garrison see her when she was snooping around the kennel? Maybe he faked being sick. Would that have given him enough time to grab a bow and several arrows and shoot Kate? She tried to imagine Garrison Fordyce killing Jesús and Travis. Garrison would know about the back roads. He would know about the cemetery. But what about motive? Guy was Garrison's meal ticket. If anything happened to Guy, if he did anything to lose the ranch, Garrison would have nothing. Blackmail. Fences left open. Expensive cattle poisoned. Guy's greyhounds dying on the track. Molly's greyhounds stolen. What did this all mean?

Then something clicked. Fences left open. Cages left open.

Had someone intended to steal Guy's cattle as they had stolen Molly's dogs? Cattle rustling was lucrative, but dogs? Kate felt that she was getting nowhere. A lot of suspicions, but not much else. She finished her wine and pulled out the note she had made for the market—*pork roast—5 lbs. at $7.99, or steak—5 lbs. at $5.99*. She stared down at the figures. Suddenly a feeling of déjà vu took hold. She remembered writing these numbers down before…but where? Had Olga mentioned similar numbers in her recipes while discussing the catering for Rosa Linda's wedding? No, specifics weren't mentioned. It had been sooner than that. A couple of days ago? Where had Kate been that she was thinking of price per pound?

Then it struck her like a sharp slap on the face. She fumbled in her purse for the cellphone. The waitress came to see if Kate wanted another glass of wine just as Kate pulled out the gun instead. Startled, the waitress turned around and ran back in the restaurant.

Shit. That's all I need. She replaced the gun and found the phone. She punched Brad Gates's number and prayed that he would answer.

"Dr. Gates."

"Thank heavens you're there."

"Kate, what's up?"

"Do you know anything about the pharmaceutical company in San Marcos called Stanley Institute?"

"Not really. Why? What do you need to know?"

"Do they run tests on animals?"

"The greyhounds."

"Right. Travis Landon left school today to go to Stanley Institute."

"I'll make some phone calls and find out. What clued you in?"

"Something that was written on Wayne Brody's calendar. I copied it down, but after my swim two nights ago, I forgot. The note is probably a paper wad in the

261

pocket of my jeans. Something about sixty-five pounds or sixty-five pound average at .40 = 26 X 75 = 1,950. There was another figure, almost identical, but I can't remember. Call me tonight at Olga's, or better yet, call this cellphone number."

Kate hung up and called McCrae.

He answered immediately. "Sheriff McCrae."

"Where are you?"

"I'm on my way to the Fordyce Ranch. Why?"

"It's not Garrison. It's Wayne Brody. I'm sure of it. Travis was working for him. I have yet to know why Jesús was involved, but I'm sure I'm on the right track, and I'm sure Brody killed Travis. It's possible that they were selling the dogs to the Stanley Institute. Travis must have gone back to the institute to see if he could get Molly's dogs back..." She explained what she had learned from the note on Brody's desk.

"Stay away from that ranch, and that's an order," he growled. "I'll keep in touch."

Kate started to leave, but decided to make one more phone call to the police department in Alpine, Texas. It was a long shot, but if it panned out, she'd have her connection. Five minutes later, Kate had her motive. As she hurried to pay her bill, the waitress and a guy, who Kate assumed was the manager, were head to head in a fearful discussion. They immediately stopped talking when they saw her. The guy's hand shook a bit when he took the money from Kate. As he handed back her change, he glanced at the phone on the counter.

Kate smiled. "Don't worry. I've called the sheriff, and he knows I have a gun."

She walked out of the restaurant, called Olga, and gave her the news. She would have to cancel her plans for therapeutic cooking. Kate was going straight to Molly's.

Kate climbed in the Explorer and as she started the engine, the phone rang. She reached in her purse and grabbed the gun. "Damn!" Kate took the gun, stuck it in the console, and then answered the phone.

"Yes."

"This is Brad. Wayne was bunching dogs."

"What?"

"It's a term used for someone who gathers up several dogs and sells them to a lab. I tried calling Stanley Institute. All I got was a message saying to call back during office hours. Then I called a vet friend of mine in San Marcos. He was very familiar with the company, and yes, they most certainly buy dogs for testing. Let me see here. I wrote this all down. They especially like greyhounds because they are calm and don't bark much. He says that because greyhounds have very little fat and hair, it's easy to tap into their nervous system. They also have a high tolerance for pain and a universal blood type. Their large heart and perfect skeletal system make them great for dissection, and—"

"Don't tell me any more. Can someone make a lot of money selling the dogs?"

"Seems so. About thirty dollars a dog. Bunchers usually bring in seventy-five or eighty dogs at a time. That would add up to more than two thousand dollars a delivery. There's your formula."

"Molly will be crushed. Is there any way to prove that the dogs were stolen?"

"I asked that. Are you sure you want to hear this?"

"No, but tell me anyway."

"As soon as the dogs come in, they cut off the ear

with the ID number tattooed inside so that they can't be identified later."

"Oh, my God. Molly's own greyhound, Gracie, was one of the stolen dogs. We've got to get to the labs and find out for sure. What about the details on the Bertillon Cards?"

"That might work, except that it is easier to get into Fort Knox then into this lab. They're careful about hiding their practice. They have a slew of lawyers that jump in whenever there's a complaint. And, according to the law, they are not doing anything illegal."

"Cruelty to animals is illegal."

"Not in the name of medicine."

"Bullshit. What are you doing tonight? I'm on my way to Molly's to break the news. If I know Molly, she's going straight to the lab as soon as she finds out. I'd feel better if you were with her."

"I have nothing to do here. The bank foreclosed yesterday."

"Oh, Brad. I'm so sorry."

"Tell Molly to locate all the Bertillon Cards on the missing dogs. It's probably too late for the ones that were stolen a few months ago, but maybe we can save the dogs that were stolen Tuesday evening. I'll meet you at her kennel. Oh, one more thing."

"I'm listening."

"The sheriff's office sent over a copy of the autopsy report on the dead greyhound. It came in a little while ago."

"And?"

"It was not epilepsy. It was poison. There were traces of cardiac glycoside in the blood."

"Meaning."

"Oleander. It appeared to be emulsified, probably added to the dog's food. What I can't understand," Brad continued, "is why the greyhounds ate the stuff. That plant is extremely bitter."

"Honey."

"What?"

"Wayne disguised the taste with honey."

Chapter Eighteen

The sun had slipped behind the hills as Kate left town. She stepped on the gas as soon as she hit the highway. She wanted to see Molly and get back to the Rodriguez ranch before Jack called. There was a big piece missing, and maybe his clear head could work in place of her muddled thinking.

Kate replayed the conversation in her mind of the first time she and McCrae talked about Jesús's murder. Guy and Jesús had been arguing. Nora heard them. Guy admitted that much. Jesús was asking for money so he could bring his family over from Mexico. Guy refused him. After the argument, Jesús stormed out of the house and Guy followed. Did Guy chase Jesús down and kill him as he drove to meet Kate and Rosa Linda? Did Guy know where Jesús was going?

And what about the photos? Kate showed them to Guy the afternoon she visited him, and they were stolen from the Jeep the night the dead greyhound was left there. Were Guy and Wayne working together? But Guy surely would not sell his dogs to a pharmaceutical company for money. Kate's frustration level had reached an all-time high.

Only the right lane of Spoke Hill Road had been paved from Ranch Road 12 almost to Molly's drive. The county road trucks were pulled off to the side and parked for the evening. She rounded the last curve before she turned into Molly's drive, and noticed two sets of headlights right behind her—Brad Gates and following him, a patrol car. McCrae had sent one of his deputies to accompany Molly and Brad to Stanley Institute. If the authorities at the lab refused to cooperate, the presence of an officer might change their minds. Kate was grateful for McCrae's assistance.

As Kate explained to Molly what had happened to Travis, Kate became aware that this was the second time today she came bearing bad news. Again, Molly calmly listened.

Outwardly, she held up well, but Kate suspected, seeing Molly clenching and unclenching her fist, that inside she was struggling to keep it together. Then Kate delivered another blow and told Molly what had happened to her missing greyhounds. Molly had reacted as Kate had predicted.

"I'm not leaving that place until I get my dogs."

"Bring the Bertillon Cards," Brad said.

Molly and Brad climbed in the patrol car with McCrae's deputy and left for Stanley Institute. Kate stayed behind to check the kennel before she left, and to make sure all locks were secure. Over the barking, she heard the cellphone ringing inside the car. At the same moment, Molly's phone buzzed across her outdoor speakers. She ignored Molly's landline, and rushed to the car.

"Yes."

"Sweetheart, are you okay? You're out of breath."

Hearing Jack's voice was what she needed. "Yes, I'm fine. I'm worried about you though."

"I'm not the one in trouble. Listen to me, Kate. I'm afraid Jesús's murder may be tied to Rosa Linda and

Daniel."

Kate's joy over her husband's voice turned to fear. The same idea had been forming in her own mind, but she refused to believe that Rosa Linda and Daniel were involved.

"What have you found out?"

"Jesús's two brothers and cousin left for the Fordyce ranch about ten days ago. No one has seen them since."

"How do you know this?"

"I was of no use to Max who doesn't understand the word listen. He's been dealing with his lawyers since we arrived. Anyway, as soon as Rosa Linda and Daniel left the courthouse, I decided to keep them in my sight. I took Max's car and followed them. They drove across the border to Nuevo Laredo, parked, and went into a restaurant through a back door. I walked in the front in time to see them go into the kitchen. I didn't want to look too obvious, so I sat down at the bar and ordered a beer. The guy was hesitant about serving me. It was clear that I was in a place where I didn't belong."

"Damn, Jack—you're telling me I should be careful."

"Hold on now—I'm fine. Anyway, I convinced the bartender that I was with Rosa Linda and Daniel. He seemed satisfied or he decided that he didn't care, one way or the other. I pretended to go in search of the men's room. As soon as I walked to the back, I heard a woman scream, and I rushed into the kitchen. Daniel was trying to hold the woman. She was hysterical, pounding her chest with her fists. She was Jesús's mother. They had just broken the news to her about Jesús's death."

"Oh, Jack. That poor woman."

"That's not all. Seems like Mrs. Flores lost all three

of her sons."

"What?"

"Jesús's brothers, Enrique and Arturo, and his cousin, Umberto, had become impatient for their visas to come through. They fled across the border with the intention of meeting Jesús in Wimberley. They never arrived."

"And my goddaughter was responsible?"

"Yes and no. Much to her credit, Rosa Linda was trying to get these three across legally, and it looked like everything would work out. Smuggling in this case wasn't necessary. But in the meantime, the boys had gotten into some kind of trouble here. They had sent a message to Jesús. He arranged for the fake papers and for their trip to Texas. He paid a thousand dollars for this service."

"Paid who?"

"It was Diego Gomez, Guy's foreman, the one who died a few days before we arrived."

"Sounds like we've stumbled into another hornet's nest."

"Right. Kate, I know how you like to handle things yourself. You get pissed and all good sense evaporates. But promise me that you will stay with Olga. All four of us are on our way back."

"I'm at Molly's, and I'm headed for the ranch now."

Kate went into the kitchen to turn off the lights and lock the door before she left. All was quiet. Freda and Lupe were asleep in their baskets. Kate snapped off the light, locked the door, and ran for the SUV when she heard Molly's landline ring again. It was McCrae and Kate had never heard him sound so excited. "Get the hell out of there. I'm at the Fordyce ranch with Guy and

Garrison. Brody knows we're on to him, and he's dangerous."

Kate slammed the door and ran to the car. Wayne had proven that he could turn up anywhere, and Olga was alone. Kate peeled out of Molly's drive. Less than a quarter mile down the road, she rounded the corner and almost ran head on into a huge machine illuminated with yellow blinking lights. The county road crew was back on the job. Kate slowed the Explorer almost to a stop. She eased over to the left lane, and the driver of the truck stopped and climbed down. He motioned for Kate to proceed as he started to direct her between the machinery. In the yellowing flashing lights, Kate saw him turn and smile. His gold-cross earring caught the reflection from the light.

She gunned the engine to swing around the maintenance truck.

Blocked.

Wayne had parked his pickup in the left lane. She slammed on her brakes, threw the SUV in reverse, and backed far enough to make a U-turn before Wayne reached the car. As she sped down the road, she looked in her review mirror.

Wayne stood there for a few more seconds and then walked to his truck. If he was coming after her, he was certainly taking his time. With a head start, Kate was certain that she could outrun him the three miles to Ranch Road 12 where the traffic, even at this time of night, was steady.

As Kate passed Molly's house and Cemetery Road, she saw a hazy glow in the distance. She crested the hill and slammed on her brakes. Wayne had set up a second roadblock with the road crew's barricades, and, as added insurance to trap Kate, he sat the barricades on fire. Now Kate understood why Wayne was in no hurry to follow. He had Spoke Hill Road blocked off in both directions. Her only choice was Cemetery Road. If he had blocked that route as well, Kate was done for.

She sped toward the cemetery, searching for a place to pull over and hide the Explorer. If she could buy herself a few minutes, she'd call McCrae.

Suddenly the Explorer sputtered.

She looked down at the gas gauge.

Empty.

"Shit! Shit! Shit!" she shouted, pounding her fist on the dash.

It had been near full when she left the ranch earlier that day. Wayne obviously was not stupid.

She abandoned the Explorer in the middle of the narrow road. She would not make things easy for him. If he came flying over the hill, there was a chance that he'd collide with the rear end of the SUV. But Kate knew that Wayne Brody was in no hurry. She was the one who would have to run. She was the mouse in his cat and mouse game.

Kate grabbed her purse and bolted down the road in the dark, searching for a place in the thick vegetation, along the roadside in which to hide. But the road on both sides was strewn with barbed wire over which tightly woven vines had grown. If she attempted to crawl through, especially with a bum right arm, she would end up hooked and tangled on a barb like a scared rabbit, like one of Wayne's rabbits, wounded, bleeding, and hanging there like a lure on a racing pole staring down the throat of a predator.

Except that Wayne would make sure that Kate was

dead: like Jesús and Travis, another shot in the head, another blow to an already crushed skull. Kate saw it in his eyes on that day she was alone with him in his office. How could she have been so stupid? She had ignored her number one rule for survival: never question her intuition.

She was used to seeing the kill in a killer's eyes as with the predators on the African plains. It was impossible to hide. Her binoculars would be focused on the eyes of the big cats—lions and cheetahs motionless in the grass, leopards crouched in trees. Their prey would see it too—an instinctual fear would shoot through the air like a bolt of electricity. It was survival in its most raw form. Prey who misread the signals did not survive.

Wayne's motive, if Kate guessed right, was steeped in a growing hatred. A killer could lie, deceive, and even charm his victims, but he could never hide that look in his eyes.

Kate had ignored all the signs.

Her only choice now was to keep running and hope for an opening in the brush. She had only a few seconds before Wayne's headlights would appear over the hill. Suddenly, her foot caught, and she tumbled head-over-heels. She felt the stitches in her arm separate. And as she struggled to her feet, she heard the pickup. No longer able to run, Kate stood her ground.

She had the gun. She'd shoot as soon as he got close enough. Kate groped around in her purse for Olga's gun and came up empty handed.

Then she remembered—the gun was in the console of the Explorer. There was no time to go back.

Wayne Brody drove past the Explorer and moments later slowed to a stop a few feet from Kate. She stood there, like a defiant deer in the headlights.

Wayne stepped out and walked in front of the truck, staying out of the glare of the headlights. He rested his foot on the bumper. In his right hand, he held the .22.

Despite falling into the trap of a madman, Kate felt a smidgen of hope. The cat wanted to play.

"You goddamned, fuckin' bitch. You tried to ruin my plan—I always land on my feet. You're a minor inconvenience, lady."

"I've already talked to McCrae, Wayne," Kate said. He's on his way.' She knew it was a weak attempt.

"It doesn't matter. I'll be done with you and out of here before that asshole finds you. Drop your bag on the ground and kick it over here."

"That's pretty low, Wayne. Draining the gas tank while I was enjoying my glass of wine." She kicked her purse into the bushes on the side of the road instead.

He was too calm, too sure of himself. Kate would push him a little farther.

An angry killer makes mistakes.

Wayne threw his head back and laughed. "Yeah, and that roadblock worked better than I had hoped. I had to do something since my other warnings didn't work. You finally made things easy for me tonight, Dr. Caraway."

"How about Travis and Jesús? Did they make things easy for you also?"

"Jesús almost ruined everything, but I turned that mess around to my advantage." He flipped open the gun and checked the cartridges. "And Travis, like you, was a nuisance."

"Why did you have to kill the boy, Wayne?"

"The little shit threatened to go to the police when he found out about my petty-cash scheme."

"Killing people over a few thousand dollars from bunching greyhounds is rather excessive, don't you think, not to mention cowardly?"

Wayne stiffened, and pointed the gun at her head. "The only goddamn coward around here is Guy Fordyce. I'm going to make him pay with everything he owns. I started with his slut daughter and then his worthless wife. But I'm not finished."

In the glare of the headlights, Kate saw the sweat forming on Wayne's upper lip. All she had on her side was time. "You were the one who wrote the blackmail note and put it on Guy's desk? And Jesús was your pawn, wasn't he?"

"Jesús got in my way. But I kept my eyes and ears open. Turn around and walk."

"Are you taking me to the cemetery, Wayne? You don't have much time. McCrae will be here before you know it."

"Shut up and walk."

Kate did as he told her. *Keep him talking*, Kate told herself. Once they left the main road and disappeared into the trees along the pathway to the cemetery, all hope would be lost. As they came over the next hill, the hill where Kate had stopped earlier that day and envisioned a picnic with Jack, she saw the cemetery entrance up ahead, no more than a few yards away.

"You were the one supplying Meredith with sedatives. I saw the note on your desk the night you shot me. Meredith needed more. Right?"

"Something like that. The cemetery was our special little meeting place. Whenever Meredith had a little gardening to do, I'd meet her here with my medicine chest."

"You were the one who attacked her a few weeks ago."

"Self-defense. The crazy bitch said she was going into rehab. When I laughed, she slapped me."

"Shame on you, Wayne, beating up on women. I should have known that was your style."

Wayne laughed and shoved Kate between her shoulders, causing her to stumble to her knees. He grabbed her by her hair, pulling her back up to her feet.

"She had the nerve to threaten me!" He put his face next to Kate's right ear. "She was going to tell her big, rich husband everything, see to it that I landed in jail! So I confessed."

"Confessed?"

"I told her that Fordyces and pills were a family affair."

"Victoria? You supplied her with drugs as well."

"That's not all I supplied Vicky with. She was the easiest piece of ass I ever had. Meredith got so upset when I told her. She lost it and attacked me—what's a guy to do?"

"You're a real fuckin' coward, Wayne."

Lights flashed around Kate's head, blinding her as she fell. Her face struck the road with such force, she lost all control of her movements. Her head spun and bile from her stomach rose up in her throat. She waited helplessly for the second blow, almost welcomed it, for the pain in the back of her head felt as if her skull had cracked.

But the blow didn't come. Instead, Wayne jammed his knee into the small of her back, grabbed her arms, and using his belt, tied her hands behind her back. Her wounded arm, now free of stitches, bled freely. Then he jerked her up on her feet, but Kate was too woozy to stand. He shoved her hard against a tree to catch his breath, and Kate was sure the skin on her left cheek was in shreds.

Wayne stuck the .22 in the waist of his jeans. He got behind her and grabbed her under the chin with one hand, and with the other, he grasped her wrists. He shoved her forward.

"Walk! You stupid bitch!"

Kate would not make this easy on him. She had to keep him from dragging her into the cemetery. The spinning in her head began to slow, but she refused to pick up her feet and walk. Instead, she let her knees buckle. Wayne clamped his hand across her throat to keep her up on her feet. Kate gasped, but his grip was too tight, and now she couldn't breathe. If Kate didn't get him to loosen his grip, she'd die. She couldn't move her head and her arms were pulled tight behind her. But she could move her legs. And she sensed him weakening. When he relaxed to get a better grip, Kate let her entire body go limp. As he jerked her up, she threw her right leg between his legs. He tripped and fell on top of her. Kate's breath was knocked out. She tasted blood.

Together they stumbled down the road. She fought, but could not shake him loose. She butted her head back and caught him hard on the nose. He cried out and lost his grip on her neck, but managed to hang on to her hands. With a sudden burst of energy, she kicked him in the shin and he finally let go.

But not having the use of her hands, Kate could not get up. Instead, she continued to kick at him to keep him away. Wayne got to his feet and steadied himself. Then he came round from behind, away from her legs. He reached down, grabbed her by her shoulders, and pulled her to her feet.

"Stand up and walk!"

Kate swayed. Wayne lost his patience and struck her left temple with the handle of the .22. Lights flashed again—red, yellow and green—they shot through Kate's skull with such intensity she knew she would die. She dropped to her knees. The lights disappeared and she saw nothing.

Kate knew she was alive—every square inch of her body burned with pain. The ringing in her ears sounded as if a microphone was held near her head and the volume turned up. She tried to press her hands over her ears, but she could not move. She dropped her head and concentrated on breathing. After a few moments, the ringing subsided, and she slowly opened her eyes, but the left one had swollen shut. Trying to focus hurt too much, and she closed her eyes again. *Breathe*, she told herself. Oxygen circulated and brought on a sense of her surroundings, then she felt something hard poking at her back. She was sitting on the ground in the cemetery, and someone's words were flying swift around her head.

"You think you're such a fuckin' heroine, always doing the right thing, always coming to the rescue."

Kate struggled to move. Her hands were still tied, and now so were her feet. She was sitting at the base of the cross. She couldn't see him. But she heard him not far behind, thrashing through the woods.

"Remember Joan of Arc? Here's your chance, Dr. Caraway, to go out in a blaze of glory."

Terror struck and melted whatever resolve Kate had left. He was gathering firewood. This madman planned to burn her to death. Cold fear turned her insides to liquid as her voice rose from deep inside, "Wayne, listen to me. You can't do this! It's not too late!"

He ignored her plea as he arranged the kindling to his liking. "Do you know where I learned to do this? The same place I learned archery. I was a few tasks away from making Eagle Scout—a few weeks away from graduating high school. When I turned twenty-one, the Brody ranch would have been mine."

"Wayne, listen. I know what happened in Alpine."

"Shut—the fuck—up!" He stormed up to Kate and came within inches of her face. "Guy killed my father. He stole everything. I came here to make him pay."

Wayne reached in his pocket and pulled out his cigarette lighter. He looked down at Kate, but didn't see her. It was as if he had stepped into his anger. A cold calm engulfed him.

"Guy Fordyce ruined my family," he whispered.

Kate felt his breath on her cheek.

"He swindled us out of our land. My father put this gun in his mouth, and I watched as he blew the top of his head off. We lost everything. The Fordyce Ranch—big, wealthy Guy Fordyce built the place with what he stole from me. I came here to take everything away from Guy Fordyce, like he took everything away from me. Jesús almost screwed it up, but I fixed that. Then you came."

Kate knew that he was beyond reach. Her pleading would go unheard. The old adage was wrong. In the face of death, one's life didn't flash before one's eyes. Instead, all of Kate's petty worries, her ego she mistook for righteousness, her selfish causes that ruled her life, all stared her in the face, and she would die knowing what a fool she had been. And now in her last moments, she failed again. Too consumed with her own inadequacies, she could not offer even one prayer for salvation.

Wayne stepped back to survey his work. "You know, if you don't have the kindling just right, a fire won't burn the way it's supposed to." He looked around and not finding what he wanted he stepped over the fence and moved into the brush.

Kate listened as his steps grew fainter. She had only a few minutes. She must do something, but her mind was frozen. Her ears still rang. She felt as if her head was floating through mud. As she leaned back against the cross, a memory of earlier that day shot through her mind like a lifeline. It was her only chance. She raised her knees up to her chest, leaned forward for leverage, and slammed her back into the cross. It gave several inches. She was too numb to feel any pain. Adrenaline surged through her blood. She slammed her back against the cross a few more times, and she felt it loosen at the base. It now leaned to the side, but hopefully Wayne was too intent on killing her to notice.

He stepped from the woods carrying another armload of brush. He was smiling. "These will work fine. All I have to do is fill in some of the gaps around the back and it should burn nicely."

Kate heard him rustling around behind her. She heard the click of his lighter and smelled the smoke before she felt the heat. He was using a cedar branch as a torch, igniting the brush along the edge. Kate feared she had waited too long. She looked over her right shoulder and saw him bending down to shove the torch underneath the pyre. With one last spike of energy she shoved her back onto the cross and the heavy structure crashed down, knocking Wayne onto his own torch. The belt binding her hands had loosened and she rolled away from the flame. Wayne stood up as the flame traveled up his jeans and soon caught his shirt. The look of shock on his face was momentary, then he began screaming.

"Throw him to the ground!" Someone shouted and Kate turned to see McCrae running over.

Kate raised her head in time to see Guy stomping out the fire, and McCrae's deputy pulling Wayne away from the flames. McCrae walked over to Kate and helped her sit up.

"I told you to stay out of trouble."

"Yeah, well, if I don't listen to my husband when he tells me to stay out of trouble, why the hell should I listen to you?"

"Damn, I'm glad she's not my wife," Guy said. He bent down to untie Kate's legs.

Chapter Nineteen

I can't believe you did that. How did you manage to get Max to agree?" Kate said.

"He didn't have a choice. I proposed the idea to Rosa Linda, and she immediately became my cohort," Jack said. He had loosened his tie and unbuttoned the top button of his shirt. "Max was in the shower, and Daniel went to the motel office to check out. I told Rosa Linda to hop in Max's truck while I went back inside and grabbed his keys. If Max wanted to make it back to Wimberley that night, he had no choice but to ride with his son-in-law. Four hours on the road would seal their fate, one way or another."

"You did good." Kate straightened the sagging rosemary sprig attached to Jack's lapel.

"What are best men for? Now that the ceremony is over, can I remove this dried up twig? I smell like an Italian meatball."

"It symbolizes a healthy and long life for the bride and groom," Kate told her husband.

"Health and longevity is no problem. These newlyweds need a herb for peace and family tolerance."

"What about the newlyweds?" Rosa Linda interrupted. "I heard something about tolerance."

"Kate was giving me suggestions for my toast," Jack said.

"You look like your mother in that dress," Kate said.

"Looking like my mother is a good thing. Now, if I could only learn not to act like my father. Come on. Dinner's ready, and Dad's starting to grumble."

With all that had happened, Rosa Linda's suggestion to have a small reception on the verandah was met with no opposition. Along with the immediate family and a few close friends, Rosa Linda and Daniel repeated their wedding vows during a private mass at St. Francis's Church. They'd planned to honeymoon in Laredo during their court appearances. Kate laughed to herself at the thought of the wedding pictures. Max, not yet ready to admit that he was growing fond of his son-in-law, scowled at the photographer—a disgruntled face forever frozen by the camera. And there was Kate—arm in a sling, stitches tracing her hairline. The disappearing rings of yellow bruises around both eyes were still visible, giving her the appearance of a *Friday the Thirteenth* survivor. Kate's second stay in the hospital prevented her from assisting Olga in the planning and preparation.

An honest-to-god cool front had drifted across the hills and stayed for several days. Not strong enough to deliver a promise of a true fall, it nevertheless provided a little hope, and for Kate, brought a flood of memories. She loved this time of the year—perfect baseball weather. Even though the Cubs were rarely in the playoffs, the excitement of the sport and the realization that the season was ending made every game exciting. Kate had to admit she missed Chicago in September.

Jack was right. For all her education and training, for all her successes and accomplishments, her good intentions and noble causes, once Kate became intent on changing the world, good judgment was often lost in a moment of passion. Two disasters on opposite sides of the globe in little more than two weeks were red flags she could not ignore. At her age, she knew that making promises to change was a setup for failure. Her return to the states was meant to be a time for recovery from the tragedy in Kenya—instead, she had been shot, beaten, tied up, and singed. Okay, she could take a hint.

The second round of stitches in her arm itched like a bad rash, and she could not take a deep breath without twinges of pain from her broken ribs. Sitting in the stands at Wrigley Field would be good medicine. Watching Jack strut around in his baseball uniform would be an added treat. Tomorrow the three of them were leaving for Chicago, and Kate was ready.

Olga was placing candles on the table, as the guests gathered around. With only ten people in attendance, including the bride and groom, the only stranger to Kate, or so she thought, was McCrae's wife. When they were introduced, Kate was surprised to discover that Lisa McCrae was the police dispatcher to whom Kate had spoken several times during the investigation.

"Your husband never mentioned that you are his dispatcher," Kate said.

"That man," Lisa responded, rolling her eyes. "Sometimes I have to remind him myself."

During dinner, they talked around the Brody/Fordyce incident. Murder was not exactly proper conversation for a wedding supper, although the subject hung in the air like a bad stench. Finding a topic that didn't rankle was not easy, and polite talk about the ceremony was becoming tedious.

Max took the lead. "What's going to happen to Guy now? I mean, they will go easy on him since he confessed."

"It's out my hands," McCrae said. "When I arrived at the ranch to question Brody, Guy had just returned. Spending those few days at Santa Rita Center clinic with Meredith in therapy gave him a chance to think about what he had done. It was eating away at him. All three men were dead when he found them locked in the back of the van."

"Guy had been under so much strain lately," Max replied. "He's a good man. How much can anyone take? He snapped. Besides, it was Gomez who was responsible."

Kate was about to say that whether Guy snapped under stress and strain, it still did not excuse his actions. She stopped short. Who was she to talk? As if reading her mind, Jack picked up her hand and held it.

"We know that Jesús had paid Gomez to go to Laredo to bring Enrique and Arturo and their cousin here," McCrae explained. "Unfortunately, as soon as Gomez arrived on the ranch, he must have started having chest pains. Guy found him outside the van. As best we can figure, Gomez turned off the engine, got out of the van, and before he could let the men out, he collapsed. The three men were trapped in the back. There were no windows in the van, but it was rigged with air conditioning as long as the engine was running. The temperature inside must have risen quickly. Jesús's brothers and cousin died from heat exhaustion.

"When Guy found their bodies, he panicked. After losing Victoria and watching his wife lose her grip on reality, he figured another tragedy would ruin him. Probably even send him to jail. He could lose everything. He couldn't let that happen. So he buried the three men in the orchard."

"All we can do is keep them in our prayers." This was Olga's polite way of putting an end to that discussion.

Jack took her hint to heart and attempted to change the subject. "So, Brad, how do you like working for your new boss?"

"She keeps me too busy, but I'm not complaining."

"I'm afraid that Brad got more than he bargained for." Molly laughed. "I asked him to spend a couple of hours each morning at my kennel. But that was before I inherited half the dogs from Stanley Institute."

"And Guy's entire stock of greyhounds," Rosa Linda added.

"Heaven knows those dogs needed treatment—" Molly stopped short.

The pause was brief, but obvious enough that Kate knew she had not imagined it.

Molly gave Jack an apologetic look and continued, moving the conversation in a slightly different direction. "Until we finished out the new kennel yesterday, Brad spent his mornings tending to the dogs, and his afternoons helping with the construction."

"I have room at my facility to house the new additions until their permanent homes are ready," Brad said.

"But I thought the bank foreclosed on you property?" Kate said.

"I was able to work things out after all, with Molly's help," Brad said.

"I'm buying Brad's pasture land, and he's keep the house and vet hospital," Molly said.

"That's great news. I'm happy for both of you. But

how about the dogs Wayne sold to the B and C class tracks?" Kate asked.

She had a nagging feeling that she had not received the entire story. During her stay at Wimberley General, Jack refused to let her use the phone and had it removed from her room. Kate thought she had foiled him, remembering that she had Rosa Linda's cellphone in her purse. Determined to get the entire truth from Olga, Kate pressed the phone's call button only to discover the battery was dead.

She finally gave in. If Jack could delay his first day of work on her account, she could try to concede to his wishes. After all, he had gone to the library and checked out every Rex Stout mystery on the shelf. He had also purchased a current copy of *Food and Wine*, *Bon Appétit*, and *Baseball Today*.

So, for several days Kate slept, read, and tried to convince Jack that a high-rise on Lake Shore Drive would be more practical than a brownstone near Wrigley Field.

Maria started serving the main course. Kate's only contribution to the shindig was her Pescado Veracruzana recipe served with white rice and mango salsa. McCrae was seated across from her, and when Maria sat his plate down, he whispered something in her ear.

"If you smother my Veracruzana in catsup," Kate said to him, "you're gonna wear it."

McCrae raised his hands in surrender. He called to Maria, "Cancel the catsup—bring Tabasco."

Before Kate could comment, he jumped in to answer her question. "Although Guy didn't know Wayne was selling his dogs to owners racing at lower-class tracks, the sales were legal. It will take a while to sort that one out. But Guy is determined to get them back. Even though he's out of the greyhound business, he wants Molly to have those dogs as well."

"Didn't Guy know the dogs were missing?" Olga said.

"Actually no," McCrae continued. "Guy left instructions for Wayne to donate the dogs to Molly whenever they started losing, which wasn't often. Guy's greyhounds were bred from a pretty good stock. That's when Wayne decided to slow them down. He didn't intend for the oleander to kill them."

"What I mistook for epilepsy was oleander poisoning," Brad said. "Some of the greyhounds were more affected than others."

"These were the dogs in those horrid pictures Jesús had taken?" Kate asked. "Surely someone on the ranch would have noticed them."

"I don't think so. The dogs in Jesús's photos weren't just sick, they were emaciated. As best we can figure," Brad said, "those were some of the discarded hounds Wayne picked up from other tracks in Louisiana. They were in pretty bad shape when he got them."

Silence fell over the gathering once more. Everyone looked down at their food again and started eating. This time Kate was positive that the avoidance was not her imagination.

"What?" Kate said. "There's something else. What is it?"

"Olga, you'll have to get this recipe from Kate," Max said. "This cruzana is better than your mother's."

"Max Rodriguez! You skunk. Stop trying to change the subject," Kate said.

"Glad you're feeling better," Max responded.

Kate punched him in the shoulder.

"Stop it." Rosa Linda laughed. "You're right, Kate. There is something else."

"Let's hear it," Kate said.

"Go ahead, Sheriff," Rosa Linda said.

"When Wayne decided to ruin his employer, he pulled out all the stops," McCrae replied. "The cattle poisoning, that was Wayne's doing also. And when he found out that we were on to him, he mixed up a large batch of oleander juice in that blender of his and tried to poison every dog in the kennel before he went in search of you."

Kate sat her fork down and slumped back in her chair. "Oh, my God."

"We lost a few dogs," Brad said. "But most survived. I had some mighty sick pups on my hands for a few days."

Kate reached over and gave Molly's hand a squeeze. "I'm sorry, Molly."

"Hey, I have my own personal vet and forty-seven more dogs. And if you and Brad hadn't figured out that Wayne was bunching greyhounds, we'd still be in the dark. And I'd have lost Gracie for good."

"I wish you could have been with us, Kate," Rosa Linda said. "Daniel and I arrived back in Wimberley just as Molly and Brad were heading out to Stanley Institute. I was ready for a full scale protest, but with half of Hays County law enforcement there, that wasn't necessary."

McCrae laughed. "Sorry to disappoint you."

"Thanks for all your help, Holden," Kate said.

"Are you kidding? With Molly and Rosa Linda I would have had the biggest uprising in the county if we didn't get into that lab. So, I sent a few extra patrol cars."

"How's Gracie?" Kate asked Molly.

"She wouldn't speak to me until the next day," Molly said. "She's fine now. But I can't stop thinking about Travis. I should have paid more attention to him. I mistook his melancholy for bashfulness. I should have realized something was going on."

"It wasn't your fault," McCrae said. "Travis was a smart boy. He knew better than to get involved with Brody."

"It's not that easy," Molly said. "If I had known how difficult things were for him, I could have helped."

"I don't think he realized what he was getting into with Wayne," Kate offered.

"What made you call and check on Wayne's background anyway?" Rosa Linda asked.

"Once I realized what Wayne was up to, I knew there was more to it," Kate said. "There had to be a motive. I remembered Wayne mentioning to me that his mother was in a nursing home in his hometown, and that his sister took care of her. His sister works for Sul Ross University. It's located in Alpine, the town where Guy is from. It took a few phone calls, but I found out Wayne's secret. The Brody family hit on hard times and the bank foreclosed on their property. Guy Fordyce owned that bank. Wayne's father began drinking and eventually put a gun to his head. Mrs. Brody ended up in a nursing home. Wayne held Guy responsible for his father's death and the loss of their land."

"I came to the ranch to arrest Wayne for stealing the dogs and he came unhinged, pulled a gun on me, and took off." McCrae added. "I didn't know at the time that he had killed Jesús. Deputy Caraway here had not yet told me what she had learned from the Alpine police."

He shot Kate and exasperated look. "Identifying yourself as one of my detectives qualifies as impersonating an officer."

"And accepting baseball tickets to look the other way can be construed as taking a bribe," Kate retorted.

"Baseball tickets?" Jack said.

"Oh, didn't I mention that?" Kate said. "With all that's happened it must have slipped my mind." She flashed Jack a quick smile and turned to Holden. "How did Wayne know about Guy burying the bodies?"

"Wayne was in the orchard getting rid of the lures when he saw Guy," McCrae continued. "It was just what he needed. He was biding his time. Turning Guy in would be too easy. Like you said, he wanted Guy to suffer, to lose everything—his family, his ranch, everything that made Guy Fordyce a well-respected rancher and candidate for state senator. An eye for an eye.

"Then on the morning Jesús was to meet Rosa Linda and Kate, he caught Wayne adding the oleander to the dog food and confronted him. Wayne laughed and told Jesús to mind his own business. Jesús became furious and told Wayne about the photos that were taken of the poisoned dogs and the ones Wayne had stolen. Jesús was going to tell Guy. Wayne saw his plan of revenge dissolving, and he quickly turned the tide by telling Jesús that his missing brothers and cousin were dead, and that Guy was responsible. It worked like a charm. Jesús stormed into Guy's office, accused him of murder, and said he was going to the police. That was the argument Nora heard, but she wasn't the only one. Wayne overheard as well. He watched Jesús, and then Guy leave, went into Guy's office, and took his gun. He then left the blackmail note and rushed out. Needing to get to Jesús quickly, Wayne cut across a feeding trail in the south pasture and met Jesús head on. One lucky shot through the windshield and Wayne Brody's master plan was almost complete. He tossed Guy's gun into the pasture. Then he pulled Jesús from the wreck, threw his body in back of the pickup, and left the ranch."

"That was what Jesús had called me about that morning I came to the bungalow to get Kate," Rosa Linda said. "He was calling about his brothers and cousin, not about the dogs."

"It wasn't Guy's fault. He was a victim of this entire mess," Max said.

"None of this would have happened if Guy had gone to the police when he found those men," Rosa Linda said. "Jesús would be alive, and so would Travis Landon."

"You listen to me, young lady," Max began.

"Stuff it," Rosa Linda said.

Kate heard enough. They had finished dessert, providing her with a perfect opportunity to slip away. "Hope you'll excuse me. I need to check on our girl."

****

The greyhound was asleep upstairs in Rosa Linda's room, and although she was beginning to walk a bit, she was still unsteady. The pin in her hip was doing its job, but her injured leg was still wrapped and pretty much useless. When Kate walked in, she lifted her head and thumped her tail against the pillow. Kate laughed and sat down beside her dog.

"Look at us. Don't we make a great pair? You with your useless leg, and me with my useless arm."

When Molly had visited Kate in the hospital and suggested that she take the greyhound, Kate did not need her good arm twisted. Jack thought it was a great idea as well. He missed having a dog as much as he missed playing baseball.

Kenya laid her head in Kate's lap. Less than a month ago, Kate was content with spending the rest of her life in Africa. The memory left a deep ache in the pit of her stomach. Letting go was something she did not do well. She hoped to return soon, but for now, she conceded to give herself a break and take things as they came.

Kate was roused from her reverie as Kenya looked toward the bedroom door.

"You ladies look as if you could use some company. You look way too serious." Jack walked in and joined them on the floor.

"Now that you mentioned it, we could use some cheering up. Kenya was telling me that she was growing fond of that gray-haired guy with the great body."

"She didn't ask for baseball tickets to the Cubs/Astros game, did she?" Jack slipped his shoes off, stretched out his legs, and leaned back against the bed.

"No. But only because she expects a prominent position next to you in the dugout."

"Maybe a dog in the ballpark will bring the team good luck." He reached down and gently patted Kenya's rump. "Think she'll be able to walk again?"

"She young and in good health. Let's hope for the best."

"How about you? Are you going to make it?"

Kate sat in silence.

Jack tapped her knee. "Hey, don't do that."

"What?"

"Get lost in your thoughts."

"I keep thinking about what started this entire thing.

Guy ruined Wayne Brody's family."

"No, he didn't, Kate. Guy was a banker. Wayne's father couldn't pay the bills. Guy foreclosed. It happens every day and normal, healthy people don't retaliate by killing someone."

"What did I do—chasing down those poachers and shooting them?"

"You had the authority to protect those elephants. Had you not taken action, those guys most likely would have killed you."

"Maybe."

"There's no maybe about it."

Kenya let out a long, slow yawn and licked Kate's hand.

"See, our girl agrees with me."

"Are you two going to gang up on me every time I feel sorry for myself?"

"That's the plan."

A yell from downstairs caught their attention.

"What's going on down there?"

"Molly, Brad and Olga, were dangling their feet in the pool when Daniel put on a shit-eating grin, stripped down to his boxers and jumped in. Do you want to hear the conversation between Max and Rosa Linda?"

"I'm ready for a laugh."

"Max was lecturing her about spreading herself too thin with school, her involvement with the greyhounds, her smuggling business, as he calls it, and now adding to all of that, the responsibilities of marriage."

"I'm sure Rosa Linda sat up and took notes."

"Actually, she told Max to mind his own damn business. Max told her that she was his damn business. She corrected him saying she was now Daniel's damn business then corrected herself, saying she was her own damn business."

Kate laughed. "Olga was right. We've been away too long."

Author's Note

To all you baseball fans, the book was written when the Houston Astros were a National League Team and before the Chicago Cubs won the 2016 World Series.

A word about the author...

Kathleen Kaska is the author of The Sherlock Holmes Quiz Book, which has been updated and reissued by Rowman & Littlefield Publishing Group. She is the founder of The Dogs in the Nighttime, the Sherlock Holmes Society of Anacortes, Washington, a scion of The Baker Street Irregulars.

Kathleen writes the two awarding-winning mystery series: the Sydney Lockhart Mystery Series set in the 1950s and the Classic Triviography Mystery Series. She also writes the Kate Caraway animal-rights series.

When she is not writing, she spends much of her time with her husband traveling the back roads and byways around the country, looking for new venues for her mysteries and bird watching along the Texas coast and beyond. Her passion for birds led to the publication The Man Who Saved the Whooping Crane: The Robert Porter Allen Story (University Press of Florida).

Kathleen was the writer, editor marketing director for Cave Art Press. Her collection of blog posts was released under the title, Do You Have a Catharsis Handy? Five-Minute Writing Tips. Catharsis was the winner of the Chanticleer International Book Award in the non-fiction Instruction and Insights category.

Kathleen Kaska is a writing coach who helps new and emerging writers discover their unique voices. With sensitivity and passion, Kathleen guides her clients as they learn the craft of writing and the art of storytelling. You can reach her via her website:
https://metaphorwritingcoach.com/
http://www.kathleenkaska.com

Thank you for purchasing
this publication of The Wild Rose Press, Inc.

For questions or more information
contact us at
info@thewildrosepress.com.

The Wild Rose Press, Inc.
www.thewildrosepress.com

www.ingramcontent.com/pod-product-compliance
Lightning Source LLC
Chambersburg PA
CBHW070054030726
47506CB00002B/463